T0355040

Opportunity

William Tucker

Archway Publishing books may be ordered through booksellers or by contacting:

Archway Publishing
1663 Liberty Drive
Bloomington, IN 47403
www.archwaypublishing.com
844-669-3957

ISBN: 978-1-6657-7248-8 (sc)
ISBN: 978-1-6657-7249-5 (e)

Library of Congress Control Number: 2025901500

Print information available on the last page.

Archway Publishing rev. date: 01/24/2025

Chapter 1

Once upon a time. No best of times worst of times. No. In the beginning. No. Jack is not sure how to start this novel. It's a sunny day in Vancouver, British Columbia and Jack is a bum on the side of the street. He is writing this novel to one day give him better days. He's been homeless for well over 6 months and yet he never gets used to it. Staying alive is hard work. He has a cup out for donations mainly to buy something to eat.

He must renovate his "cardboard palace" every other week. And twice a week when it rains. And then there is the stench that follows him even after he showers.

Jack is originally from Fayetteville, North Carolina. He earned a PhD in Neurobiology from Duke University. His dad is a biomedical engineer at Fort Bragg, North Carolina and has earned 5 master's degrees. Jack's mom is a microbiologist at DeNovo: a biotech company in Fayetteville. A distinguished family indeed.

Jack worked for Panacea Pharmaceuticals in Rockville, Maryland. A suburb of Washington, D.C. he made great money there, but he invested a lot of his money in real estate. He was so sure of his investment that he quit his job. Unfortunately, the market crashed.

What money he had left over went to his ex-wife Beth. She divorced him as soon as he quit his job. His reputation preceded him on the east coast of the United States. So, he ended up living with a friend in Vancouver. Jack's incident traveled even across North America. He couldn't hold a job in his specialty. His friend had to move so Jack had no place to stay. His family shunned him so he couldn't go back home. His family supported Beth's decision to leave him. So, he hasn't seen his son, Brent, in quite some time.

Today is a new day, Jack reminds himself. Once I finish this novel, the cash will roll in. These daydreams keep his spirits up. Which allows him to function in such a pitiful existence. Jack works on his novel for another hour. Then his stomach begins to growl. The inevitable pangs of hunger. He checks his donation cup. Yes! Enough money for a decent meal at McDonald's.

Jack hates fast food. But usually that is all he can afford. The restaurant is only a few blocks away so Jack walks there. He hopes no mischievous kids will destroy his cardboard palace. Jack orders a couple of Big Macs and some fries. As he orders the meal, Jack notices people backing away from him.

It must be my foul odor. I'll eat outside on this nice bench. It's a beautiful day. Jack is happier than most about the weather. Since a warm day usually leads to a night that isn't unbearably frigid. While eating, Jack wonders what he will do today.

Should I go to the thrift store and acquire more clothes since I stink? Where can I take a shower? When first becoming homeless, Jack had enough money to spend some nights in a cheap motel. The motel was in the seedy part of town. People talk about how rough of a neighborhood it is. But he never saw anything suspicious. But the motel seemed terrible at first. But now he dreams about it like it's the Hilton.

He checks his donation cup-only enough money for a few more days of fast-food meals. Jack almost chokes on some fries because he is eating too fast. That's what happens when you are extremely hungry. Jack finishes his meal in about eight minutes. And he is still debating on what to do today.

He decides to go to the public library to read newspapers and books. Jack wants to walk to the library, but it is just too far away. So, he rides the city bus. He hates traveling on public transportation because of the dirty looks he receives. Oh well. They just must deal with my stench today.

Jack boards the bus and stands near the back. Purposely distancing himself from the other passengers. He is excited about going to the library. He looks forward to learning. Reading is one of the few things he looks forward to every day. As usual at mid-day on a weekday: the public library is practically empty. Which Jack loves because he can read newspapers without having to wait for someone else to finish reading them.

Plus, during the winter the library is such a warm sanctuary. I wish I could stay here overnight. Once in the library, Jack skims the local newspaper. Nothing major is going on. Same ole local stories. Then after this, which took about ten minutes, he reads The New York Times. When Jack was younger, he always dreamed of being retired and reading The New York Times front to back.

Timc goes by quickly and now Jack is hungry again. People that don't have to worry about where their next meal is coming from, don't experience hunger pangs quite like me. Tired of fast-food, he buys food from a sub shop. As soon as he enters the shop, the aroma causes his stomach to growl even louder. To the point that he figures everyone in the store can hear it. Jack spends a few minutes counting money in his donation cup. I shouldn't buy this expensive meal, but I'll find money somewhere. Yes! I can buy a large cold cut sub, chips, and a big 32 oz drink. And after I finish the sub, I can still buy a cheesecake.

The sub is more to handle than Jack thinks. But since he has no fridge, he doesn't want to waste food. So, he stuffs himself to the max. Jack overdoes it and must walk bent over. He must lie down somewhere. He goes back to his cardboard palace. Since it's summer, he doesn't need blankets for the night. He still has a few dollars in his donation cup. So today is a good day.

The tomatoes on the sub give him weird dreams about aliens. The aliens abduct him, and he fights them off with a cane. The dreams seem so real that Jack keeps waking up every other hour. At midnight, he goes for a walk to calm himself down. Along the way to the historic part of town, he notices some kids in a parking lot smoking. They are smoking marijuana right out in the open with no fear.

Noticing Jack's attention, one kid says, "What you are looking at bum?"

Jack put his head down and walks at a brisk pace.

"That's what I thought," the kid says.

Jack continues his journey and observes how many pharmacies he comes across. We are taking drugs for everything. But if had the money, I would take drugs for my ailing knee. I would no longer walk with a limp. He keeps walking down the same street and really likes the smell of this city. It doesn't smell like a typical city. A streetsweeper rumbles by stirring up dust- the only time the streets are not squeaky clean. Jack covers his mouth as the machine passes him on the street.

Once in the historic part of town, he sits on a park bench and almost dozes off. This walk does a good job of making him sleepy. Strangely, a few bars are open on this weeknight.

He left his donation cup in his cardboard palace, but he has some dollars on him.

Jack contemplates going to a bar. To order a nice glass of wine and maybe a few shots of liquor. They say a little alcohol is good for the body as a faint smile comes across Jack's face. He hasn't had a drink in a long time. Not because he gave up alcohol, but because with his meager income drinking is expensive. He would have to choose between food or liquor.

He shakes the feeling of enjoying some firewater and walks around historic Vancouver. After about 5 minutes of walking, he is ready to return to his palace. The cobblestones are really penetrating his worn-out shoes. Which makes a comfortable walk impossible.

Chapter 2

So, Jack heads back home. The walk home takes forever. Jack is so sleepy that he could lie down on the side of the road right now. But he manages to wait until he is home to rest. Once there, he dozes off immediately.

Jack sleeps for about 11 hours- it's not like he has any obligations to be somewhere at a certain time. He isn't that hungry so; he empties the money currently in his donation cup and hides it in his cardboard palace. Then he saunters to a busy street and begins begging. By noon, Jack collects 20 dollars. He is hungry by this time, but again he doesn't want fast food.

He orders an Italian sub with the works and a huge drink from a local vendor. Jack sits on the nearest bench and gorges himself. The onions are so strong that their odor is coming through his pores. He finishes half of the sub. Takes a break and then quickly chomps down the final half.

Jack is being greedy. The sub already fills him up. Yet he orders a sundae from Dairy Queen. He takes four bites of it and throws the rest of it away. What a waste. He just can't consume anymore food. Jack sits in the restaurant for a good 15 minutes until he doesn't feel as stuffed. I don't want to read anything right now.

He goes back to his cardboard palace- grabs a pen and his novel and decides to write at the beach. Unfortunately, to get to the beach he must take a boat across the water. Which requires money. It's worth it so Jack uses some money from his now full donation cup. He arrives at the beach and fins a nice picnic table to write on. It's a weekday so the beach front area is not packed. A perfect place to relax and write. Jack is still stuck on how to begin this novel.

He hasn't done creative writing since college. He wasn't considered a gifted writer back then. He remembers one teacher who heavily criticized his work. She told him he was a terrible writer. I would have liked to critique her writing. Anyway, he blocks the negative out and comes back to the present time. It takes him awhile, but Jack finally knows what he wants his novel to be about: a basketball player. Jack brainstorms on how he wants the plot to go. He does this before writing anything down. Because that's what the great writer Virginia Wolfe did.

She thought about how a story should go before just writing everything on paper. I may read some of her work for inspiration. Jack gets back to writing his story. I t's a rags-to-riches story taking place in Maryland in the near present. Jack writes about 2 paragraphs and then brainstorms. This isn't as easy as I thought- creating an original novel. He takes a break. He goes into the beach bathroom and takes a shower. He doesn't have clean clothes or good soap. So, the hand soap with running water must do something. He looks at the grime coming off him and he immediately becomes a shade lighter. Since the water Is free, Jack stays in it until his skin prunes. He uses a towel that looks clean even though it was left over by someone else. I feel better now.

I'll sit at this picnic table and work on my novel. He writes for a long time. He puts together 20 pages. Which is pretty good since he sometimes suffers from paralysis of analysis. Meaning, he is uncertain of what sentence to write next.

Jack does not know the time, but his stomach lets him know it's time for food. Jack wants to eat healthful food, but when you are broke: extenuating circumstances.

I'm tired of McDonald's, but where else can I go? I'll try the soup kitchen. Jack drops his novel and writing utensil off at his cardboard palace. Then he heads to the soup kitchen for some vittles.

The smell of good food travels blocks from the kitchen. Which makes him even hungrier. By the time he gets to the soup kitchen, he is more than ready for a great meal. He eats there for about 20 minutes. There are other people there, but Jack ignores them and heads home. It's a lot easier to walk with a full stomach.

Some young guys in an Escalade are eyeing him. Jack avoids eye contact until they rev up the engine at the redlight. As Jacks looks up, one of the passengers gives him the middle finger. This happens to Jack every-now-and-then. Young kids with nothing better to do then to harass homeless people. Jack quickens his pace with his head down. Luckily, the guys just laugh for a bit and drive off.

Jack really could not have defended himself because he has no weapons. He gets to his palace and lies down. He managed to find a good flashlight about a month ago. He contemplates working on his novel but decides to just sleep. Even in a cardboard box, the right temperature and a full stomach make for an easy night of rest.

Chapter 3

INSIDE OF HIS PALACE the streetlights are no longer visible. Jack has a dream about Beth, his ex-wife. He comes home from work, and she wants a divorce. Sadly, this really happened after Jack quit his job at Panacea Pharmaceuticals. His parents were so embarrassed that they shunned him. He had no place to go with family. Jack pushes this reality out of his mind.

Before he knows it, the sun is coming up. As usual, once he gets up his stomach is growling. So, he walks to the nearest fast-food establishment. He wants to clean up a bit. So, once in the bathroom, he puts soap under his arms and nether regions. Then he wets a paper towel and cleans his whole body. He hates the smell of cheap hand soap, but it is better than the stench of body odor. After 15 minutes, Jack is done bathing and leaves the fast-food restaurant.

I guess I'll beg for a few dollars because I'm running low on cash. He walks to a busy street, Robson, picks out a high-traffic area and commences to begging. Most people look at him with disdain.

One man walks up to Jack and says, "Get a job like the rest of us!"

Then the man promptly walks away. He doesn't know what I've been through. Jack isn't even mad at the guy. Then Jack recalls his family disowning him.

"You are not my son! You're an embarrassment to us. You will never step foot in our house again!"

His dad's voice resonates in his head.

I can't stop these tears. I hate you dad! I'm relaxing now. I'm back to being calm. It's better to be a bum than live with hypercritical people. I'll get back to the present.

Jack holds is donation cup out and wonders what he'll buy with the money left over after he eats. It's summertime so I don't need any blankets. I need new shoes. I loved Michael Jordan' shoes when I was younger. I felt like the most popular kid in school with them on my feet. But someone always steps on them during the first day of school, I can't buy Jordan's now so I must settle for fish heads.

They aren't comfortable nor are they stylish. But they offer basic protection. After picking out a multi-colored pair of shoes, he pays half the cost in loose change. He is so excited. He can barely hide it. Then Jack treats himself by going to the bookstore across the street.

He stays in the bookstore for a long time. Because it has a Starbucks inside and the smell of coffee is intoxicating. Jack reads a lot of articles from a newspaper. His eyes glaze over from reading so much. His vision is blurry. Regardless, he buys a novel and reads it until dusk.

The age-old problem of hunger creeps into his mind. He contemplates digging in the trash to save a few dollars. He rarely does this because he got sick from eating a half-rotten sub a few months ago. Jack walks by a Mexican restaurant and decides he wants an authentic taco. He sits down in the shop for a few minutes. Then the manager approaches him. Jack is so hungry that he isn't thinking straight. He is ignorant of how he looks. But everyone else is not.

"Can I help you, senor?"

"I'd like a beef taco please."

The other customers are still staring at Jack, and he feels uncomfortable. Maybe I should get this taco to go. Well, the waiter isn't acting funny, so I'll stay.

It takes 45 minutes for his food to be ready. However, the aroma of this taco makes Jack forget about any complaint. The taco is extremely big. The meat is juicy and the vegetables in the taco are very fresh. The whole meal costs a whopping 15 dollars. Jack had to pay the last 6 dollars in loose change. Sleepy with a full stomach, Jack heads to the mall to sit in a plush chair to relax.

Some kids are playing videogames in an arcade. I used to love going to the arcade. Too bad there aren't many around now-a-days. Bored, Jack heads to his cardboard palace and goes right to sleep.

He is awakened by construction occurring a few streets away from his palace. The workers are tearing up the road. The jackhammers make sleep impossible. There is no way I can doze off through this. Somehow, he blocks out the noise and works on his novel. So consumed with writing, he loses track of time. He skips breakfast.

By the afternoon, he is hungry. He digs in his stash for money and wonders what and where to buy something to eat. So low on cash and famished, he goes against his commonsense and browses through the garbage of a popular eatery.

The food in the trash bin smells good. This sandwich has not even been bitten into. I'll take a small bite. Mmm. Very tasty. In the bag next to the sandwich are some potato chips. They taste good too. Wow! This is a decent meal.

Oh no! Negative thoughts flood my mind. Jack recalls his last conversation with his ex-wife before she left him.

"You quit your job? You practically gambled away most of our money on your real estate scheme! I'm done with you!"

"But Beth, you still have a decent amount of money in savings. We can tap into that until I find another job."

"No. You're too stupid. I'm divorcing you. See you in court."

Jack writes a poem on his ex-wife Beth:

> Beautiful face, ugly heart, her appearance had me from the start, later though her character I understood, it was all about looking good, don't tarnish the family name, always maintain a kind of snobbishness to those not as educated, respect for the poor, must at least have to have earned an undergraduate degree, to even talk to me, her parents are well-off, they have financial security, as well as my family, yet I'm humble mostly, I see with my eyes, but more so my heart, loving others like we were brothers from the start,

Tears stream down his face. I need to get these bad feelings out of me. Although having not been to church regularly since his high school days, he tries to recall the 23rd Psalm. I feel no different. Maybe watching the ocean will be soothing.

I do feel relaxed now observing nature. Those whitecaps on the mountains make me want to ski. I've never skied, but it may be as relaxing as watching the sea. As usual, hunger hits him, and Jack decides to go to the soup kitchen.

Instead of sitting by himself, Jack sits at the table of those he's seen frequently at the soup kitchen. They seem to be very friendly because as Jack sits down, they nod and smile.

"Hi, I'm Curtis. How are you doing?"

"I'm fine. How are you guys?"

They all say ok.

Jack looks up a few times and then digs into his plate. The meat is a little tough, but the vegetables taste great- especially the collard greens. The greens are so great that Jack can't remember ever tasting greens like these.

Jack finishes eating in what could be a Guiness world record. He gets seconds and finishes this plate quickly. Then he wonders how to talk to the people at the table. Jack doesn't want to offend anyone, so refrains from asking where they live or if they have jobs. I'll come up with a topic that's non-intrusive.

"So, what do you think of the food?"

"Well, I've had better roast beef, but you can't beat the potato salad and the vegetables," Curtis replies.

Then another person at the table, who has been looking at Jack intensely, says," Hey, I remember seeing you before at the beach. You are always writing something."

"Yeah, it helps to clear my mind. It's therapeutic. Maybe I'll share one of my great poems with you one day. As a matter of fact, I'll recite short poem that I've memorized right now:

> Why can't I get what I want now, instead of waiting around, my patience can only last so long, I'm aware of how short life can be, I can't believe, I'm already forty, seems like just the other day, I went away to college, a lot of late nights, studying until daylight, I was so disciplined, I knew exactly what I wanted then, a degree, now I want big money, I'm not a fortune teller, so I can't see into the future,

> God's got me, but I can still hear the whispers of Lucifer, do whatever it takes, take whatever you want, you are accountable to yourself only, by any means, do your thing, get that bling, yet I know not to go with the flow,

"So, Curtis, how long have you been struggling?"

"It's been about 2 years. I just can't find a great job. I've been working wherever I can and I'm just barely getting by." Curtis says while holding back tears.

Everyone tells their story. Jack realizes he isn't the only one hurting. Their stories don't really make him feel better about himself. In fact, he spaces out and wonders what will happen tomorrow. He doesn't want to go back to his cardboard palace. He just wants to go back home. Unfortunately, none of his family would greet him. He's an outcast. Now Jack envisions living in a mansion with exotic cars in his driveway.

"Jack! Jack!" Curtis says.

Jack snaps from his daydream. He looks at Curtis like a person who just woke up from a deep slumber. Jack looks confused.

"What's wrong Jack?" Curtis says.

Not wanting to tell the whole truth, Jack says, "I'm just ready to live like a normal person. I'm tired of struggling."

Everyone at the table nods.

"I just want to do well and not be in survival mode."

Feeling a bit uncomfortable with these questions, he excuses himself. He decides to head back "home" to sleep with a full stomach. His stomach hurts from stuffing himself. And from walking at a brisk pace. I don't remember the walk home taking this long. Jack gets a pain in his side and must take a little break.

Wow, this I really hurting me. Luckily, the pain subsides, and he can walk again. I'm ready to lie down. As Jack rounds the alley of his palace, worry strikes his heart. It looks as though his palace has been ransacked. The palace is hanging together loosely, but nothing that can't be repaired. However, as Jack looks inside, he's been had! A thief! All his money from begging is gone.

Jack had saved up to about 300 dollars. He had big plans to buy decent clothes. Now with nothing left, all he can do is shake his head. More so out of disappointment than anger.

What am I going to do? He holds back tears. Well, the dorms for the homeless are a long walk away. At least the thief didn't steal my duct tape. So, he repairs his home. It takes quite some time because he doesn't have a lot of tape. He must be efficient.

Jack is now exhausted. His fingers are sore from pulling tape. He's so tired to the point that he isn't sleepy. He lies down anyway, and his mind wanders into all kinds of strange thoughts. This may have come from some type of food he ate at the soup kitchen. I'm on a big yacht in the Mediterranean Sea. I'm in a desert in Saudi Arabia riding a camel.

This mind-wandering continues for about 2 hours and Jack still can't sleep. No big deal. It's not like I work. I get up when I wanna. Then Jack becomes angry about his money being stolen. I'm going to figure out who is the thief.

Maybe I should question some of the drug addicts I occasionally talk to about a block away. Jack is jumping to conclusions now. However, deep down, he believes he'll never find the thief. The city is just too big. Jack is no longer angry and manages to get some sleep. He sleeps well throughout the night.

As usual, his empty, growling stomach is his alarm clock. Since I have no money, I'll do some begging and eat a fast-food joint. All that grease may hurt my stomach, but at least I will be full.

The fast-food restaurant is close to his sleeping quarters. I'll beg for a few minutes to buy a couple of sandwiches. So, he puts on his dirtiest shirt to create even more sympathy. He collects 5 dollars. At the restaurant, he scarves down all the food he can buy. Now I can think clearly.

That's one thing about this life- once you get some food, there is almost nothing to do. What should I do now? I'll try to read my poems for pocket change. I'll read my works on the main street.

He picks a popular corner that gets a lot of foot traffic. I really want music to each of my poems, but I don't have any musical talents. I'll make do with what I have. Jack has a sign reading "Great poet struggling. Deposit loose change for inspiration." Jack has a couple of inquisitive minds staring at the placard.

One person deposits a dollar and asks, "So, are you any good?"

Jack replies, "You be the judge."

He clears his throat and reads one of his poems "Places":

> Places to go, people to see, writing helps me
> deal with poverty, maybe with the change I
> collect, I should play the lottery, no, I'll take
> my chances writing about my circumstances,
> not to evoke pity, but to show I'm witty, my
> lines smooth never gritty, or I can switch it
> up with a poem so poignant, it will leave you
> teary-eyed, I know what I'm doing, I've got

hooks like a truant, a great poet the world
will be pursuing,

Jacks looks up after reading this poem: observing the body language of this middle-aged man. The man claps and then drops a 5-dollar bill into Jack's donation cup. The man has a smile on his face. The clapping draws even more attention to Jack's enterprise and Jack is delighted.

People deposit money into his donation cup as Jack reads more of his poems for a good part of the day. And when he is done reading them, he has a decent amount of dollars.

Maybe I'll start reading my short stories. Having eaten a few hours ago, Jack is ready for the night. I might as well sleep now.

Jack is up early before rush hour. He decides to go for a stroll; not sure of where he'll end up. With money in his pocket, Jack wonders if he should buy something nice. He heads to the shopping district. He's looking for anything that catches his eye.

He enters one shop that looks as though anime books are sold there. There is a sign indicating the entire collection upstairs. Jack is on the ground floor and sees some music albums. One of the artists albums is an Asian reggae singer. Jack listens to a few songs. Not bad.

Still browsing on the first floor, he spots some special type of Far East Asian candy. Jack is hesitant to try it because it doesn't resemble any candy he has ever seen. Maybe another time. Jack walks upstairs.

The store has an amazing anime collection. Wow! He spends 45 minutes paging through some anime classics. The store owner approaches Jack and looks at him suspiciously. Jack ignores the owner and continues to read to his heart's content.

After about 45 minutes, the owner says, "So, what you buy?"

Jack looks down at the price of one magazine: 20 dollars.

Jack replies, "No. I'm just looking."

"Well, you need to buy something."

Jack reads one more page and decides it is time to leave this place. Where to go next?

Jack counts the money he made yesterday and plans to save it for a rainy day. He goes to the park to gather his thoughts. It's such a beautiful day. Not a cloud in the sky. It takes time to get to the park and it is crowded. It's not that relaxing with so many people around. Dogs are barking. Kids are crying. Everything is just loud. Jack tries to tolerate the noise by spacing out.

He wonders if he'll ever have a family again. He recalls reading to his son, Brent, every night with Classical music playing in the background. That music is supposed to make children smarter. Brent was a decent student before the divorce. Tears come to his eyes remembering Brent's first steps. Then a dog jumps over the bench where Jack is sitting. The dog is chasing after a tennis ball. This knocks Jack to the present and he walks in the park.

He carefully avoids animal dung and observes people playing tennis. The players aren't highly skilled, but at least they look to be having a great time. In fact, none of the tennis players look that serious. This brings a smile to Jack's face. He keeps walking- seeing some kids feeding fish in the stream flowing through the park. The fish are big, and the kids just love watching them swim. Jack continues strolling around the park until he must take a break.

His feet hurt because he isn't wearing his good shoes. Luckily, that thief just wanted hard cash. Jack rests for an hour and then he is back strolling in the park- enjoying every moment. Now Jack is bored out of his mind. He doesn't want to read or write anything. I just want to do nothing. So, he goes back to his cardboard palace and takes a nap. He naps for a long time. He wakes up around midnight.

Chapter 4

JACK JUMPS UP AND hits the local corner store for some grub. He eats a couple honeybuns and drinks 2 pints of milk. I'll probably have a stomachache later, but I need something to eat. Sure enough, an hour later he is lying down with a lot of pain in his stomach. Jack is thinking about going to the hospital, but then the pain subsides.

It's too dark to read and most stores are closed. So, Jack lays down with his eyes wide open. His mind begins to wander. Negative thoughts pervade his mind. He wants to buy alcohol-he knows it will clear his mind if only for a day. But he fights this urge because he realizes that is what the average bum would do. This last thought leaves Jack incensed at his own failures. He starts cursing at every negative emotion that overcomes him. He is now steaming mad that he can't control his emotions. He's a wreck. Suddenly, these thoughts fade away and life isn't unbearable at all. Jack remembers seeing children fishing at the park. Brent, I love you. Then he slowly falls to sleep.

As usual, his growling stomach wakes him up. He is calm now, but Jack is thinking about why he is a bum. It's been a long time. He has no running water or toilet. No electricity. Strangely, what he misses the most is not those things, but just some quiet. When you live on the street, there is always noise. Whether it be: people talking, cars whizzing by, or construction going on.

Today is no different. Some loudmouths walking by are arguing about who is better: Kobe or Lebron? These guys are really getting into it. It's like they are getting louder to make their points. Jack is really annoyed and thinks about saying something. As soon as he sticks his head out of his cardboard palace, the guys lower their voices. Not out of respect, but because other people on the street are staring at them. Jack is relieved because he truly dislikes interacting with people when he is mad.

He calms down immediately, and food is back on his mind. He grabs the donation cup and begs for money on a busy street. Jack contemplates reading some of his writings for money, but at the last minute he just takes his cup. He begs until he acquires enough money to buy breakfast at a fast-food joint. But first he needs a shower.

He buys cheap soap from Dollar General and goes to the beach. Because there are showers there. These shoers are intended to just wash off sand, but Jack uses them for good hygiene. Jack is as clean as a whistle. He thinks about acquiring decent clothing.

Breakfast is very good. So, Jack is fully satisfied. I really need a decent job. He thinks about this as he browses the drugstore. Everything is so expensive. Maybe I should go back to Dollar General. Jack digs in his pocket. He is delighted to find a twenty-dollar bill. He buys some essentials: toothpaste, a toothbrush, soap, shampoo, and hair tonic. Razors are not that cheap. So, Jack must dip into his pocket again to pay for the razors.

Unfortunately, Jack needs and wants a haircut. But getting one would hurt his pockets. He thinks of buying scissors and going for broke. No, that would really look messed up. He decides to keep his hair long. Jack heads to the restroom and uses the toothbrush and toothpaste immediately. What a relief.

Jack walks back to his palace with a limp. His shoes are so worn out that he can feel the pebbles beneath him- not just the rocks. He changes shoes immediately and then counts his money. Time to make more. Jack gets ready for his hustle by looking over some of his writings. He selects what he believes to be his best short story. Jack rereads it a few times; making sure it flows well. He also studies a couple of his poems. And he wonders if he should write more poems or edit the ones he has written. I might as well do both.

Jack walks to a convenience store and drinks green tea. He's making sure his vocal cords are warmed up and ready. The warmth of the tea goes from his mouth to his entire head. He's totally relaxed and is optimistic that he'll make good money today. He believes there may be some literary agents looking at him doing his craft. Jack strolls to a spot on a busy street. It's a beautiful day. The sun is out and it's about 65 degrees. Just warm enough to be comfortable outside without a heavy coat or jacket.

Jack is reading his best short story. As usual, most people ignore him. As he reads the 4th and 5th paragraph, one person stops to listen. The short story takes about 7 minutes to read. One person deposits 3 dollars for Jack.

"Thank you. You are giving to a good cause."

Now he is in the mood to read one of his poems. He rifles through one of his poetry books searching for a great poem. This takes quite a bit of time. Here's a great one:

> You can lose a lot of things, but never lose hope, especially in yourself, you must maintain good mental health, no matter the situation, even though things look bad, they could be worse, I get a burst, of energy, thinking of

> how good life can be, even as a bum, I believe, everything happens for a reason, things may look up in the next season, the tides of life are just that,

When he finishes reading the poem, a small group assembled around him claps. Jack is so proud of himself. Well, time to eat. With this money in his pocket, Jack wants to eat at a decent restaurant. Instead of consuming unhealthy fast food. Riding high, Jack goes to an Italian restaurant.

It's a few blocks away so, he hails a taxi instead of walking. The taxi has that new car smell which smells strange to Jack. He hasn't been in a taxi in a very long time. The cab driver is taking his time by going up the main roads instead of taking shortcuts. This longer ride doesn't bother Jack. Since he's high on life right now. Jack is spaced out during the ride. The driver has to say something to snap Jack back down to Earth.

Jack strolls up to the classy restaurant and is quickly escorted to a fine table. He looks around slowly. Taking everything in. Counting his money mentally, Jack decides to go all out and buys a 5-course meal. He orders some mussels as an appetizer. Jack tries to be calm as he eats the seafood. He hasn't had a truly 5-course meal in a very long time. Since he published a paper in a scientific journal. Jack savors every bite because he wants to enjoy what he pays for.

Next, Jack orders a big plate of chicken penne pasta. The pasta is so well seasoned that Jack wants to give his compliment to the chef. After this great entrée, Jack feasts on a tiramisu for dessert. It's made just right- it has a little tart taste, but it is still sweet. Jack is now stuffed. He pays for the meal and drops a handsome tip.

He leaves the restaurant with his head held high like he

won the lottery. It's almost dark now and he isn't sure what to do next. It is far too early to go back to his cardboard palace and go to sleep. He feels too old to celebrate at a nightclub. Plus, he hasn't been to one in a very long time.

I'll go to the mall and maybe buy something that doesn't cost too much. The mall isn't crowded. Jack starts limping again. But this time he has his good shoes on. Jack is very concerned. What if I need surgery? I can't even afford to go to the emergency room. Oh yeah, I'm not in the U.S. They say everyone gets treated for free in hospital in Canada. There's got to be a catch. I can't imagine free health care. I'll just head to my cardboard palace to rest my leg.

Jack lies down for an hour but is then bored. He wants to walk around, but his leg throbs in pain whenever he moves it. I need a good bath. The pain subsides, but he doesn't want to get up yet. Jack sings some well-known songs to lift his spirits. Surprisingly, this makes him feel better.

Then Jack drifts off to sleep. He wakes up in 30 minutes-his leg is back hurting. It's impossible to relax when experiencing this throbbing pain. Jack pops a painkiller. Jack can't sleep yet since the pill doesn't work instantaneously. But in a few hours, he drifts back off to sleep. Jack dreams about playing basketball with his son Brent. They are playing one-on-one.

Brent is getting the best of him on a sunny, cloudless day with a slight breeze. Well, Jack isn't playing his hardest. Although losing, Jack is having the time of his life. Both are smiling ear-to-ear and doing a bit of showboating. Jack tries a crossover, but Brent picks his pocket. Brent then checks up, blows by his dad, and makes a lay-up. Jack applauds the move and then gets the ball after Brent misses a long shot. Jack drains a jumper. All net! Boom! The Earth shakes, but Jack is no longer dreaming.

Chapter 5

He opens his eyes to find three teenage boys standing over him grinning. Still a bit groggy, Jack is then at full attention when he is kicked in the ribs. As he struggles to catch his breath, the boys laugh hysterically. They must have no conscience to pick on a homeless man.

"Get a job!" One of them yells.

The boys keep laughing and taunting Jack. Jack isn't mad but scared. He's heard of people roughing up homeless people before. He thinks about running and then they kick him again. Right in the solar plexus. They don't stop kicking him until they get tired. Luckily, they only stomped his body and left his head alone.

"You are worthless to society!" They yell.

Then they walk away looking side-to-side to make sure no one is watching them. Jack has never broken a rib, but his side hurts every time he breathes. How can I sleep now? Fortunately, he is not spitting up blood. Meaning, he is not bleeding internally.

I've got to get to a hospital. Jack can barely move. Maybe the pain will subside in a few hours. He is right. 3 hours later, Jack is not only breathing without pain, but he can stand up without any problem. Jack walks around the block without any pain. Not even his leg hurts. He's happy.

Then he becomes angry when he recalls what those boys did to him. He contemplates moving his cardboard palace elsewhere. But his current spot is usually safe. I'll think about moving another day.

It's not too cold today, but there is a certain crispness in the air. Jack is walking around with a light coat, but the cold doesn't seem to bother him. In fact, his torso feels warm from the throbbing pain from being stomped. The sunrise is beautiful with the mountains in the background.

Jack takes all this in and says under his breath, "What a beautiful morning. Everything is going my way."

He tries to cheer himself up. Jack walks back to his palace and composes this poem:

> Put down by society, uplifted by my own mind, as I climb to reach the peak of just being happy, from getting beat up to being praised, just because of how I can phrase, any emotion or feeling, so my poems are appealing, to all who hear them, I'm sure even in the next life or realm, my ability, skill with the pen, my mental agility, will make any audience love me,

It took Jack 45 minutes to write this short poem. I'll read this poem today. I know I'll make money doing this. Jack gathers some of his writings and heads to a main street to beg. But today, there is little foot traffic. I guess it's a holiday. However, Jack is still confident that he'll make a lot of money today.

He lays down a towel to put his writings on. He is ready to begin. Jack looks around. And as usual, gets the evil eye from passersby. Having encountered this many times before, he is in no way intimidated. Jack gulps down a bottle of water, clears his throat and reads this poem about overcoming obstacles:

> From prince to pauper, I've experienced what this world has to offer, a big house, a couple foreign cars, now I'm far, from having money to spend, yet I'm confident, I'll overcome, no adversity is realistic to me, no doubt what I've been up against, is a mountain not a molehill, yet still, I'll scale whatever is in the field, of my dreams,

This poem is riveting and catches the ear of a lot of people. Once Jack finishes reading it, he attracts a small crowd. Some in the crowd drop a few dollars for him. They are eager to hear much more from this wordsmith.

Jack asks the crowd, "What do you want to hear, a poem or a short story?"

"The story takes place in ancient America involving a conflict between two tribes. One tribe dominates one side of the river, and the other tribe dominates the other side of the river. Both tribes are rather small. So, there is no competition for natural resources like trees and animals. Particularly fish captured from the river. Yet the chiefs of these tribes have had disagreements for well over two decades.

Surprisingly, no one has been killed- just a bunch of posturing and exchanging disrespectful words. Finally, after pleading to one of the chiefs, a young man crosses the river to negotiate with the other tribe. Scared out of his mind, this brave man canoes right towards the hub of the other tribe. But not without shaking from the fear of death. Luckily, he is not shot with an arrow or even beaten. The other chief welcomes him into the tepee and they have a discussion.

Neither tribe seems to want land, but only respect. The chief offers a peace pipe to the young man to smoke tobacco. Still wary of this tribe, the young man smokes reluctantly-believing he will be scalped. But not a hair on his head is harmed. The chief makes a few jokes and the young man canoes back to his chief. He tells the chief everything that happens. So, now it seems that the tribes will get along.

Later that night, the young man has a dream. He dreams of a time with never-ending food. An abundance of fish in the river and small mammals throughout the forest. He wakes up with a smile on his face and wants to tell his chief this vision. But as he approaches the chief, he knows something is wrong. The chief has such a grave look on his face that anyone can see.

The young man finds out that the truce has been broken and the chief's son is a hostage. His son was kidnapped as he was canoeing for leisure. The other tribe demands meat and goods made from deerskin. They say if they do not get these things, the chief's son is a goner. Obviously, this frightens the chief, and he is more sad than angry. Some in his tribe believe they should wage war. But the chief reminds them that it's been 7 generations since their tribe battled over anything. The chief wants to appease the other tribe in pretty much any way.

So, the tribe gives fur coats and moccasins, but to no avail. The other tribe takes the gifts and now wants land on the other side of the river. The chief holds a meeting. Many of its members want to send a small group to sneak across the river and seize the chief's son. Still against any form of war, the chief thinks by himself for a few hours. After smoking the peace pipe, ironically, he decides on war.

Some in his council state that if we win, we should take the other tribe's land. This makes the chief nervous that many in his tribe are so greedy. He just wants his son back. He wonders what will happen if his tribe wins and he refuses to split up the conquered land.

This thought keeps the chief up all night. Before attacking the tribe, he tries for peace one more time. He sends one of his diplomats to the other tribe. This diplomat comes back shocked at how callous the other chief is. Wide-eyed, he tells his chief that his son has already been killed. So, now the chief sends his best warriors to destroy the other tribe.

Livid as any father would be, the chief doesn't calm down until the war is over. His tribe is victorious, and he personally scalps the other tribe's chief."

"The end." Jack says.

A man then asks, "What is the moral of the story?"

"Don't make waves in a calm sea. Meaning, when things are going well don't always change something. Even for the so called better because it may not be to your advantage. So, be cautious of change."

The man is impressed and drops a few dollars in Jack's donation box.

"I need a break," Jack says.

The crowd disperses for a bit as Jack wets his palate with water. Maybe my writings will sell. He smiles, clears his throat and spends the rest of the day reading his short stories out loud. Finally, the sun sets, and Jack is very tired and hungry. I'll go to the soup kitchen to save money. While walking to the soup kitchen, he drops his writings off at home. Back at home, he hides his writings, believing that they may be stolen just like his money not too long ago.

Chapter 6

HE CATCHES THE TIME from a screen in front of a bank. The soup kitchen closes soon. Jack picks up his walking pace and is almost jogging. He can smell the food before reaching the kitchen. It smells like lobster. He can't remember the last time free lobster was an option. But sure enough, there are plates of steamed lobster.

Jack looks around and sees Curtis sitting in his usual spot with his usual group of friends. Jack waves at Curtis and is glad to find a familiar face. Jack's stomach rumbles and he heads to the line. He sees scallops and shrimp. Surprisingly, the line is not long- meaning Jack may be able to get seconds. The smell of food makes him even hungrier. He wants to cut in line to quickly get some lobster.

"Hey Curtis," Jack says once he has a plate of seafood.

Curtis looks shocked at Jack's friendliness, but responds calmy, "Fine."

Then Jack cracks open a lobster shell dives in. But he still minds his manners and doesn't go caveman on his food. Ironically, the more lobster Jack devours the hungrier he feels. Only after his 4th lobster does he feel full.

Then he wants to talk. Jack hasn't said much to Curtis or anyone at the soup kitchen.

He strikes up a conversation saying, "So Curtis, what did you do for a living?"

"Well, I was a carpenter for some time until I was laid-off. I've been out of steady work for about 2 years. I'm just glad my kids are grown. So, I don't have to raise them in my current state. In fact, I wanted to stay with one of them, but I feel embarrassed. I'm a man. I should provide for myself.

Curtis's answer shocks Jack. Jack did not want to talk about anything deep- just small talk. As others at the table share their stories, Jack realizes his own misconceptions about the homeless. They aren't lazy people: they've just fallen into hard times. This kind of makes Jack feel better about himself. Now Jack no longer wants to live away from everyone. So, he asks about any living quarters at a local shelter. It's not a real house, but it's better than my current situation.

Usually, Jack leaves the soup kitchen when he finishes his meal. But he stays there conversing with folk- these people are making him happy because he doesn't have to go at it alone.

Jack follows them to the shelter. Fortunately, it is not far from the soup kitchen. So, the journey does not require money for public transportation. Jack looks around on the way to the shelter. He notices that the roads aren't quite as clean as the center city roads. And the buildings are dingy on the outside. There is also a stench in the air emanating from something Jack can't quite figure out.

At the shelter, Jack is assigned a relatively plush cot and a quilted blanket. He is glad to be here, but he worries about his belongings back at his cardboard palace. He is especially worried about his precious writings. Plus, reading some of them out loud puts some money in his pocket. I'll get them tomorrow. I'll stretch out on this cot now.

He looks around and Curtis is already snoring. Good

meals don't make Jack sleepy. As the lights are dimmed, he is still wide awake. He is contemplating how well he has been treated. Finally, after about an hour of being on the cot, Jack fades into dreamland. When he awakens, Curtis and the others are cleaning their cots.

"You must've had a long day," Curtis says.

A worker at the shelter tosses Jack cleaning supplies and Jack rubs down his cot. Jack looks up at the clock. It's 10:00 AM.

"Breakfast is ready!" One of the workers exclaims.

Jack doesn't smell sausage or anything. And a few minutes later, he finds out why. It's nothing but a continental breakfast. This does not satisfy Jack. He tells Curtis he is heading to McDonalds's down the road. He is addicted to their breakfast.

McDonald's may just be fast-food, but their breakfast is excellent. Especially for a man wanting something filling. Jack pays for his meal in one-dollar coins and some quarters. He buys a large orange juice and three sausage egg McMuffin sandwiches. By the time he is done eating, his stomach protrudes, but he feels good.

Jack walks back to the shelter and there is no sign of any cots. Everyone is socializing until a worker directs some people into a room. Where they begin reading books on different subjects.

Jack is wowed by this and is glad when a worker signals for him to enter this smaller room. He notices that this room isn't just for reading, but for learning. They teach homeless people to read and to write. Once Jack tells the workers he can read, they hand him a book. It's a classic novel, and they tell him to read to a homeless man. Who doesn't read well. Jack happily obliges and spends an hour reading aloud. Until the homeless man interrupts him.

"Son, you seem very smart. Why are you here?"

Not wanting to go into detail about his personal life, Jack replies, "Hard times."

The homeless man can hear the tone in Jack's voice and says, "Please, keep reading."

Jack continues reading until his voice is raspy and he becomes hoarse. The homeless man is extremely grateful and Jack drinks a bottle of water. After drinking H20, Jack's voice comes back. A worker notices this but decides that Jack has read aloud long enough. So, he hands Jack a book for leisure. Jack reads for 45 minutes until Curtis interrupts him.

"Hey Jack, what do you think of our training program?"

"Well, it's great, but I need money. Is there any way I can get paid to help others?"

"You should talk to the boss. I'll take you to him now."

"Hey James, I have a new guy for you," Curtis says.

James looks indifferent and says," Hey."

Jack doesn't care much for this type of attitude, so he replies without any emotion, "Hey."

"So, what can I help you with?"

"I'd like to read to people to earn money," Jack says.

"You should know we don't pay much. By the way you talk I can tell you are educated. So, you can teach people to read better. You'll make minimum wage. You can start as soon as we get the paperwork done."

Wow! I won't have to beg on the street. A mile comes across Jack's face. Curtis and Jack walk out of the office and decide to celebrate. They go to a seafood restaurant.

The waiter asks what they want to eat, and he quickly responds, "Lobster."

Before he was homeless, Jack ate lobster all the time. Because he could afford to. After the meal, they go to the mall to window-shop. Jack loves new clothes and shoes and stares at an outfit. He promises to buy it when he acquires more money. They head back to the shelter and Jack is eager to read to someone.

Jack is given a history book to read to a homeless woman, Anna. Anna is very tall and has a model-like body. She is very reserved- she only looks up to Jack for a few seconds before dropping her head.

Jack asks, “Why do you want me to read a history book?”

“Because that is what my dad used to do before he passed away.”

The subject matter is a bit dry; the book is about French kings, but Anna listens intently. The book is thick and after about 70 pages, Jack’s voice is giving out. He drinks water and takes his time to regain his concentration. Jack reads the entire book to Anna, and now it’s time to go to the soup kitchen for dinner. Jack remembers eating lobster there and wonders what they’ll serve tonight. Hopefully some pasta because it’s one of his favorite meals.

Fortunately, that’s what is for dinner- baked ziti and ravioli. He always loved ravioli as a kid, but this isn’t canned ravioli. It’s fresh, homemade ravioli. Once again, Jack finds himself salivating from the pleasant odor emanating from Italian food. He has never had homemade ravioli- he has never had ravioli not in a can. So anxious to try something new, he walks quickly to where a line is forming.

It doesn’t take long to get the food and Jack digs in immediately. The smell matches the taste, and he is thoroughly satisfied.

Curtis snickers at him and asks, “You aren’t hungry, are you?”

“Oh sorry. I love this type of food.”

Curits chomps on the ravioli and says, "Wow! This dish is good."

"Yes, they are good, and I haven't had homemade ravioli."

After dinner, they walk back to the shelter. The staff at the shelter set up Bingo as entertainment. Jack isn't all that fond of the game but participates anyway. Bingo is one way to pass the time. Before they know it, it is time for bed. Jack didn't come close to winning a single game.

The next day, Jack reads The Hobbit to a homeless man. The man listens to every word. You can tell by his eyes that he is paying close attention. This motivates Jack to continue reading. Even though he is exhausted from reading so much. In fact, it's now afternoon and Jack wants to take a nap.

He tries to shake off this feeling and tells the guy, "I need a break."

Jack finds a plush chair and dozes off. He dreams of living in a mansion somewhere in the Caribbean. Jack walks on the beach while sipping on a smoothie. Then he stretches out in a hammock taking in the sun. Jack naps for a good hour until he feels a tapping on his knee. He opens one of his eyes and James is standing over him with his arms crossed.

"This is not what I pay you for. Rise and shine. Get back to work!"

Still a bit groggy, Jack says under his breath, "Best of times, worst of times."

Chapter 7

JACK GETS ON HIS feet and notices the homeless man that he read The Hobbit to is nowhere to be found. Jack panics some not knowing what to do next. Because he wants to appear busy in case James comes by again. With nothing to do, he tries to find Curtis in the shelter. After walking down a few hallways, Jack spots Curtis on a computer. He's working on his resume.

"Hey Curtis, what kind of job are you looking for?"

"Well, I want a decent-paying job just to have money to move into a real house. I've been searching for a good job for a while, but to no avail," Curtis replies.

Jack feels sad because Curtis seems to be a good guy. He lost his job due to downsizing and could no longer support himself. Jack wonders if he himself will ever find gainful employment. Working at the shelter put some money in his pocket, but not enough to live comfortably. Jack misses his privacy and there is always some noise at the shelter.

Curtis is now looking for a job in Marine Construction that is based at the local dock. It pays a good salary, and the hours aren't that bad. He just must get up early in the morning.

While filling out an application, he asks Jack, "Why don't you try to get a job with me? It's hard work at times, but you'll learn a lot. And you'll gain skill in working with your hands."

Jack contemplates this. He is getting tired of being in the shelter practically all day. Plus, there is nothing like fresh air.

Jack replies, "You know what? I might as well try it. Even though I've never worked with my hands. Let alone doing so for an extended period."

"I'm sure you'll get this job, and we'll work together. It will be fun," Curtis says.

Jack finds an unoccupied computer and fills out an application for Marine Construction. Some questions are difficult to answer- seeing that he doesn't know the terminology used in this line of work. He manages to fill out the application with Curtis's help. After submitting the application, Jack searches on the internet. He studies Marine Construction.

Then, he thinks about his true love- writing. He hasn't been writing for quite some time. He's been focused on his job at the shelter. In fact, Jack hasn't been thinking about writing until now. Jack does have a locker containing his writings. He plans to at least look at them before the day is over.

Right now, Jack wants to sleep because he didn't sleep well last night. The food from the soup kitchen hurt his stomach. This is unusual since the soup kitchen food tastes very good. This is the first time anything from there gave him any trouble. Not even indigestion. That was short-lived. Jack's stomach does not hurt now.

Just as he gets up from the computer, James approaches him and asks, "When are you going to read to somebody?"

Jack replies, "Well, I can do that now. But hopefully I'll start a job soon in Marine Construction."

"Until then, we can still use a reader. So please, help again with another homeless man. He loves Mark Twain so read Tom Sawyer to him when you get a chance."

Jack nods his head. When James walks away, Jack rolls

his eyes. Yet Jack is smart enough to not tell anyone about his discontent for James too much. Because James will eventually find out. Living in the shelter is way better than that cardboard palace.

A homeless man looks to be waiting. This man's eyes light up when he sees Jack coming closer. Jack is already a bit of a legend around here. Because he is such a good reader. A lot of people literally line up to hear him read classic novels. The man waiting has his hands gripped on Tom Sawyer.

He eagerly hands Jack the book and says, "Read!"

Of course, Jack begins to read and finds himself enthralled in this classic book. The book seems even better when read aloud. Jack reads so long that the homeless man falls asleep and snores lightly. Jack, immersed in the book, doesn't notice that the man is sleep. He continues reading until his eyes cross and only then does he notice the man I sleep. The man is really sleep because he is drooling. Jack closes the book and puts it on the man's leg.

Jack is now bored. Yes, he could work on his writings, but his eyes hurt from reading so much. He walks around the shelter wondering if there is any activity he can do. Jack doesn't want to socialize and he's neither tired nor sleepy. He decides to take a stroll outside. It's a beautiful night.

It's still a few hours until dinner. The neighborhood is nice. Even though he is downtown, the city does not smell like a city. The area he is walking through smells good because of a flower shop nearby. Jack is walking slowly. After about a block, he takes a turn. He plans to walk one block, turn right and then walk back to the shelter.

Some shops are still open, and he peers into the window of a clothing shop. The shop has nice jeans on display along with stylish shoes. Jack wants these shoes, but they are way out of his price range. I'll buy these shoes when my writing career takes off. Jack stares at these shoes for a while. He fixes a mental picture of them for motivation. Then Jack keeps strolling down the street- not thinking about much.

Jack then realizes it's time to go back to the shelter. Because it's time for dinner at the soup kitchen. As soon as he arrives at the shelter, everyone lines up and begins the journey to the soup kitchen.

He catches up with Curtis. Who says, "Where have you been? James has been looking for you. You aren't gonna quit, are you?"

Jack replies, "No way. I enjoy reading aloud. I needed fresh air."

Then from behind James says, "Well, get air when you are off. But when you work, I want you reading."

Jack responds, "Ok" and wonders why he allows James to talk to him any old way.

I mean I'm not a kid. Next time I'm saying something.

So, they walk to the soup kitchen. Jack is still mad at how James talks to him. Even at dinner, Jack remains tense.

Finally, Curtis asks, "Hey, what's going on?"

Jack tries to play it off with a smile, but then says, "You know James is getting under my skin. I'm ready to take a shot at him. I won't, but doesn't he irritate you?"

Curtis responds, "Of course. He is very condescending, but to live in this shelter you've gotta block him out. Just try to ignore him. And don't take it to heart when he's sarcastic. And once you get the Marine Construction job, you should have enough money to move out in a couple months."

Jack takes a deep breath and is calmed by the thought of having his own place. He devours his meal and feels better now with a full stomach. He sips some soda. It's very strong- stinging this throat like no other. Then Jack contemplates his life in that cardboard palace.

I could've been killed out there. I'm not putting myself through that again. Jack wonders what his son and other family members are doing. I may contact them one day soon. Jack has been telling himself that for years. In fact, he feels worthless and a deadbeat for not being there for his son. Even though his family shuns him, Jack wants to go back home. Jack tears up over this thought, but then forces this idea out of his mind. The hard knock life. Jack joins the conversation at the table. They are talking about the best books they have read.

As the discussion continues, Jack gets animated and says, "War and Peace is the best book hands down."

Jack recalls reading this book in college. It's a large one, but reading the entire book is very satisfying. To his surprise, no one at the table had read the novel. He advises them to check it out. Reading kept Jack alive during those rough days. The escape from enduring the life in his cardboard palace made living bearable. Jack smiles to himself; he realizes he'll probably never have to live on the streets anymore. Although in a way Jack liked privacy, he had which living on the streets.

Then people at the table talk about their favorite foods and then some random things. Attempting to take his mind off harrowing thoughts, Jack chimes in- stating lasagna is by far the best dish out there. He talks about a restaurant in the city that serves excellent Italian food. He promises to treat everyone at the table to a free dinner. Once he has some money saved up. Jack really means good. Although he isn't sure when he'll be able to do that. I need this construction job.

The group talks for a good two hours and then James says, "Well, dinner is over. Time to go back to the shelter."

There is a lot of groaning. Because most people are relaxing and enjoying having some space. The shelter is overcrowded. Everyone walks back to the shelter. Jack cannot look at James without having ill feelings. His fists are clenched, but he calms down after remembering what Curtis told him. Jack has always been laid-back, but James is really under his skin like no other person before. Well, then Jack recalls his ex-wife. Which proves false his previous thought. He chuckles at this.

I need to get back to writing. I haven't written much since staying in the shelter. I'll get to it soon. As soon as Jack relaxes at the shelter, reading a good book, James comes by.

James doesn't even say hi, but says, "Well Jack, I've got someone who wants to be read to."

Jack doesn't look up from his book.

And then James taps him on the shoulder and says," Hey, I'm talking to you!"

James glares at Jack as if he's ready to do him bodily harm. In fact, James seems like the one being antagonized- his face twitching with anger. For some reason, Jack is surprisingly unfazed by James like he is a Buddhist monk. Jack doesn't care about how annoying James has been.

He calmly looks up to James and replies, "Ok."

This demeanor seems to irk James. As if he doesn't know what to do. So, he walks away. Jack even surprises himself with how nonchalant he is.

Chapter 8

"SO, WHAT IS YOUR name?" Jack asks the man he is about to read to.

"Well, I'm Harry. I just learned to read a month ago. My dad always told me to read Charles Dickens's books one day. So, I want you to read Oliver Twist to me. And then I'll read this wonderful novel myself.

Wow! For him to be basically illiterate so late in life. Jack feels sorry for the guy and decides to read to him right now.

"Great! Let's get started Jack!"

"Ok. Um humm."

Then, Jack begins reading. After about the tenth page, Harry closes his eyes. Jack stops reading for a second. Figuring that Harry is tired. But then Harry opens his eyes.

"I'm just visualizing every phrase. Go on." Harry says impatiently.

So, Jack continues reading. It is now 10:00 PM: time for bed. As soon as Jack stops reading, Harry opens his eyes, and a tear drops from one of them.

"I always wanted my father to read this book to me before he passed away from cancer. I know he's looking down from heaven smiling at this moment."

Jack chokes up and then recalls reading to his son Brent

many years ago. He wants to call Brent now. Before Jack goes to sleep, a few tears fall on his pillow.

Wow. I need more rest, Jack thinks as he wakes up in the morning. He slept all through the night, but he's still sleepy. He gets ready for the day. And everyone at the shelter is ready to walk to the soup kitchen. Jack walks over to Curtis- who appears to be in a good mood.

"Hey Curtis, you seem so happy."

"Yeah. Everything seems to be going my way. I talked to my family, and they want me back home."

This news makes Jack mad. He doesn't have the courage to call his relatives. His sense of shame is too great. And his family has made no attempts to contact him.

"That's good to hear Curtis. So, when are you leaving this place.?"

"Well, I'm not exactly sure. Hopefully within a few weeks. My family is trying to find me a decent job. I can't believe they still love me so deeply. Especially since they pushed me away a while ago."

"Sounds like my family," Jack replies.

Jack really wants to leave with Curtis. He is the only friend Jack has at the shelter. Yes, the food at the soup kitchen is great, but there is something missing.

"We should celebrate!" Jack says.

"Yes, we should. But what are we going to do?" Curtis asks.

"I'm not exactly sure. I'll think of something," Jack replies.

On the way to the soup kitchen, Curtis can't stop talking about his home. Most people would be annoyed by this. But Jack, although a bit jealous, is happy for him. Jack can't see himself living in the shelter for a long time. This must be like prison, Jack thinks. At the soup kitchen, Curtis is still talking.

Jack doesn't want to be rude, but he finally says, "I'm happy for you, but calm down."

"You are right. I guess I am somewhat annoying. I just can't wait to live like a normal person again. This is going to be wonderful."

Curtis is smiling from ear-to-ear. Jack isn't that hungry and only eats a bowl of cereal. After breakfast, James announces something new for those at the shelter to do.

"I know we don't usually do this, but since the community supports us, we must support the community. So, we will build houses in impoverished areas of the city. Starting tomorrow, we will help those who need a good home. Hopefully, some of you guys will move into some of these homes one day," James says.

This news excites Jack. He dreams of living with more privacy. The homes aren't in the best neighborhoods. But Jack has seen a lot worse over the years in the USA. I wish had friends to live with. Oh well. I'll find more friends, I guess.

Jack is a little sleepy. And with a full stomach, struggles to keep his eyes open. Of course, cereal isn't exactly all that filling, but it is doing the job this morning.

Everyone walks back to the shelter, and Harry approaches Jack. He wants Jack to continue reading Oliver Twist immediately. With nothing else to do, Jack decides to read to him. After a few hours and a couple of breaks, Jack finishes reading the entire book.

Harry is so excited that he says, "You don't know how much this means to me. I hope to one day read this book to my grandkids. If I ever see them again."

Jack wants to ask why Harry hasn't seen his grandkids but doesn't want Harry to become sad due to nostalgia. Cleary, Harry has struggled with some type of drugs because he has missing teeth. And the left side of his face twitches involuntarily.

Harry says goodbye and now Jack is bored. Then a grand idea pops into his head- I should work on my writings. So, Jack goes to his locker and pulls out one of his poetry books. He thumbs through a few pages. He is pleased with how good his poems are. He reads a couple of poems and that inspires him to do some writing right now. Jack brainstorms a bit, and the words just flow on the paper. These are two of my best poems:

> I just sit down and it comes to me, am I genius, likely, the million dollar lifestyle is for me, no more financial worries, I won't have to get up early, to punch in at a job, so more fun surely, my body is still, but my mind goes around this world, thinking of how to bring in more dough, rags-to-riches story, I'm sure will be the title, of my biography, money talks, and it could never lie to me, no fake cash from monopoly, wealthy, I'll definitely be,

> My Spanish teacher used to say," Poco un poco.", meaning, little by little, don't try to learn everything at once, I want my riches and Maserati now, but I've got to settle down, my dream will be my reality, I've also found true joy in this shelter, peace of mind, so calm, I feel like a yogi at times, I've made it through the hardships of living on the streets, but I hardly say a peep, about what I've seen,

> plenty of scenes, more entertaining than the
> latest action flick, not to seem like a tough
> guy, but if can make it through that, living
> like roaches and rats, basically in the sewer,
> being called a loser, I'll use words to maneu-
> ver, to live in a mansion, no bills outstanding,
> everything paid for, even the Bentley 4-door,
> poco un poco,

Jack looks at the clock. He has written 20 poems in a couple of hours. Well, my hand is tired. I can't write much more today. It's bedtime anyway. As usual, James announces "lights out." Scientists claim doing something intellectual before bed helps you sleep well. This seems to be true because Jack doesn't wake up until the morning.

Jack is so well rested that he gets out of bed and writes poems until breakfast. Jack finishes up a poem just as everyone begins walking to the soup kitchen.

"C'mon Jack, let's go," Curtis says.

Curtis can sense Jack seems distracted and asks, "Are you ok?"

"Yeah. I'm thinking about my writing. I need to perfect the art of poetry. Hopefully, I'll get there soon."

"Well, you know I'm leaving the shelter soon. I want to read a couple of your poems before heading back home." Curtis says.

Jack had forgotten that his best friend here would be gone soon. However, Jack still plans to do Marine Construction if his application is accepted. He enjoys reading to others, but he seriously needs more money. Especially to buy clothes. Because items from the thrift store wear out quickly and don't look stylish. Jack plans to expand his wardrobe soon. All these thoughts are going through his mind until he's about a block away from the soup kitchen.

Jack smells the breakfast food from the soup kitchen, and he can't think of anything else. His stomach is rumbling and he's salivating like a dog. Usually the food is decent, but it doesn't always smell this good. Jack gets the answer to his question as he walks into the soup kitchen. He sees real chefs in the building.

They are here every now and then. The chefs are from 5-star restaurants across the city. Sometimes they cook so much food that there are leftovers the next day. I'm not sure who coordinates these events, but James always takes credit. To no one's surprise. They really are the best of the best.

Jack's omelet is better than what is served at a typical restaurant. It's too big and Jack can't eat all of it. And he ate too much anyway. He feels miserable. I may not eat anything else for the rest of the day.

He looks to his left and sees Curtis, devouring blueberry pancakes. Wow, he's working hard like he never ate anything before. But Jack understands why he is eating like this- the food is that good. In fact, Jack has never had a better breakfast.

It's better than mom's cooking. The stomach pain subsides, and Jack feels like taking a nap. A full stomach: what can be better than that? Then Jack starts feeling jealous of Curtis. He gets to rejoin his family. Jack doesn't know who he will hang out with once his best friend leaves the shelter for good. Jack tells himself that he is happy for Curtis. But deep down he knows this is a façade. Now Jack goes from being jealous to being angry.

Jack thinks about everything he hates about the shelter. Curtis continues stuffing his mouth with as much food as possible. Jack calms himself and thinks about what he'll do today.

He's looking forward to reading to others at the shelter. He tells himself it could be worse. Jack feels better and wonders how long he will continue reading to people. Breakfast is now over, and everyone walks back to the shelter.

Jack decides not to let James get to him, but to stay positive and enjoy the day. Jack heads to the chair that he usually reads to people from.

A young man comes up to him and asks, "Will you read a Harry Potter book to me?"

"Of course. So, you can't read at all?" Jack asks.

"Well, I can make out most words, but as far as reading an entire book- not really. I was in school, but I had to drop out to help take care of my ailing mother. I don't know much. But I'm willing to learn."

"I'm not a teacher, but I'll do the best I can to help you. I'll read slowly to help you pronounce certain words. And I want you to look up words you don't know."

Jack adds, "And Frank, when I finish reading this book, I'll read more books until you can read by yourself."

Frank's eyes light up and he can barely contain himself.

"Well, let's get started!" Jack says.

Jack clears his throat and begins reading to Frank- who listens intently. Jack is not familiar with any J.K. Rowling book, yet he enjoys this novel. So immersed in this novel, Jack loses track of time. Although he has lost most of his voice, Jack is happy to please Frank who is very humble.

Jack then hands the book to Frank and says, "Now it's your turn."

Frank opens the book and tries to read it. He stutters a lot and mispronounces a lot of words.

"Take your time. You'll get the hang of it," Jack says.

Frank looks embarrassed. Like when he tried to read in school. Frank is disheartened but presses on. He reads for 20 minutes and seems to be relaxed and confident.

Jack says, "Good job. You'll get the hang of it soon. Well, it's time for lunch. Talk to you later," Jack says.

"Thanks," Frank replies with a tear in his eye.

Just as Curtis said, the chefs are still in the soup kitchen. It's evident a block away from the kitchen when the smell becomes captivating. Jack isn't sure what type of food he smells, but it's got to be good. Sure enough, the chefs cook steak. Jack can't remember the last time he ate steak.

So, when it's time to eat, he picks the biggest steak. The food is so exquisite. The vegetable is collard greens- which Jack loves. Before long, Jack is stuffing his face like Curtis. The steak is so tender that he doesn't need a knife. Jack gets seconds.

Unlike breakfast though, he knows when to stop eating before his stomach hurts. Curtis on the other hand, is now miserable; he is moaning from the pain. Jack laughs to himself about Curtis's problem.

I can't wait until dinner to see what these chefs can put together. How can you outdo steak? Now it's time to walk back to the shelter.

Chapter 9

ONCE AT THE SHELTER, Jack walks straight to James's office to get paid. For some reason, James seems to be in a good mood and doesn't heckle Jack at all.

Instead, James says, "Here is your pay for the week."

It isn't much, but with free rent and free food, it amounts to having some spending change. In fact, Jack wants to go to the store to buy new clothes. No hand me downs, but a collection from Ralph Lauren- Jack's favorite American designer. When he worked at Panacea Pharmaceuticals, he would buy clothing by Ralph Lauren all the time. Jack wonders if he'll ever be able to do this again.

Jack hasn't been shopping much since living on the street. He bought a blanket one winter. His other blanket got wet from precipitation. So, he needed new cloth to avoid becoming sick from frigid conditions. Jack has this new blanket in his locker. It's clean and in good shape.

Surprisingly, Jack liked being homeless in some ways. He misses his privacy. Practically everything is shared here, and he can't do anything without someone knowing about it. Also, he never had someone like James hounding him most of the time. Jack managed to stay clean sometimes by washing himself in a restroom by the beach.

Obviously living in the shelter has its benefits. I eat good meals and socialize a lot. Well, it looks like I won't read to anyone right now. What should I do? I should exercise. I've put on weight since living in the shelter. I wasn't starving on the streets, but all that walking kept me thin. The shelter does not have a gym.

Jack heads to James's office anxious to find a place to exercise. James is reading an important document as Jack enters his office.

Hearing footsteps, James looks up and says, "What can I help you with Jack?"

"Well, James, is there a place where I can exercise? I need to get into shape or do something."

"There is the Aquatic Center. It has: a large Olympic-size pool, a sauna, a jacuzzi, and a weight room."

"That sounds expensive James. I would love to go there, but I need to save money."

"The price isn't high, and you will enjoy this center." James says.

"Thanks" Jack replies.

He is totally shocked that James is so agreeable right now.

Jack sees Curtis in the computer room and must tell him about this incident.

"Hey Curtis, guess what?"

"Hey, what is it, Jack? You seem happy. "I am. James found a place for us to exercise. He seems so nice right now. I can't believe it."

Curtis replies, "Yeah. That is strange. Maybe he is realizing life will be better with a positive attitude."

"Maybe. I think something good happened to him recently. Nobody can change that fast," Jack says.

Curtis shrugs his shoulders and brings his attention back to the computer screen. Jack wants to use a computer, but they are all taken. So, he's wondering how to spend his time. He isn't scheduled to read to anyone. He is bored.

There is some open space in the shelter. So, he decides to do pushups. Jack does 15 repetitions and it's just too much. His chest and arms are very sore, and he is breathing quite heavily. As Jack stands up for a second, he feels like he is going to pass out. After a few minutes of rest, he is no longer disoriented. Jack feels better than before exercising.

Now, he's very sleepy. He takes a nap. He dreams of living in a mansion in California. Overlooking the water with exotic cars in his garage.

He is cruising in a sports car down a winding road when someone yells out, "Jack! Wake up!"

He opens his eyes to find Curtis shaking him.

"What is it, Curtis?"

"We are all going to the movies in a few minutes. James is paying."

Still a bit groggy, Jack says, "Huh?"

"C'mon Jack, you heard me. We are going to the movies."

Now fully awake, Jack says, "Wow, what are we seeing?"

"An action film made in Hollywood. You'll like it. Everybody likes this actor."

"All right. Let me washy my face to get ready," Jack says.

Like most of the places they go to, they must walk. The movie theater isn't a long walk from the shelter. They arrive there with plenty of time before the movie starts. Jack wants to order a Freeze Frame drink and a large bag of popcorn. But his pockets have rabbit ears: no money in them. Plus, he's still full of steak.

The theater is monstrous. All the people from the shelter can fit inside with no problem. Jack sits in a good seat- not too close to the screen, but not too far where he must squint to see the screen. Of course, the previews come on which Jack totally ignores. He thinks about whether the movie will be great or not.

Halfway through the movie, Jack is pleasantly surprised. There is a ton of action, and the plot is very believable and intriguing. Really, Jack doesn't want this adventure to end. Unfortunately, the film does end, but in a way no one could foresee.

Some from the audience clap when the credits are rolling. Jack is one of them. After leaving the theater, everyone talks about their favorite scene. And what they thought would happen. Even Curtis is a bit giddy and babbles on and on about how the movie ends.

Jack remains quiet, but on the inside, he is hyped up from this wonderful film. When the group reaches the shelter, everyone is still buzzing. Then James has another surprise for the people at the shelter.

"It seems as though everyone enjoyed the movie. Now we'll celebrate. An ice cream shop has a bowl of ice cream for everybody," James says with a big smile.

A few minutes later, workers from the store hand out creamy, thick ice cream. Jack tastes the dessert, and it is of high quality. The ice cream is as good as Ben and & Jerry's. Jack finishes his bowl and looks for more. But there are no seconds. Because everyone loves this ice cream. The bowls aren't big, but they contain a sizeable portion of the dessert. Now it's time for bed.

Jack can't fall asleep. The ice cream hurt his stomach. He tosses and turns for about an hour and just lies in his cot with his eyes wide open. He tries to count sheep, but to no avail. Then he visualizes being back home. He only concentrates on the good memories. He can sleep now- remembering throwing a ball with his son. Jack sleeps peacefully for the rest of the night. He is awakened by James. It's time for breakfast.

Still groggy, Jack says, "Ok" and lies back down for a minute.

Until he realizes that he'll be hungry if he misses the early meal. Jack hops out of bed and walks to the soup kitchen. There are no world-class chefs this morning. So, Jack eats a bagel and cereal. At the table, the conversation focuses on exercise. Everyone seems excited about being able to use the Aquatic Center that is not far away.

Jack doesn't say anything. He listens to everyone. One woman claims exercise will benefit everyone because it helps you to fall asleep easier. Another person says using the center is a good idea because there will be more space in the shelter. As people go to the center to exercise, there will be fewer of them at the shelter- allowing others more privacy. Jack nods his head.

Then Curtis says, "I heard they have a weight room. I know I won't be here long, but I will take advantage of that."

Jack was in decent shape living by himself. Because he couldn't just stay still in his cardboard palace. He has put on a substantial amount of weight living at the shelter. He has a pot belly now. It takes effort to tie his shoes or bend over for any reason. Jack thinks about swimming. He heard it's the best type of exercise because it works the entire body. Anyway, Jack is very excited by the prospect of exercising.

After breakfast, Jack gets back to his job. He reads Shakespeare to a woman at the shelter. He reads Taming of the Shrew to the woman, Shirley. She listens with her eyes closed. She is envisioning every scene by this brilliant playwright. Jack has only read a few plays by Shakespeare. But he must admit that this play is deftly written.

It takes some time, but Jack finished reading this play. And Shirley wants him to read more plays. She is a bit pushy, and Jack's throat is getting sore from reading so much. Instead of reading another play right way, Jack tells Shirley he'll take a 15 minute break.

Jack's mind is all over the place. Reading Shakespeare has made him think about writing more novels. Right at 15 minutes, Shirley is eager to hear another play by one of the greatest playwrights of all time. So, Jack dives into another play to Shirley's amusement. Jack finishes the play just in time for lunch.

Shirley walks with Jack to the soup kitchen. She goes on and on about different books. She is really into English Literature and is very knowledgeable about the subject. This really surprises Jack. She seems smart, but why is she homeless? Hard times, I guess. Jack gets his food and now she is talking about American Literature. Once again, she is very knowledgeable about this genre.

Jack zones out after she goes on and on about Mark Twain. He knows a lot about Mark Twain, and she doesn't say anything new. Curtis looks tired of hearing her too. But he is too nice to say anything. He pretends to listen. After talking about Walt Whitman, Shirley looks around at the table and realizes she is doing all the talking. She's not embarrassed but decides to be quiet now.

Jack is thinking about his own writings when he notices that Shirley is now silent. Jack doesn't know Shirley that well. So, he isn't sure if he wants to be around someone that talks so much. But then again, once Curtis leaves, who else will he hang out with?

Plus, when she isn't going off on a rant, she is cool. And she is smart. Jack laughs to himself. He happens to look up and see Curtis's face. Curtis looks disgusted by Shirley. It's obvious that he wants to get away from her as soon as possible.

Other people at the table seem to be oblivious to Shirley. They continue eating their food. There is a long silence and Jack prays that she doesn't start talking anymore. In fact, Jack thinks about saying something to end the awkwardness. Jack wonders what to talk about. He loves discussing books, but he's sure no one except Shirley wants to hear that right now.

Jack says, "So what did everyone do before being in the shelter?"

Kenny's eyes light up and he replies, "I was a high school teacher until I was laid off due to budget cuts. The schools really need good teachers, but what can you do?"

Curits sees Jack is in his own world and approaches him on the walk back to the shelter.

"What's wrong?"

"I want my old job and my old life back. I really miss my son Brent."

Jack has tears in his eyes knowing he may not see Brent for a very long time.

"Why don't you find his number and call him? I know you don't get along with your ex-wife and most of your family. But I'm sure Brent misses you too?" Curtis says.

It's been such a long time. Jack doesn't know how Brent is doing. Brent lives with his mother. Jack hates her and it's hard for Jack to get past that fact. Of course, with technology, he could easily find Brent's information on the internet.

"You know, I may get in contact with Brent today. It's just hard to overlook how my ex-wife treats me."

Curtis replies, "Well, I've never dealt with a mean ex-wife before. But just keep Brent in mind when you think about your past."

That's sound advice. Now I know why he is such a good friend. After this talk, Jack seems to be in a good mood. He reads to Shirley, and she notices his pleasant disposition.

After reading part of a play by Shakespeare, Jack goes on the computer. And the search is on for Brent's contact information. Jack finds his email address and sends a message to his son.

He writes, "Hello, I haven't contacted you in a while. How are you doing?"

This doesn't sound that good. I'll send it anyway. A tear runs down his face. Jack is glad he has the courage to do this. And thanks Curtis for keeping him focused on what is important.

Pumped up now, Jack feels like he can work on his writings all day. Jack walks to his locker. Because he wants to write a poem. He pulls out one of his journals and brainstorms before writing one line of a poem. As Jack brainstorms, his mind begins to wander. He daydreams of fancy cars. How will I get these things? This causes him to focus, and he writes this poem:

> We do it practically every night, it's like our minds take flight, escaping normal thought processes, to the land of endless opportunities, our dreams, but my dream is not about fantasy, or dragons or weird things, but relaxing, on a beach, with clear water, south of the border, in Miami or another cool destination,

Then he writes this poem:

> Will my novel ever sell enough so I can live well, the road to riches, seems like a trail, a

> bumpy journey with so many distractions, it's hard to gain traction, but I'm on this path until the very end, writing is my passion, plus it can pay me trillions, just from stories so I'm feeling, confident, that I may retire soon, so those on the best seller's list, make room for a man with a strong will, head hard as an anvil, there's no stopping his progress,

Jack reads both poems aloud and is pleased. Then Jack goes to the computer in hopes of submitting this poem to win an award. He has never submitted any of his writings. The grand prize at a particular website is a thousand dollars. This amount doesn't seem like much, but to a homeless man, this money can go a long way. In fact, Jack has been saving the money he makes from reading to people. He hopes to live in a nice place by using this money. He really wants to go with Curtis to Curtis's hometown. But Jack believes being around another man's family like that can be awkward. So, I'll stay here.

Jack continues searching the internet. He is looking for more poetry contests. He can't find any more contests that pay. Yeah, the acclaim would be great, but I need help financially. Just thinking of winning the award and money has Jack very enthused. Tired of sitting still, Jack leaves the shelter to go for a walk.

As he strides down the block, Jack's legs feel better from this little bit of exercise. Jack rarely exercises let alone walk a great deal of distance. I really need to train a lot at the Aquatic Center. Other than walking to the soup kitchen for meals, Jack is sedentary. So, it isn't surprising that he is winded after walking for 20 minutes. But he doesn't want to turn back yet.

He debates whether to take public transportation to look at parts of this beautiful city. He comes to part of the metropolis with restaurants lined on one side of the street. The street smells so good. An Italian restaurant is putting out the strongest aroma. Jack looks in his wallet to see if he has enough money to eat there. Yep. I could buy a meal here, but wow, that would hurt my pocket. I'll eat here another time. Jack heads back to the shelter. Just in time for the walk to the soup kitchen for dinner.

Chapter 10

WHILE AT THE SOUP kitchen, all Jack can think about is winning that award for one of his poems. If I can just get started, I'll make it out of here. Then Jack remembers his application for the marine construction job. I should check my email soon. This job wouldn't make Jack rich, but it pays more than reading to others at the shelter. However, this job requires working with your hands. Also known as manual labor. Jack had never worked in construction before. I'll try my best.

Fortunately, Shirley is sitting halfway across the soup kitchen. She is probably annoying somebody. Jack sits with practically the same people, including Curtis. Curtis looks to be in a good mood.

Curtis says, "Well everyone, I'll be leaving soon to try my luck with my family."

"I hope you do well there!" Jack says even though he is upset at Curtis.

Now I must deal with living here without my best friend. Jack begins to think about James and his antics. And the downsides of living in this shelter. No privacy. Little income. But it is better here than living on the street. Jack reminds himself. He doesn't miss living alone and being unsure if he'll make it through the night. Either from disease or some unknown force.

At one time while living on the street, Jack had a terrible cough and thought he was very sick. Luckily, his cough went away after about a month. Of course, had he gone to the hospital, he couldn't pay for the medicine. If he had been in the United States. But he didn't know how health care works in Canada. What a scary time. I'll never go through that again. I guess living in the shelter isn't as bad as I initially thought.

Jack gets on the computer to check his email. No word from the marine construction company. This deflates Jack. Who is starting to believe he won't even get an interview for this job. Well reading aloud is easy, the construction job pays a lot more. Plus, he'll be moving around instead of feeling cramped like at the shelter. Maybe I should read in different locations. I'll ask James about this now. Jack walks to James's office and knocks on the door.

"Come in."

"Hey James. I enjoy reading to people, but I'm kind of tired of doing it in the shelter. Could I possibly do this in the park or along the beach?" Jack asks.

"Of course you can Jack. I don't see any problems changing places. The people here like what you are doing now. So many of them ask when you can read to them. Reading aloud has become rather popular around here. And I see you are having fun too."

Jack replies, "Yes. I love learning. I'm gaining knowledge from reading great literature. It's also rewarding watching people getting so excited from my readings."

What will I do if I get the marine construction job? I'll deal with that when I must.

"Any other questions Jack?"

"Not really James. Talk to you later."

Wow! That went well. What to do next. No one is on

schedule to read to, so I'll read poetry. Jack opens his locker and pulls out a book by Chinese authors. He has never read this book. He bought it from an antique bookstore a few weeks ago. It was cheap. Jack has heard of Confucius but is not familiar with most authors that are not American or British.

Jack cracks the book open. After reading a couple poems, he realizes this book is a collection of maxims. Maxims that you would find in fortune cookies. Most of the poems have a moral to the story. Which is fine with Jack. He loves to read philosophy books and wise sayings. Jack recalls leafing through the book of Proverbs in the Bible in his younger days. He reads poems for 45 minutes. I may read more of this book tomorrow.

Jack is very relaxed- something that reading does to him. Maybe too relaxed. He is ready for sleep. It's not long now until the lights are cut off. Jack sees some people playing chess. I'll check this out. Jack knows how to play, but he isn't good. He could never beat the artificial intelligence on one of his computers. He was always frustrated by this. The guys playing now look good. They seem to think through every single move. And they are concentrating on the game like only experts do.

Jack follows the game for a while. Then guys start to play fast- aware that the lights will be cut off soon. Jack walks to his cot and closes his eyes just as the lights are turned off.

Jack has a weird dream. He is on a ship during a horrible storm. This is odd, because he's never been on a ship during a storm. Other than fishing a few times, he hasn't stepped foot on a boat. Well, in this dream he falls off the vessel. He is close to drowning even though he is treading water.

Most people would wake up then, but Jack remains sound asleep. Next, the ship is sinking, and members of the crew are screaming for help and flopping their arms. When this happens, Jack wakes up in a cold sweat. Why am I dreaming this? Certain foods can give me nightmares. But I haven't eaten anything odd lately.

Then, he becomes fearful about the marine construction job. How far out to sea may I travel? Will I have a life jacket? Jack is unsure if he should pursue this type of employment. I'll think about this later. I'm going back to sleep.

As the lights are turned on, Jack gets right out of his bed. He is eager to start the day. He goes to his locker and pulls out one of his poetry books. He writes this short poem on dreaming:

> Can dreams tell the future, or are they useless,
> just my subconscious running wild, nothing
> important to note, like I dreamt of falling
> off a boat, is this a warning to not do marine
> construction, a job that's extremely risky, at
> least I can swim, better yet tread water,

Now it's time to go to the soup kitchen for breakfast. Today's breakfast is a continental breakfast. Meaning, there isn't much hot food- just a bunch of bagels and cereals. Jack doesn't really care about the food. He is back to thinking about the marine construction job.

He remembers from the application that he may have to work long hours even on the weekends. He never works long hours at his current job. I'll wait until I hear from the marine construction job before making any decisions. Jack tries to enjoy the food. He'd rather eat at an IHOP or something. Jack sees this food as only a filler. Just something to stop the stomach rumblings.

After breakfast, James announces that everyone at the shelter can use the Aquatic center practically for free. Jack is excited about this: he needs to work off his gut. The gut he developed since living in the shelter. He plans to go to the center today.

After reading for a couple of hours, Jack heads to the center with Curtis and a few others. The facilities are outstanding: new weights, new pool, and a new building. Jack didn't bring any swimming trunks, so he plans to run for cardio.

Curtis, who is strongly built, goes to the weight room and Jack follows him. Curtis lights up once entering the weight room- ready to do some lifting.

He turns to Jack and says, "What body part do you want to work on?"

"My stomach. I want to see my abs soon."

"All right, no problem. Let's do inverse crunches on this weight bench."

Curtis gives Jack a demonstration on how to do the exercise. Then Jack does crunches. To Jack's surprise, he does 20 crunches before muscle soreness kicks in. Jack gets off the weight bench only to see Curtis do more crunches.

Then Curtis says, "Your turn."

"My turn, I thought I was done."

"No, that was just the first set. Two more sets to go."

Jack acquiesces and can only do 5 crunches for the second set. Now his abs are tight, and he is breathing quite heavily.

Curtis gets back on the bench and completes the final set. He is so smooth doing crunches. It's obvious that the exercise is not hurting him.

Jack tries the final set and can only do 4 crunches before exclaiming, "I'm maxed out!"

"That's good Jack. Eventually you'll be able to do more crunches. Now you know what to improve on," Curtis says.

I guess Jack thinks. After doing more ab exercises on different machines, Jack runs on the treadmill for 30 minutes. Sweat is literally dripping off him. Walking is now challenging, and Jack doesn't think he can walk much farther. And then the time is up. Jack believes he has accomplished something. The runner's high kicks in and Jack feels wonderful. But he is a little sore though.

Curtis sees Jack struggling and says, "You'll be fine later. Everybody goes through this when starting out. Your body will adapt."

Yeah right. Strangely, this soreness doesn't seem as bad as one would think. Jack can move rather well and hasn't lost any range of motion. Jack is done exercising.

Curtis continues to lift weights for another 30 minutes; he's lifting weights that Jack can only dream of. And Curtis isn't straining. As they walk back to the shelter, Curtis shares workout secrets with Jack.

"The key to lifting weights is to use weight that is heavy, but not too heavy. You want resistance, but lifting too much weight will cause injury."

Jack nods his head since this all makes perfect sense. Today, Jack feels like he used too heavy a weight. I'll probably be sore for many days.

Then Curtis says, "Cardio is very important. It helps lower body fat. I used to only lift weights. But when I started doing cardio, I began to look a lot better and have more energy."

"So, how much cardio should I do?"

"I would day as much as you can. Because it can't really hurt you. As far as losing muscle. Unless you run a marathon or something like that. So, in two days we'll come back here, and I'll help you work out again."

Once they get back to the shelter, Jack takes a shower and

plops down in a chair. He is worn out from head to toe. I'll do some writing. Instead of writing a poem, Jack works on his novel. Jack brainstorms for a while- getting his thoughts together. Then he writes and writes.

Jack has been writing novels since becoming homeless. He believes he is a good writer. I know I'll make it big one day. But until then, I'll work where I can. Jack writes for a couple hours. He writes until his hand is too tired to continue scribing.

Jack puts his writings back into his locker and visits James. Jack is extremely bored now and wants to read aloud to someone. So, James finds Chris- an older gentleman who surprisingly loves Harry Potter. Not many adults ask to hear these books to be read aloud. Not judging him, Jack reads part of the first book to Chris until dinnertime. What a good, productive day.

At supper, Shirley sits with Jack and some other people. She quizzes them on trivia dealing with English Literature. No one knows as much as her. She seems to enjoy this. Shirley is aggravating everyone. Jack is glad dinner is over so that he can get away from her.

While walking back to the shelter, Curtis says, "You want to go to the aquatic center now?"

"Back to the center? I can barely walk. No thanks Curtis. I'm so sore that I need a break."

"Well, you could do a light workout. But I guess rest is best. However, I'm going to lift weights now."

Jack decides to read some more of Harry Potter to Chris. After about an hour, Christ begins to nod off. It's clear that he can't pay attention and follow the storyline. It is getting late, and Chris is old: Jack understands. So, Jack checks his email.

He has a message from the marine construction company. The company wants him for a job interview. Jack is happy and sad at them same time. He wants more money, but the hazards of this job are harrowing. I must face my fears.

The job interview is in a few days. Jack is preparing mentally for the interview. He is thinking about what he'll wear and what he will say. He is confident that he'll get this job.

"That's wonderful Jack. I hope you get it. You need to get out more, instead of being in the shelter most of the time. You know, I leave soon to go to my true home. We had fun times, but it is time for me to live a normal life," Curtis says.

Jack understands all of this, but still wishes Curtis would stay. It is what it is. Life goes on Jack thinks.

"Wish me luck Jack. I might need it."

"I wish you the best," Jack says.

They play Monopoly until lights out. In the morning, they head to the soup kitchen for breakfast. It's a humid day and the sun is out- beaming down on all who are outside. Jack loves the sun beaming down like this because it helps him to wake up. Jack is fully awake when they reach the soup kitchen. To everyone's surprise, professional chefs are in the kitchen- ready to whip up gourmet meals.

When everyone is seated, James says, "Well, today is very special. One of our own, Curtis, is leaving us to go back to his family. This is what the shelter is all about. Keeping those afloat until they can get back on their feet. I'm very proud of Curtis. Who could've given up, but he refused to let his situation get the better of him. C'mon Curtis, speak a little bit."

Curtis is in tears when he realizes how much everyone here cares for him.

"Thank you, James. It has been a while since I've lived in a house and I'm ready to do so now. You guys are cool to hang out with, but I feel like I need my own space and privacy. I may visit you guys now and then. That's all I have to say. Thanks to everyone for your continued support. Now let's eat!"

Everyone claps, and then the chefs get busy. Jack orders an omelet: a very big 4-egg omelet that covers his entire plate. Curtis on the other hand, orders pancakes and Shirley orders crepes. The omelet is excellent and filling. Jack is stuffed and wants to go back to his cot. But he refrains from thinking about this. Instead, he focuses on what exercises regimen he'll do later at the gym. Curtis is talkative at the table. He is still excited about going back home.

Jack is jealous. He is not in contact with his family. And he has no idea when he'll leave the shelter. Well, I've just got to deal with it.

After breakfast, Jack goes to the gym with some people he associates with. Although none are his friends. The center has air-conditioning, and it is frigid in the weight room. Jack's muscles don't seem warmed up, so he stretches first and then hits the weights. Jack lifts light weights since he is sore from the other day. Surprisingly, after a couple of minutes of working out, Jack's muscles are no longer sore. So, he decides to add more weight to his exercises.

Jack feels like a pro because he understands how his muscles work. After lifting weights, Jack hits a heavy bag for cardio. He then hits the bag lightly for 15 minutes until he is extremely tired. After this, Jack thinks- wow what a workout. He is dripping with sweat. Yet, he feels good.

Back at the shelter, Jack hangs around Curtis for the last time. Curtis will take the bus to the airport in 30 minutes.

Curtis says, "I may send you an email every now and then. We'll keep in touch no doubt. Well, it's been fun hanging around with you. I wish you the best. See you later."

Jack shakes his hand, and Curtis leaves the shelter.

The next day, Jack sulks for a little while. He decides to take his mind off this event. H reads to a homeless woman. Linda wants Jack to read some of Virginia Wolfe: one of Jack's favorite authors. So, he really enjoys reading to Linda. Jack is happy for this distraction, so he reads until lunch.

At the end of the reading session, she says, "Thank you. Would you mind reading more of this book after lunch?"

"Of course, I love Virginia Wolfe too."

At the soup kitchen, they have "Philly Day." Meaning, the kitchen serves Philadelphian food products like cheesesteaks and hoagies. Jack has heard about hoagies tasting good. Today, he will eat one for the first time. Linda, who has lived in Philadelphia, tells him how good Philly subs are. Jack takes a bite, and the sub tastes wonderful. The vegetables on the sub are fresh.

As Jack eats the hoagie, Linda says, "You need chips to make this meal proper!"

So, Jack goes back to the lunch line and grabs a bag of salt and vinegar chips. Feeling the Italian spirit, Jack eats tiramisu for dessert. Jack used to this treat every time he ate at Italian restaurants.

"How is the sub?" Linda asks.

"Excellent. Next time I'll try a Philly cheesesteak."

"That's as good as a hoagie when cooked right," Linda adds.

Jack feels good now. There is nothing like a stomach full of great food. He chats a bit with the people at the table. And for a second, forgets that he has lost a best friend.

On the walk back to the shelter, Jack has trouble moving. His stomach is heavy. However, he manages to get back to the shelter and Linda approaches him immediately. No doubt, after a good meal, most people like to sit down and relax. So, Jack relaxes as he reads more of Virginia Wolfe to Linda.

Jack only reads for 1 ½ hours because he's starting to go hoarse. After this time, Jack tells Linda he is done reading aloud today. Then he begins to work on his writings. Specifically on his poetry. He writes this poem:

> From rags to riches, a bum to a millionaire, the never die attitude, something that we all share, I refuse to lose, no matter the issue, I don't care, I get through the headaches without any Bayer, Aspirin, I remember where, it all began, believing in myself, knowing that I will attain wealth, it's good for my health, the shelter helps, but I want to support myself,

Not the best poem I've ever written. Then, Jack reads some books by Virginia Wolfe for himself. As he reads, he pulls out a sheet of paper and attempts to copy her writing style. Jack heard that emulating a writing style improves your own writing ability. After doing this for a while, Jack searches the internet. At first, he searches for anything that pops into his mind.

Then, he reads quotes by Mark Twain. After reading about 15 quotes, Jack grows tired of being on the computer. So, he takes a nap. Jack dreams about writing books. Then he dreams of driving an exotic car through California. He is as rich as anyone who has ever lived. Jack wakes up happy and is motivated to write some more. So, he writes until dinnertime. I can't wait until I go the soup kitchen to eat a Philly cheesesteak.

At the soup kitchen, Jack is very talkative. He socializes more than Shirley. And yes, just like Linda said- the Philly cheesesteak tastes good. He also eats boardwalk French fries.

Jack can barely walk back to the shelter. When everyone is back there, James has an announcement.

"I know everyone enjoyed this meal. The chefs are the best in the city. And they are passionate about their craft. Hopefully, they'll cook many more meals for us. But on a different note, instead of just relaxing now after dinner, the staff has decided that tonight is movie night. So, we'll watch the most popular title. So please, make up your mind."

With a full stomach, Jack is ready to watch something. After 5 minutes of debating, the guys select a comedy movie. It's a good movie- evidenced by the amount of laughter occurring in the main room. After the movie, the staff passes out ice cream. What a good night.

In the morning, Jack goes on the computer to check his email. Sure enough, the marine construction company has sent a confirmation email. They want to interview him. The docks are only a few miles away from the shelter; public transportation would take Jack to company headquarters in 15 minutes. Jack is excited yet cautious at the same time. Yes, he wants to make more money and not stay in the shelter all day. However, he still worries that this type of work is too dangerous.

Jack isn't the strongest swimmer. He also never worked with his hands. But I might as well give it a try. Jack stays on the computer just reading the news and then looks up some random things. Then, he studies marine construction. I must be sharp on the subject. It doesn't seem too difficult. But Jack knows he needs to understand more. So, he continues researching this topic. After an hour of studying, he feels like he has the hang of it.

Chapter 11

By now everyone at the shelter is awake and awakened by the stomach rumblings: they need breakfast. Expecting great food, everyone is upset when they can't smell any aroma on their way to the soup kitchen. This means they will be served a continental breakfast. The grumbling stops though when everyone realizes it's better than nothing. Jack eats a bowl of cereal with cream cheese on a bagel. The bagel is good, but not great. He washes the bagel down with orange juice. Then it is back to the shelter.

Once again Jack reads to another person. This time he reads a book by a Japanese author- whom the man wants to hear. The morning goes by fast and then everyone eats lunch. Then some of them go to the gym.

Today, Jack swims, but takes a break from lifting weights. The indoor pool is lukewarm- the perfect temperature to swim in. Unsure of his swimming ability, Jack sticks to the shallow end of the pool and plays water polo.

Jack has seen water polo being played on tv and it didn't look that interesting. But he is having a ball playing it today. Jack plays this game for about 30 minutes then he swims. It doesn't take long for him to get tired. After 20 minutes of swimming, he is ready to exit the pool and read a book. Jack decides to stay in the pool a little while longer to play water polo. By now, his legs are sore from moving in the water so much.

After the last game, Jack gets in the sauna. He heard the sauna helps you lose weight. So, he stays in the sauna for 20 minutes and feels drained. It's like all the water has left his body. However, the warmth relaxes his muscles. He drinks water and wonders if should jump in the jacuzzi. Maybe next time.

At the shelter, Jack keeps going back to the water fountain. He can't seem to quench his thirst. So, he walks to the nearest convenience store to buy a sports drink. Experts claim sports drinks are better for rehydration than plain water. While in the store, Jack looks for a quick snack. On the health tip, he grabs a bag of mixed nuts instead of a chocolate bar. The mixed nuts really complement the sports drink.

Back at the shelter, Jack has free time, so he works on his writings. He edits his novel for an hour. Then, Shirley approaches him with a book to read. She hands him Les Miserable.

"What a thick book!" Jack exclaims.

Jack has never read this classic before. Shirley just nods to signal for Jack to begin reading. Jack clears his throat and reads the book out loud. He takes a few breaks and stops reading with about an hour before dinner. During this time, Jack takes a short nap and dreams about doing marine construction.

The dream starts off pleasantly with Jack working on a dock. Then, he dreams he falls in the water and his foot is caught on something. He is drowning. Jack wakes up in a cold sweat. All these omens are telling me to leave this job alone. But I want to at least try this job.

Wow, it's time for dinner. Jack eats an open-faced turkey sandwich, which tastes ok. Well, I'm hungry. Shirely explains

Les Miserable to everyone at the table. No one tells her to stop. But it's obvious nobody is interested. They aren't even paying attention. However, she doesn't know this. It seems like she doesn't understand most people don't want to hear what she talks about.

Oh well. At least she is a good person. Even Jack zones out- wondering what he'll read or study after dinner. I'm tired of writing my novel for now. So, I'll read some of it. When he gets back to the shelter, Jack does exactly that. He is happy with his progress. I'll write some poems now.

> I'm saving money in case of a rainy day, even though housing is free, I still have to pay for nice clothes, but I hope these writings sell, because being poor is its own hell, it's just me, yet I have trouble making ends meet, oh well, I know I will prevail, I think hard times are behind me, at least I'm no longer on the street, no more garbage-digging, I've got plenty to eat, plus I have friends now, and I hardly have any PTSD, I'm looking forward to tomorrow,
>
> My family abandoned me, for standing up and trying what I feel, I never wanted to be in science, I studied this subject, because I was reliant, on the so called wisdom of my parents, they said study in a field of STEM, Science, Technology, Engineering, Math, then you'll always have, a good paying job, so it's odd, that when Panacea Pharmaceuticals had bad years, hundreds were laid off, the

> CEO didn't shed a tear, it's what's best for the company, he said as the stock price shot up, his stock went up, in value, but that's the way of the world,

He's really putting in some work and is tired by bedtime. The lights are turned off and Jack is fast asleep. Jack wakes up in the morning, bent on writing more of everything. Jack is in the zone. He writes until it's time for breakfast. Even he is surprised at the ease at which he writes. Once again, he daydreams of one day being an acclaimed author living in a mansion.

He grew up in a suburb. His parents have advanced degrees. Jack had everything a child needs for a great upbringing. He went to a special high school that required high test scores for admission. Then, we went to Duke University for his undergraduate degree and PhD in Neuroscience.

That's why it is strange to him that he is suffering so much now. Life isn't supposed to be this hard when you grow up privileged. I deserve better. All my high school and college friends are successful. I'll get there. I was deemed to be the smartest in my high school class. Anyway, I'll eat breakfast now.

He enjoys pancakes with sausage and eggs on the side. The meal is good so Jack can't complain. The professional chefs did not cook this meal. But no one could cook it any better.

After breakfast, Jack reads to Shirley, and then they walk around the city- bored from just reading and listening to books. The temperature is about 72 degrees. Which is perfect for walking in the city.

Shirley doesn't look in shape, but she keeps up with Jack

no matter the pace. And they walk a long way from the shelter. Jack really wants to take a cab but decides to act tough and keep on strolling around. Neither one of them has money so they window shop for quite some time. However, they try on clothes and chat with employees in the stores. As if they are going to buy something. Yet Jack knows he couldn't afford some of these clothes if he had his old job. The clothes are extremely nice, Jack must admit.

Then, they browse in a sunglass store. These shades are the top of the line. They are pricey, but of high quality. Jack and Shirley are in the store for about 15 minutes until an employee gives them the evil eye. Jack gets the message, tells Shirely, so they leave the store. They window shop in the rest of the trendy fashion district.

Jack's legs are tired from all the walking, but Shirley is energetic and wants to keep going. They walk around the city for another hour before heading back to the shelter. Jack is glad that he went on this walk- just something different from the usual. Now Jack wants a nap. He takes one after lunch and now it's back to reading to someone.

This time Matt, who is about the age of Jack, wants Jack to read a newspaper to him. Matt cannot read at all. So, Jack grabs a well-renown paper and gets started. Jack reads an article in the Science section on brain cells. The article states that unlike previously thought, brain cells are created throughout one's life. Not just in infancy. Jack recalls designing a drug at his old job. It was supposed to create new brain cells for those that suffered a stroke. The drug did not work, but maybe someone could use my research to advance Neuroscience.

After reading all the articles in the Science section, Jack takes a break. But only for a few minutes because Matt wants him to read even more of this newspaper. So, Jack does this. Now Jack is tired of reading. He says bye to Matt and works on his writings. He feels like writing poems:

> I'll do anything for you, just give me a call, any time is fine, I love you more than I can express in a rhyme, remember shooting hoops, betting on a box of Fruit Loops, those were the days, I'm amazed, that was so long ago, but it is so clear, in my memory, like that happened last year, I do fear, that I may never see you again, hopefully we can be friends, before the end,
>
> I'm not technically homeless, I have my cardboard palace, but I've got to get out of this, I'm not proud of it, but right now it's all I've got, I hear the noise of the city, it's never quiet to me, rumblings of the cars and trucks, hummings of construction equipment, and mumblings of passersby, I could cry, from being so hopeless, but somehow I know this struggle won't last forever, if I'm clever, enough to earn a PHD, I'm smart enough to think myself into a better place, pride has kept me from asking for help, but after having welts, caused by the anger of teenagers, I wager, being in the shelter, definitely seems safer,

Jack has tears in his eyes when he is done writing these poems. Some tears are for Brent and some tears are for himself. Tired of sulking, Jack puts his writings into his locker. Then, he plays a board game with some people in the shelter. He just wants to get his mind off Brent. But he turns out to really enjoy the board game. He doesn't win, but giving his mind a break from worrying is good enough. Then, Jack goes on the computer to check his email. To no surprise Brent has not emailed him back. But there is a message from Curtis:

> "Hey Jack, I hope you are doing fine. I'm doing well so far. I've found a decent job, and my family seems happy to have me back. I play soccer with my grandkids every night after work. I love my life right now. Well, I hope you can stand being in the shelter a little while longer. I'm in talks with my family about you coming here to live. But they aren't sure about this. Anyway, keep your head up and keep me posted on what is happening in the shelter. Email me back when you get the chance. Sincerely, Curtis."

Happy that Curtis is having fun brings a smile to Jack's face.
He immediately replies:

> "I'm doing fine Curtis. As of now, I'm still reading books and newspapers to some people in the shelter. I'm proud that I'm giving joy to people. However, I have an interview with that Marine Construction company. I'm a little worried because I have no experience in this field. But I'll try my best. No doubt I could use the money. I'm glad you

are doing well. Maybe one day I'll join you. I
hope to see you one day. I wish you the best.
Your friend, Jack."

Jack keeps himself calm after reading Curtis's email. He doesn't want to get too excited about the possibility of living with Curtis and his family. It's understandable that Curtis's family may not trust Jack. He has no hard feelings about that. Yet, he would love the privacy of living in a real home. And not having to sleep on cots anymore. But as of now I'll make do the best way I know how.

Chapter 12

TIRED OR READING AND writing, Jack doesn't know what to do next. It's a few hours before dinner and he is no longer interested in playing board games. He sits in a chair- closing his eyes, bored out of his mind. He isn't in a bad mood. He is relaxing. After 45 minutes, Jack is tired of doing nothing.

So, Jack goes on the internet. There isn't anything specific that he is looking for. He's looking up random things. Then, Jack looks up information on marine construction. He studies this subject extensively. Finally, he understands this type of construction. Jack has newfound confidence and a lot of energy. So, he gets back to working on his writings. He writes a poem on marine construction:

> On the water, but not for a cruise, putting together decks and docks, produces excellent views, as the sun rises across the horizon, as beautiful as the birth of a newborn, people pay good money, for waterfront property, so there is always a demand for piers, yet the work isn't easy, even with machinery, to lift poles and boards, but when put together right, good pay you are ensured,

I can't wait for the job interview.

"Hey Jack. What are you working on?" Shirley asks.

"Well, I'm studying and writing about marine construction. I plan to work in this field if my job interview goes well. I could use the money. I love reading to others. But it's just not possible to accumulate a lot of money by reading to people. Hopefully, I can progress financially by getting this job," Jack replies.

Shirley nods her head and says, "Can't you do both? You are such a good reader. You've taught me so much just by saying things out loud."

"I've never thought about doing both. I may try this. I love reading so thanks for the idea."

Shirley is smart. I'll miss her insights whenever I leave this place. Jack watches a bit of television and then it's time for dinner. At dinner, all Jack can think about is writing. It's like he is obsessed with the craft. Jack is composing a poem without writing any lines down. He gets to about the fourth line and starts forgetting the previous bars. Oh well, I'll get to writing when I get back to the shelter.

Back in the shelter, a small group wants to go to the gym. I'll put off writing later so that I can go to the gym now. At the gym, Jack gets comfortable in the weight room by doing a warmup. Shirley does some stretching. She is very limber. Then, they lift weights. Shirley's legs are slightly more powerful than Jack's. His pride is not hurt because a woman is stronger than him.

After lifting weights, the small group plays basketball. What an ugly game. There are plenty of airballs and double dribbles. Yet Jack is having fun. He manages to cross over his opponent and makes a layup. Then, Shirley shoots a nice three-point jumper.

After the game, everyone is tired. They get in the sauna. They stay in it for 30 minutes. Jack is comfortable and at ease that he almost falls asleep. He wants to stay in here longer, but everyone else leaves the sauna. Then, they all take showers at the gym and head back to the shelter.

Jack is so sore that he can barely move. He did a full body workout. So, practically every part of his body hurts. Jack is surprised at this feeling because he has no runner's high. I'm just in pain- no high. But I still want to go to the gym tomorrow to get into shape. Feeling relaxed, Jack reads an interesting 19th century novel for an hour. Then sleep gets the best of him, so he takes a nap.

When he awakens, James is yelling, "Time for bed everyone!"

Jack walks to his cot and calls it a night. At about 12:00 AM, Jack gets up to use the bathroom. But struggles to do so because he is even more sore than earlier in the day. Somehow, he manages to sleep through the pain. He wakes up just before the lights are turned on. Jack spends this downtime thinking about what to do today.

He plans to visit the bookstore and the public library. He also wants to go to the gym to lift weights and maybe swim for a bit. As soon as the lights come on, Jack does some writing. He writes this poem on exercising:

> For strength and for looks, the good feeling from lifting weights, will get you hooked, which I don't think is a bad thing, watching your diet, not eating and drinking whatever you desire, self-discipline is required, delayed gratification, which we try to teach our kids, having rewards for behavior, positive

> reinforcement, so I do something I like, every
> now and then, going out with friends, getting
> into great shape, every time I go to the gym,
> also getting compliments, I really love them,

His stomach growls and thankfully it is time for breakfast. Today the soup kitchen serves a hot breakfast. This includes eggs, bacon, pancakes, and French toast. The chefs get it right. The French toast is exquisite. The aroma of this toast with syrup is irresistible. It's so irresistible that everyone at the table eats some. Jack goes back for seconds.

Shirley says, "Jack, you're going to be fat. It doesn't matter how much you exercise because of the way you eat."

Jack looks at his stomach. He has a small gut. He thinks about what Shirley says. But he ignores her and continues eating. Jack is incensed by her comment since she isn't the leanest woman. But she's a good friend so I won't respond negatively. At least not this time.

After breakfast, Jack is ready to go to the bookstore. The bookstore is four stories high. The size of the bookstore makes Jack happy. I can have fun in a place like this. He decides to browse from the top floor and work his way down. A book on the mind catches Jack's attention. He picks it up and skims through almost half of it. The main idea is that the mind is more plastic than previously thought. Even in old age it can learn new things. As a neuroscientist, I was taught that brain cells are not created after birth. Yet we were wrong. I guess you can teach an old dog new tricks.

Next, Jack picks up a book on human memory. This book teaches mnemonic techniques. Which allows anyone to remember at a faster rate than normal. He looks at the price and realizes something- he should check if the public library has a similar book. Why pay for something when you can get it for free? After going through cursory readings of several books, Jack needs a break.

So, he orders coffee. The heat from the coffee warms his entire head and throat- this is very relaxing. He sips on coffee and thinks about what to read next in this colossal bookstore. Jack gets a little hungry and orders a chocolate chip cookie. He devours it in two bites. Then, he checks the time. It is a few hours before lunch at the soup kitchen. I'll go to the public library before eating a real meal. Jack finds Shirley. She is listening to an audiobook.

They take public transportation to the public library. The library looks as good as a 5-star hotel. The computers are modern. It may be better than my college library. Wanting to improve his fitness, Jack checks out a book on bodybuilding by Arnold Schwarzenegger. Even though Jack doesn't want to be that big, he figures the book contains something useful.

He hasn't seen Shirley since entering the public library. Like the bookstore, the library is huge. He searches for her from the top floor on down. He spots her sitting Indian style reading a book on yoga. She doesn't see him approaching her.

Then, out of the corner of her eye she sees Jack and says, "Oh, Hey Jack. Did you find anything interesting?"

"Yes. I found a book on weightlifting by Arnold. I want to go to the gym immediately to try out some of his tips."

It's like Shirely doesn't hear him. She doesn't look up and probably never stops reading.

"Well, let's go," Jack says.

"Let me finish reading this page."

They check the books out and head back to the shelter. Back at the shelter, a few people want Jack to read out loud to them. But Jack wants to read Arnold's book on bodybuilding. However, he reminds himself that he gets paid to read out loud. So, Jack sets the bodybuilding book aside and reads a classic novel to a homeless man. Jack's voice is monotonous because all he can think about is reading Arnold's book on bodybuilding.

The homeless man notices Jack's lack of excitement and says, "I thought they said you were a good reader?"

Thinking that the man is getting smart, Jack replies, "Do you want me to read out loud or what?"

"Continue on."

Aware of sounding boring, Jack picks up the pace and reads out loud like he normally does. After ten minutes, the man's face lights up. He has that look that all people have when they hear Jack read. They are all astonished at his ability.

Jack is enjoying reading out loud and is surprised when it is time for lunch. Seemingly obsessed with yoga, Shirley carries this yoga book on their way to the soup kitchen. She is walking rather quickly and sits at a table to read the book right away. It's almost like she is speed reading.

The other people at the table engage in small talk as Jack eats pasta. The penne pasta is excellent. A fine restaurant couldn't cook it any better. While everyone is eating, Jame announces that people from jobs services are stopping by later. To help everyone prepare for a decent job. This is something new. Usually James talks about jobs, but no one has come in to help in this manner. Jack isn't really listening since he has the marine construction job lined up. Jack continues to eat pasta.

Shirley isn't paying attention. She is into this book on yoga. Back at the shelter, Jack gets back to reading to a homeless man. Then, he has some time to himself and reads some of

Arnold's book on bodybuilding. He compares his physique to Arnold's. I have a long way to go. He is nowhere near Arnold's size nor definition. Jack vows to one day look something like Arnold. I want to go to the gym now.

Jack asks some people at the shelter if they want to go with him. No one feels like going. Shirley, who usually loves the gym, is still into her yoga book. I'll go at it alone.

This is the first time Jack has no company at the gym and it is very boring. The walk there just feels different. Once at the gym, Jack blocks out this feeling and gets to work in the weight room. Today is chest day. Meaning, Jack only does exercises that target his chest. He doesn't have a spotter. So, he is careful not to put too much weight on the bar. Jack has been to the gym in the past few weeks, so the workout doesn't make his chest sore- well at least not for now.

After an hour of weightlifting, Jack hits the sauna. While in the sauna, delayed soreness in his chest occurs. He does a bit of stretching and heads to the jacuzzi.

Jack really relaxes in the jacuzzi. After almost falling asleep a couple times: he gets out of the jacuzzi, takes a quick shower, and walks back to the shelter. The walk back is enjoyable. His chest is no longer sore, and he feels as though he has an energy boost. At the shelter, he reads some of Arnold's book and does some writing:

> One day I'll get big, one day I'll be cut, just gotta keep lifting and not get stuck, at a plateau, no, keep pushing on, to look great, there's nothing wrong, hope to compete, in tournaments with my physique, I'll be the one to beat,

Not bad. Jack also writes this poem on marine construction:

> Waiting for low tide in order to work, digging out dirt to put rods in, to stabilize the wall, it takes all, of my strength not to fall, working so intensely, but I guess this is exercise, so it's good for me, no need to complain, just take short breaks, ignore some of the muscle pain, focus must be maintained, because the work can be dangerous, water may be deep, other crew members too anxious, and various accidents from a lack of concentration may occur,

Then, Jack writes this poem on dieting:

> I want to take sweets out of my diet, to get in better shape, I'll try to, but what else will I eat, because I don't feel full, without a treat, I gotta have the discipline of a yoga master, mind over matter, I must watch what I eat, because I'd rather be cut, than have a beer belly,

Not bad. Jack stops writing because his hand becomes tired. This happens when Jack becomes inspired and flows for a long period of time. He has downtime since he isn't reading to anyone for the next 1 ½ hours. So, he decides to play checkers against a young boy.

Jack has seen him whip everyone of all ages. Jack, who used to play this game often, believes he can defeat him. But it isn't meant to be. Jack plays 15 games and wins none of them.

The young boy just laughs and laughs. This irritates Jack. Who is now more motivated to beat this boy. But he can't. The boy is just too good.

Frustrated by the defeats, Jack reads Arnold's book. Hyped up, Jack drops down and does pushups. He can only do five of them because his chest is tight from working out at the gym. So, he reads more of Arnold's book on bodybuilding. The young boy, Kent, who beat him in checkers, sees Jack reading this book. Kent is intrigued.

"How good is that book?" Kent asks.

"It's very good. If you want to get into excellent shape. As a matter of fact, drop down and give me 20 pushups."

Kent smiles and says, "I'll try."

He starts out with perfect form. However, on the 10th pushup, his muscles begin to tire, and it's obvious that he is straining. He tries to do one more pushup, but his arms are shaking. Also, all the veins in his forehead are popping out.

"All right Kent, stop. You are maxing out. You should do more exercises to get stronger," Jack says.

Kent nods his head and drinks water. Jack is so impressed with Kent. Most young boys are not as strong as him. Kent is in great shape because he does sit-ups and runs around the city every morning and evening.

From now on Kent goes to the gym whenever Jack goes. Jack gets back to reading Arnold's book. He is already half-way done with reading the book. He feels that he has learned a lot. In fact, he is ready to hit the gym now because he is so inspired. After dinner, Jack gets right back to reading. He does not read out loud to anyone. He spends all evening reading Arnold's book. He can't believe how much he has learned about fitness.

Jack envisions lifting weights with Kent. He is reminded of playing sports with his son many years ago. Tears drop down his face. Well, it's time for bed. The lights are turned off. Jack can't wait until tomorrow.

Chapter 13

JACK WAKES UP FULL of life and writes these poems before breakfast:

> Up early I am, today will be special, as I mind wrestle, doubt of making it out, of the shelter, better than when I came here, so far I've made friends that are dear, to my heart and soul, they won't let me fold, they tell me I'm bold, as I hold on to their every word, like the Sun will shine once again, the audacity of hope, it's been an uphill climb to the mountain top, now I'm cruising down the slope, it's all downhill from now on, there's nothing wrong, with a big dose of self-belief,
>
> I've got an ace in the hole, loaded dice when I roll, only strikes when I bowl, a diamond around coal, in other words, the fight is fixed, rigged, for me come out with big, money from my poems and books, I get the audience hooked, like a skilled boxer, drunk off my words, like they're lager, my rhymes a delicacy, like lobster,

Jack talks with Kent after breakfast and they go to the gym. Kent wants to do chest exercises to look bigger. Jack teaches him exercises to work other muscles, but Kent still focuses on working his chest. After bench pressing, Kent poses in the mirror as if that exercise alone makes his chest significantly bigger. Jack laughs to himself. He recalls doing this when he was younger.

Jack does biceps curls and then works his abs. Now Kent is doing pushups. It's clearly hurting him because his body is shaking as he presses up. Jack would tell him to rest, but Jack is sure experience is a better teacher than a warning.

Sure enough, after about 4 pushups, Kent says, "I think I've worked my chest too much. It is throbbing in pain, and it hurts to touch it. I'll never work any muscle this hard again."

Jack smiles, nods his head, and finishes his workout on the ab machine. After lifting weights, Jack and Kent get in the sauna. Kent feels better and is not as sore as he once was. I'm glad he didn't work his legs Jack thinks. He wouldn't have been able to walk. Jack, having lifted weights for some time, is not sore at all. He uses moderate weight and does not strain. Jack rarely pushes himself to the absolute limit.

Kent sees Jack zoning out and says, "What are you thinking about?"

"I remember how rough it was living on the street."

Kent doesn't know that feeling. Fortunately, his parents were able to stay in shelters along with their kids. He has never gone hungry in his whole life. The only problem he encountered was being teased by a bully in elementary school. He ignores bullies now and concentrates on school. He dreams of going to college in the USA.

Jack helps him with his studies, but Kent rarely needs assistance. Kent knows nothing of Jack's past. Jack never talks about anything before becoming homeless. But Kent knows Jack is smart. Whenever Jack works on a math problem for Kent, his homework has never been marked wrong by his teachers. And Jack never turns him away. No matter the time of day or night.

Jack reads the newspaper to an illiterate man for some time. Worn out from both exercising and reading out loud, Jack takes a short nap before lunch. Instead of just a nap, he deep sleeps and dreams well, he has nightmares. He envisions himself drowning when he falls in the water. While doing marine construction. Then, he has a nightmare about weightlifting. The bar drops on his chest as he benches. This nightmare wakes him up and he can't get back to sleep. Jack is just lying on his cot.

It's now time for lunch. The soup kitchen only serves peanut butter and jelly sandwiches. Jack can't believe this. Allowing world-class chefs to make us meals and now we are down to nothing but basic sandwiches? Not wanting to get too worked up, Jack eats the sandwiches with milk.

Jack looks around as other people are enjoying these sandwiches. Shirley must be hungry. She scarfs down a sandwich like she's in an eating contest. Kent seems to be enjoying himself. Jack eats until he is full. Jack's stomach begins to churn on the walk back to the shelter. He is no longer walking normally.

"Are you ok?" Shirley asks.

"Yeah. I just ate too many sandwiches. Sometimes peanut butter hurts my stomach, but I'll be fine later."

As soon as he gets back to the shelter, Jack lies down on his cot. This doesn't help. Jack is now sweating. He gets up to walk around, but he can't stand upright. So, he takes some medicine immediately and is relieved.

James approaches him and says, "I heard you are looking for

a new job? Why aren't you happy reading to homeless people?" Before answering, Jack thinks about why James cares so much. Reading to people does not take a whole lot of skill or effort.

Jack says, "Well, I need more money. I want to leave this shelter one day and get on with my life."

"That's understandable. However, by the time you travel to the work sites and factor in other costs, you'll break even. So, it is best if you continue reading to others for money."

I knew there was something I didn't like about this guy. How can I respond to this?

Jack says, "I see where you are coming from. But I'm tired of being in the shelter all day. I need some air and space. Don't' get me wrong; I enjoy reading to others, but I want to make money another way. I cannot be persuaded otherwise."

James is quiet for a few minutes.

Then he says, "Suit yourself." And he walks away.

Jack is concerned that he made the boss angry. He may disrupt my peaceful existence at the shelter. He seems like that type of person. Jack is mad. He picks up a book to read but can't. All he can do is picture punching James I the mouth to shut him up for good.

I can't do that. I can't unleash on someone I disagree with. Jack envisions unloading a haymaker on James in his office. Then, the police arresting Jack. I can't win. Then again, excluding James's bickering, the shelter is not a bad place to live.

The people are friendly and the food in the soup kitchen is usually delicious. But sometimes the snoring of other people is unbearable. Jack goes to the computer room to check his email. But all the computer stations are occupied. What should I do now? There is a group playing card games. Jack never plays poker, so he scans the shelter- seeing if there is anything interesting to be involved in. Most of the people are socializing- Shirley is talking to friends as usual. I might as well read a book. Finally, someone is done on a computer, so Jack checks his email:

> "Hey Jack, I hope you are doing fine. I'm doing ok and I've managed to find a decent-paying job. I've been working it for a short time, but in a few weeks, I'll see if I can find a job for you there. I'm still smoothing things over with my family. So that you can stay at our house. Write back soon, Curtis."

Initially, Jack is elated, but then realizes he won't be able to leave the shelter any time soon. Curtis says it will take weeks or months for his family to think of trusting Jack. How can I deal with James for another day? Better yet for another month or two?

To calm down, Jack reads a classic novel. He reads until "lights out." Jack sleeps well and wakes up before the lights are turned on. So, Jack is in his cot thinking and planning. What should I do today? I'll go to the gym with Kent later. I may do some writing. I'm not sure how much free time I'll have because James will surely find work for me today. Jack isn't mad at this- he just gets tired of always following James's orders.

It's so frustrating. But I'll make the most of it and try not to complain. Just after this thought, the lights are on. Jack opens his eyes and is ready for the day. Breakfast is decent and Jack eats French toast- one of his favorite breakfast meals. Jack eats five slices and downs some milk to wash them down. Jack is ready to go the gym. He tells Kent they'll go as soon as they get back to the shelter.

At the shelter, James tells Jack, "Read to this homeless man immediately!"

"Can't I do that later?"

"No! I want you to read to him as soon as possible. It's important and going to the gym is a privilege not a right. I don't care what you want," James replies.

Well, my days here are numbered. I may move into an apartment soon. But I must listen to him right now. So, Jack finds the homeless man to read to. The man has a newspaper and a book that he wants Jack to read out loud. The newspaper is not that thick, so Jack reads it all in about 30 minutes.

Then he dives into Tom Sawyer. Jack has never read this book in its entirety. But he is now thoroughly enjoying reading it. With a glass of water at his side, Jack reads for 2 hours before he gets tired. Then Jack does some writing. He writes two poems:

> If pain is weakness leaving the body, then I should be stronger than everybody, mental pain is real and robs me, in my pursuit of happiness, of inner peace, stress is like putting a dog on a choker leash, you can't go far without something pulling you back, panic attacks, no matter how macho you act, complicates just relaxing,

> If I could have one-fifth the tolerance of Jesus, and his patience, I wouldn't be so anxious, to slap James or anyone, just over words, because I've heard, a hotheaded person, is always immersed in conflict, he doesn't know inner peace, yes James's attitude is getting

> to me, and if I tell him this, I risk, losing a
> decent place to live, but I can't go back to my
> cardboard palace, something has gotta give,

Emulating Jesus will help me deal with James. Jack changes his thoughts abruptly to get this man and his attitude off his mind. So, he decides to engage in conversation with the people at the lunch table. He talks to Shirley about whether English Literature is better than American Literature or vise-versa. Extremely passionate, Shirley makes a good case for both.

She explains that both are great. Jack weighs in and believes English Literature is better because it has been around longer. Shirley attacks this belief and logically it doesn't make sense. Jack recants and says that both are great. Other people at the table agree that both genres are great. Shirley should've been a lawyer. She is so articulate. She is good at proving arguments false.

Jack has never asked about her background. Whether she attended college or was self-educated. It's obvious that she is very intelligent. After lunch, Jack isn't sure if he should go to the gym since James wants him to work. So, he tells Kent that they'll go to the gym perhaps later. Without this job of reading out loud, Jack wouldn't have any money. He refuses to beg again. So, all he can do is eat at the soup kitchen and check out books from the public library. Staying in this shelter all the time would drive me crazy.

Jack gets back on his job of reading Tom Sawyer to a homeless man. The good thing about reading is that it keeps you distracted from thinking about unpleasant things. Like punching James in the mouth. Jack is really into reading out loud, so the time flies by. However, the homeless man is getting restless sitting for so long.

Jack notices this and says, "Well, I'll read more of this book another time."

"Thank you for reading to me. Hopefully you can finish reading this book to me soon."

Now what do I want to do? I'm tired of reading and I don't want to write anything. So, I'll take a nap. During his nap, Jack can only dream of one thing: hitting James in the mouth. Wow! My subconscious is really taking over. However, the dream doesn't make him hate James. Instead, Jack wants to find inner peace some kind of way.

Jack wonders if she should: go to church, take up yoga, or do anything that is supposed to have a calming effect. Maybe I should go to the gym. Maybe I should go for a walk. Jack doesn't tell anyone he's leaving because he wants to be alone.

Then his mind wanders to his son Brent. This brings a tear to his eye. As he recalls how sweet his life had been before quitting his job. He used to make six figures. But now he can't even buy a nice pair of shoes without feeling the pinch.

Jack walks into a clothing store just to occupy his mind. The clothes look way better than what Jack is wearing. But the clothes are out of his narrow price range. Jack only stays in the store for a few minutes. Because he is tired of looking at these threads. Jack walks back to the shelter- ready to eat dinner.

The soup kitchen smells of something that Jack is not familiar with. Everyone is trying to figure out the foreign smells. Some believe it is just strange spices, but everyone is shocked when the chefs tell them what the food is. The chefs prepare a Middle Eastern meal. It smells spicy and Jack decides to try some of the food. Plus, it's not like he could find quality free food anywhere else.

At first, Jack dislikes the meal. But after a few bites he loves it. He hears one of the chefs say it's an acquired taste.

Before they know it, everyone is full and looking forward to more of this type of food later in the week. Back at the shelter, Jack is bored.

With no one to read to and tired of writing- Jack twiddles his thumbs. He wonders if he should give James a piece of his mind. It's not worth it. He decides to find Shirley to have an interesting conversation. Jack finds her laughing and having fun playing a board game. Everyone seems happy playing the game- feeding off Shirley's positive energy. Jack spends the rest of the night playing this board game until the lights are turned out.

Chapter 14

A FEW DAYS LATER, today is the day for Jack's job interview for the marine construction job. Jack puts on his best clothes given to him and heads down to the docks. He has money on his mind.

After arriving at the facility, Jack waits for a few minutes until he is called into the office. The room is clean and smells of cheap cologne. The interviewer is a middle-aged man with bags under his eyes. He is wearing a bright green polyester suit which clashes with Jack's idea of a construction worker.

He greets Jack with a smile and says, "I'm glad you made it. Let's get started."

After a few detailed questions, it is obvious Jack doesn't know a lot about marine construction. And then something mind turns on and he able to answer certain questions. Jack can see the light in the interviewer's eyes as he correctly answers question after question. The interview lasts for about 20 minutes and Jack is hired on the spot. He starts work tomorrow.

After the interview, Jack heads to a clothing store immediately. He buys jeans, work shirts, and rugged boots. Jack is so happy to have this job that he tells everyone he sees at the shelter. Jack is excited that it's hard for him to eat lunch. After lunch, Jack and Kent go to the gym.

Jack knows the marine construction job requires a certain degree of strength. So, he has another incentive to lift weights. So, the gym session is intense. After sitting in the sauna for some time, both guys are sore as a board. They want to lie down somewhere and relax.

Once they get back to the shelter, Jack reads a bit to another homeless person. While Kent stretches out on his cot and goes to sleep. After dinner, Jack tucks it in early to be well rested for the first day of his new job.

The morning comes quickly, and Jack is ready to work. He dresses and puts on his new boots. Jack takes the train to the docks. He immediately sees his new boss. He must be better than James.

"Glad you are on time Jack. Let's get you acquainted with some things before you do any work," Nick, the boss, says.

So, they spend an hour going over basic concepts of marine construction. Then Nick shows Jack the equipment being used. Even though it will be some time before Jack has enough training to use the heavy machinery.

"We are going to a jobsite. I want you to get on the barge and ride it until we get to a specific bulkhead."

Jack nods and eagerly gets on the barge. Jack notices all the lumber on the barge and is not completely sure how this lumber is oriented. Then, Jack's mind wanders because he's riding on the barge for 30 minutes. He thinks about his son and plans to email him again when he gets back to the shelter. Before Jack realizes it, it is time to get off the barge and go to work.

Nick explains exact what Jack will do today. Jack carries lumber to the bulkhead line and hold the lumber until it can be driven into the ground. Having been going to the gym regularly, Jack moves the boards with ease. Jack is working too fast, and the other workers are snickering. They know he'll burn out soon from lifting boards so fast.

But Jack doesn't feel any burning in his muscles yet. They break for lunch, and Nick buys chicken for everyone. The crew talks to each other for a little bit, then it's back to work. For the first 15 minutes Jack is moving like he did in the morning. However, after working for about an hour, his muscles, especially the muscles in his lower back tighten up. His arms feel heavy and he's a little weary.

One of the experienced workers says, "You are working too quickly. We are surprised that you can even walk."

Jack thinks about this for a while. He realizes no one else is rushing to put the boards up. The workers are moving at a steady pace, and now Jack learns something. This is almost like going to the gym Jack thinks.

The workday is over, and Nick says, "Great work Jack! Hopefully you won't be too sore and come back tomorrow."

Then he pats Jack on the back.

"See you tomorrow," Jack says meekly.

Tired, Jack debates whether to go to the gym later. As soon as he gets back to the shelter, everyone asks him how his day went. He tells them all about how worn out he is. And he tells Kent that he's skipping the gym today to recover. Jack hasn't seen James yet and he's so tired he's not even angry anymore.

Jack takes a shower and then relaxes until it is time for dinner. As usual, dinner is at the soup kitchen. Man, I can barely walk right now. My lower back is extremely sore. He manages to walk to the soup kitchen.

Maybe all that work made Jack hungry because all the food smells and tastes excellent. Jack looks around and no one else is savoring every bite. Maybe the food isn't all that great tonight. Jack finishes his meal with some ice cream. He is so tired that he can barely pay attention to what Shirley is saying. All he can think about is how lovely his cot will feel. When Jack gets back to the shelter, he tries to read. He then lies on his cot and falls into a deep sleep. The lights are still on, and Jack doesn't even notice.

He sleeps soundly and then suddenly, it's time for work. After a long yawn, Jack puts on his work clothes and hops on the train. Still sore in his lower back, he really feels it when he gets off the train at the docks. The day is uneventful. Jack paces himself carrying boards, so work isn't that bad. After work, he is not tired and plans to go the gym later.

Dinner is good. The main course is steak. Jack absolutely loves steak. Especially with mashed potatoes. Which are what the chefs cook with the tender steaks.

At the gym with Kent, Jack exercises his lower back to make it stronger for work. Surprisingly, Jack isn't tired from lifting weights. So, he swims a few laps. Jack notices how swimming relaxes his muscles. He vows to swim as much as possible before or after lifting weights.

The sauna feels so good that Jack doesn't want to get out of it. Even though his skins prunes, Jack stays in the sauna longer than usual. In fact, he almost falls asleep until Kent nudges him.

Then Jack sits in the jacuzzi to relax even more. Kent plays basketball while Jack sits in the jacuzzi. Kent holds his own on the court. Basketball is Kent's favorite sport, and he loves everything about it. He's such a great player that if he keeps his grades up, he'll play in college or beyond. Since Kent's parents don't have much money, a basketball scholarship is what he is striving for. He can already dunk with ease.

Back at the shelter, Jack and Kent play cards. Until James tells Jack to follow him to his office.

"Well Jack, I'm glad you found employment elsewhere and you are on your way to being independent. I've heard that there is an opening in public housing that you could take advantage of." Jack isn't happy about this. Although public housing is a real home, it is in a rough part of the city. So, it's a lot safer to stay in the shelter.

Before Jack can speak, James says, "I know you have gotten word about public housing. I will admit that being in a rough neighborhood can be challenging, but you will have a large degree of privacy. And you won't have to deal with me. So, do you want to at least try to live like that?"

Jack doesn't want to regress. The shelter is better than living on the street. But living on the street was safer than living in a rough part of the city. So, it's safety first.

"James, we may have our disagreements, but I'll reside in the shelter."

"Suit yourself," James says.

Of course, I'm going to suit myself. So that is that. Jack leaves the office and continues playing cards. He can't concentrate because James is on his mind. Wow, he hates me for no reason. What have I done to him? Jack is glad it is almost lights out. Because he wants to get these negative thoughts off his mind. Jack sleeps well. And before he knows it, it's time for another day of work doing marine construction.

Yawning while on the docks, Jack tries to remember what he learned yesterday. He closes his eye as he recounts how to hold boards until a machine hammers them down in the water. He then recalls how to make certain measurements on the boards. To ensure that the boards are tight to each other. So that the boards hold up from the pressure from the incoming tide. At the jobsite, it's another day of putting boards down in the water.

Jack paces himself and isn't tired all day. The other workers are impressed by his stamina. Jack tries to look tough in front of them, but his back is hurting. Maybe I'm not lifting the boards correctly. Jack asks one of the veteran workers about this and he says Jack is lifting the boards properly. It takes time for muscles to adapt to this type of work.

Not tired like yesterday, Jack goes to the gym with Kent. He lifts some weights, but mainly stays in the pool because it relaxes the muscles in his lower back. Bent on getting bigger, Kent is in the weight room for an hour. Then, they sit in the sauna. Then, they sit in the jacuzzi. This must be like heaven, Jack thinks. Jack falls asleep and Kent must nudge him awake.

When they get back to the shelter, Jack checks his email to see if Curtis replied to his message. He has not. Oh well. I'll do some reading to distract myself. Jack is still upset that James wants him in public housing. Jack wants to complain to a higher up, but he doesn't know anyone above James. So, there isn't a person to report to. How frustrating. He is mad but calms down and plays board games to ease his mind. Then Jack reads a little bit of a novel, and it's lights out.

Chapter 15

He wakes up early and has time to read something before getting ready for work. He reads the newspaper but stops reading it after a few articles because it's so negative. Instead of putting boards in the ground, the crew is now making a pier for the house of a club owner.

The pier will be 500 feet long and the crew works fast. In just one day of work, the pier is halfway done, and Jack can't believe it. Jack is proud of how much work he has done. Jack screws in the deck boards. In the afternoon, Jack continues putting screws in for a few hours. His hand is tired. But it isn't that bad. After work, Jack and Kent go to the gym as soon as Jack comes home.

Jack swims in the pool for a short time and then goes to the weight room. Kent has been training hard and has already worked up a sweat. Jack sees him bench pressing. He is really getting strong. He'll be stronger than me in no time. If not already.

"Hey Kent, do you need a spotter?" Jack notices Kent struggling on his last repetition.

"Yeah sure," Kent responds as he takes a few breaths to prepare to move this heavy weight again.

Kent starts off strong. But after a few reps, he moves the bar slowly. Jack is about to assist Kent, but he shakes his head and does the last rep all by himself. The weight is 340 pounds- which is extraordinary for a 14-year-old. Kent is somewhat muscular, but no one would guess that he is that strong. After bench pressing, Kent heads to the squat rack.

Squatting is Kent's favorite lift. Because it makes you jump higher. The only bad thing about squatting is that your whole body becomes sore. Donning his weightlifting belt, Kent is ready to work. He warms up with light weight and then squats heavy weight for the next 5 minutes. Afterwards, Kent can barely stand.

Kent looks at Jack and says, "I know. I know. I'm training too hard. But this is the only way I can get strong fast."

"Maybe. But how many years can you lift like this before your body gives out? You're already waddling like a duck," Jack says.

"I can lift for many years with this same intensity. My body recovers like no other."

You'll see Jack thinks. There is no way you can punish yourself year after year.

Back at the shelter, rumor has it that James may be leaving the shelter. Jack holds his contentment inside and just nods when told the news. Supposedly, James is looking to move close to Seattle, Washington. Because the hospital there is one of the best in the world. His wife has a rare form of leukemia. Fortunately, the doctors caught the cancer early, so it's likely she will survive with proper treatment.

Jack feels sorry for James's wife but doesn't really care about James. Jack can't empathize with him because of how disrespectful he is. Jack gets in his cot and isn't sure if he should be happy or not. But then decides to go to sleep. At least tomorrow starts the weekend is Jack's last thought before nodding off.

He wakes up to a pleasant smell coming from the cleaning crew. They are vacuuming and washing the carpet in the shelter. The odor reminds him of freshly made lemonade. The cleaning crew is busy every Saturday and Jack still loves this aroma. Unable to get back to sleep, Jack washes his face and is ready for the day. Sometimes on Saturdays James plans trips for everyone. Like going to the aquarium and even a trip to a sporting event like a basketball game.

Today, however, is a day to do nothing. Tired from his first week of marine construction, Jack doesn't want to do much. Jack doesn't feel like going to the gym either. Jack cracks open the novel he has been reading lately. He is wrapped up in the plot. He finished reading the book and is now bored.

So, he finds friends and they play a board game. It's fun and this social interaction is what Jack needs. Instead of being a loner. He wins a few games, and this shocks him. He usually never wins at this board game for some reason. Whether it is luck or skill, today is Jack's lucky day. He boasts that he should play the slots. After playing the board game, Jack decides to do some writing. He writes this poem:

> At first I go blank, like my mind has stalled,
> then ideas come down, like the leaves in fall,
> I call on every brain cell, when I write, to be
> active, to create a massive, horde of informa-
> tion, then I scribble down an amazing, array
> of wordplays, designed to thrill any readers,
> and to leave them eager, to read more of what
> I have in store, in later pages,

Then he writes this poem:

> A life of contrasts, eating gourmet food, to scavenging in trash, thankfully I'm past that, but what if I never, had discovered the shelter, living while others ignored me on the streets, or picked on me, abused verbally and occasionally physically, but I made It through, not how I used to live, in a big house, yet I'm content about, having the bare necessities,

He reads these poems to Shirley.

"Great!" She says while hand clapping.

"You should submit the first poem to a poetry contest."

Jack nods and finds a website that will pay $ 1,000 to the winner. While on the computer, Jack checks his email and sees that Curtis has left him a message. Curtis is finally able to convince his family to allow Jack to move in as soon as possible. This good news excites Jack, but now he isn't sure if he wants to leave the shelter.

So, he writes to Curtis explaining his intention of staying in the shelter for an extended period. Jack takes a short nap and wakes up for lunch.

It seems lie the soup kitchen is cutting back. Because today, lunch is nothing but gruel. In the lunch line, Jack wants to go up to the servers and say "more sir" just like Oliver Twist. But he changes his mind. Because you never want to anger those dealing with your food. Surprisingly, the gruel is tasty. Jack goes back for seconds. Everyone comments on the food and has the same sentiment as him.

Some of the people at the shelter are going to an art museum. I might as well go. This art gallery is amazing. Even though Jack is no expert on art, he can see the skill and detail in it from the outset. There are works by famous artists and some works by relatively unknown artists.

Jack is fascinated by DaVinci's artwork. The curator explains Davinci's masterpieces. Jack likes every painting in the gallery. Jack has an appreciation for art and wonders at how creative people can be. After about 2 hours in the gallery, the group heads back to the shelter. At the shelter, all the kids are explaining how marvelous the art gallery is to those that didn't go. This brings a smile to Jack's face.

Feeling inspired, Jack writes this poem on art:

> To each his own interpretation, when judging art, if one can even judge art, artists may not have a message in their work, they just flirt with different themes, and commit to none, they just make something that's fun, something that may not last a generation, being skilled in the art of writing, I liken portraits to essays, to the point, with only what's essential,

Jack shares this short poem with Shirley.

"Wow! This is good!" She speaks.

Jack blushes and says, "It could be better.

Always the perfectionist, Jack revises this poem 15 times. Still feeling inspired, he writes 6 poems and a substantial number of pages of his novel. At dinner, Jack spaces out: only thinking about what he wants to write next. After the meal, he rushes back to the shelter and continues to write. Now he must stop because of soreness in his hand. Proud of himself, Jack goes to sleep with a smile.

It's now Sunday and a priest is at the shelter preaching.

Jack usually stays away from religion even though he was raised in the church. Whenever he thinks about Christianity, he thinks of religious leaders explaining "Fire and Brimstone." They try to make him feel guilty about everything. But this priest is different.

The sermon only lasts 15 minutes, yet it is so impactful. Jack studies scriptures associated with the sermon. These scriptures explain how you should never hate anyone. And always love thy neighbor. Wow. Treating James like this will be challenging, but I'll try. After reading some scriptures, Jack and Kent go to the gym for an afternoon workout.

There aren't many people in the gym. This is great because no one is on the equipment Jack wants to use. Jack works his abs for most of his workout and then exercises his chest. Kent works his back and then works his abs. Since they both go to the gym regularly, they rarely get sore from lifting weights. After lifting weights, they play basketball. They run the floor for a while until Jack is tired.

Being young, Kent isn't breathing hard when he says, "Jack, are you ok?"

Jack tries to catch his breath, but he can't talk right now.

Jack holds up his hand and finally says, "I don't know if I'm ok. But I'll never play this hard again."

Eventually Jack is fine. He feels normal after coming out of the sauna. When they get back to the shelter, Jack falls on his cot and is fast asleep. He doesn't sleep long and is up reading to someone. This time he is reading to an illiterate who wants to be great at chess. So, Jack is reading a book on chess to Antonio.

After about an hour, Antonio says, "That's enough for today. I need to understand what I've heard."

Jack shakes his head- perplexed that this illiterate person can play a mentally demanding game such as chess. Antonio walks to a chess board and practices the moves that Jack read to him. Jack watches Antonio talk to himself as moves the chess pieces. Then Jack reads a novel by Oscar Wilde. It is so good that Jack must stop himself from reading anymore. Then he decides to socialize and walks over to people playing Connect-4.

Everyone seems to be in a good mood. Eddie, a great Connect-4 player, taunts Jack before the game starts. Eddie is a known braggart. Boasting doesn't matter to Jack. He tunes everyone out- he is trying to win. Eddie destroys Jack in the first 2 games and of course, talks more trash.

Eddie says, "Hey college boy, what are you gonna do now?"

"You'll see," Jack replies calmly.

Sure enough, Jack wins the next game and that ticks Eddie off. It rare for anyone to beat Eddie. And Jack, who barely plays, of all people, defeats him. Eddie takes a few deep breaths to settle himself down. He is ready to play again. After winning the next game, Eddie is back being confident. Jack is trying his best, but he can't beat Eddie anymore. After 10 frustrating games, Jack resigns to his cot and reopens that novel by Oscar Wilde.

Jack isn't upset over losing, just a bit disappointed. The book distracts him from this feeling as he is totally immersed in this book. The time flies by and it's time for bed. Man, Sunday went by too fast. I have work tomorrow.

Jack sleeps soundly all night and then is up ready for work. Riding on the train to work, Jack usually doesn't pay attention to what is around him. But this time he observes how beautiful the city is. The skyscrapers are accompanied with nice apartments and squeaky-clean streets. The people walking about seem friendly and no one appears rude. This makes Jack smile, who sometimes feels that no one notices or cares about him.

Then Jack thinks about his son Brent. He probably feels like I don't care about him. Well, I'm not sure. I email him every once and awhile. But he never responds. Maybe one day he'll let me into his life. Jack believes once Brent becomes a man, his mom, who hates Jack, will have less of an influence. And their relationship will be repaired. In the meantime, I'll just stay optimistic and email him periodically.

The train conductor announces the next stop, so Jack puts his mind in work mode. Marine construction isn't super difficult, but you must be focused because it can be dangerous. Today is no exception. A mishap occurs while loading boards onto the barge. The chain holding the boards snaps from repeated stress. Fortunately, no one is hurt. Yet this is a close call. Had the chain snapped 4 feet to the left, Jack would've been seriously hurt.

This mishap alone makes Jack think about quitting. And go back to reading to the homeless back at the shelter. I don't know. The money is decent, so I'll try to stay longer. But if another accident occurs, I'm out of here. The rest of the day is rather uneventful, and Jack is glad to be off. He doesn't go straight to the shelter but stops in a coffee shop.

I just need something to calm me down. All Jack keeps replaying in his mind are the boards dropping. He has not told anyone that he is concerned. He didn't tell any of the guys at work. They would see him as being soft. He wonders if he'll tell Shirley. But she would worry, and he doesn't need that. I'll think of something. Jack heads back to the shelter with a stomach full of coffee- read to do some reading.

Jack is comfortable on his cot reading a magazine when he sees James approaching him. Jack pretends not to see him. Jack can sense he'll probably have to do something he doesn't like.

Sure enough, James, without saying hello, says, "Jack, I need to speak with you for a minute in my office."

Jack nods his head and follows James to his office.

James says, "We have a problem. The government wants to expand the shelter soon. But only disabled individuals can stay here. All able-bodied people will be moved to public housing."

Jack wants to say something to James, but he is so mad nothing good could come of it. So, Jack storms out of the office and paces around the shelter to calm down. After settling down, Jack talks to others at the shelter.

They say moving isn't that bad. It might be better since James will continue running the shelter. James won't have anything to do with public housing. Shirley checks on Jack after about an hour. He is no longer incensed.

"Jack, I know you are ticked off. But living outside of the shelter is not that bad. We'll still be around you. Plus, you can still go to the gym," Shirley says.

Jack nods his head. He recalls living on the street. Barely getting enough to eat. What was my life expectancy then? Indeed. It could have been a lot worse. No more Cardboard Palace. Dire need is the words James emphasized. Is not living on the street dire? No need to be upset. There is nothing I can do. Fortunately, furniture and kitchen appliances will be provided in public housing.

Jack does a bit of writing and before he knows it, it is time for bed. Then morning comes. Reluctantly, Jack gets up and heads to work. Today is a hard day. The weather is bad. Rain makes it hard to grip the boards properly and it's also challenging to have good footing. Thankfully, no one got hurt. Everyone is moving slowly just to be cautious. By noon, the rain was gone, and the crew was very productive.

But Jack can't focus on work. He keeps thinking of how he is tired of James. His blood pressure rises with the mere thought of living in public housing. The shelter is so comfortable. Well, I've got to think of something else. Jack thinks about the good times he has had at the shelter. Playing board games with Kent and others. Reading to a little girl who is learning to read. She is more advanced than her parents.

Which is sad since they'll probably never find good jobs. I hope I can find a great job again. It's challenging to find someone to put a good word in for me for a top job. I would rather work than live in a shelter. But I can only do my best. I'll get on my feet soon. I'll continue to work in marine construction to save up money. Then, I'll move back to the United States. The workday is now over, so Jack heads back to the shelter. Jack isn't that tired, so he goes to the gym.

He hits the heavy bag just for cardio and now he is physically tired. But Jack knows his energy will come back because he is in good shape. Now Jack lifts weights.

Right now, he's working his arms by doing biceps curls and triceps extensions. He is using moderate weight to not get injured from lifting weights. His arms ache after moving the weights. Then Jack goes back to hitting the heavy bag. Now his arms feel numb. He isn't sure if he wants to lift anymore today. He is exhausted. Jack goes back to the shelter- ready for a shower and some rest.

Chapter 16

AFTER SETTLING DOWN, JACK decides to read to someone. Shelby is 4 years old. She approaches him with one of his all-time favorite books: The Cat in the Hat by Dr. Seuss. Jack clears his throat and begins reading. He really gets into it and doesn't take a break as he reads the entire book. The little girl is happy that he did this and thanks him repeatedly. Jack nods his head, holding back the joy he feels. Then it's like something in his body kicks in and he can barely keep his eyes open.

He sees people playing a board game and he gets on his cot and falls asleep. He has pleasant dreams- typical of a day of physical exhaustion. Jack sleeps the entire night and hears the unfortunate sound of his alarm clock. Time for another day of work. Jack breathes deeply and gets ready for work. He wonders how much work they'll do since the boss has other things to do.

At work, the crew is tidying up the work area by picking up wood, plastic and cut-offs from metal bolts. This is an easy task and is not physically demanding. They finish work by lunch.

The boss says, "Well, that's all for today. Have a good day and see you all tomorrow."

Jack stops by the bookstore. He browses the new fiction section. He imagines being a best-selling author. A smile comes across his face as he visualizes people reading his book. He sees a very interesting book and checks his pockets. Well, I don't want to spend $30. So, I'll wait a few months until the book is available in the public library. What should I do with all this free time.?

The public library is on the other side of town. Jack doesn't feel like riding there on a bus or train. But I don't want to go back to the shelter yet. Jack decides to watch a movie. The ticket itself is reasonably priced, but the food costs way too much. I'm glad I'm not hungry. What movie should I see? A great action movie catches his eye. He chooses that movie. As advertised, the movie is engaging and keeps Jack's attention for the whole film. That is a great piece of escapism.

Jack changes his clothes at the shelter and walks to the soup kitchen for dinner. At dinner, Jack chats with Shirley. She is elated that he stopped at the bookstore- her favorite place to shop. She asks what new books are in print. She wants to visit the store during the weekend. Kent wants to go there too.

Jack tells them about the movie, but they want to talk about books. Jack is tired of the subject, so he zones them out. He concentrates on the food he is eating. Which is easy because the meal is exquisite. Then he zones back into the conversation.

Kent talks about lifting weights. These people don't lift weights for the most part. So, they have no idea what being strong is all about. Oh well, he's young. Then Kent talks about how strong Jack is. Jack is embarrassed. Then Jack imagines how strong he would be had he never been homeless. Before leaving his old job, Jack went to the gym regularly. He also exercised at home. He even ran around the block consistently. So, he was in excellent shape.

After dinner, Kent runs around downtown. Jack's left knee

is hurting so he opts to stay in the shelter and do some reading. Well, Jack tries to read a novel, but people keep asking him to read to them. Jack rejects them all and focuses on the novel. He reads until his eyes are tired and decides it's time for bed.

The morning comes quickly, and Jack doesn't feel like getting up. But work is work. Jack leaves the shelter a few minutes early to grab a cup of coffee. The stimulant does the job. Jack is fully awake. By the afternoon, Jack is outworking everyone and still feels pretty good. Jack is so pumped up he plans to go to the gym after work. Well, once Kent comes home from school. Jacks plays a few card games until Kent comes home.

As soon as Kent walks in the shelter, Jack asks, "So, how was school?

"Pretty good. I learned about U.S. History and how it shapes our view of the world today."

Kent goes into more detail as Jack listens intently. Jack loves Kent like a son. So, he is paying attention to every word Kent says.

"I'm amped up! Let's go to the gym," Jack says.

"All right. Let me eat a snack right now and then I'll be ready," Kent responds.

Jack decides to eat a little something before working out too. Jack devours two granola bars, and they are off to the gym.

Kent plays basketball to warm up while Jack swims. After a few laps in the pool, Jack pumps iron. His muscles, warm from swimming, allow Jack to set a personal best in squatting-500 pounds. Squatting heavy weight no longer hurts his lower back. Because his body is used to moving a substantial amount of weight.

Kent exercises his arms and then goes back to playing basketball. Jack wants to play, but a lot of running sometimes hurts his left knee. So, Jack just spectates. Kent is very fast and can shoot well from everywhere on the court. Jack must applaud when Kent crosses up a defender and then dunks. Then on a fastbreak, Kent does a beautiful finger roll. Once again Jack must applaud another play by Kent.

Jack is so happy for Kent. He knows that if Kent can stay healthy, he will be a basketball star in college and maybe even make it to the NBA. Yes, he is that good. After a couple of games, it's obvious that Kent is truly gifted. The opposing players don't want to play basketball anymore.

Jack and Kent get in the sauna. The sauna relieves the pain in Jack's knee. So, he wants to stay in this warm place for a long time. But as his skin prunes, he realizes it is time to get out. They then sit in the jacuzzi to avoid dehydration. His skin resembles a raisin and now being in the jacuzzi is no longer soothing. So, Jack and Kent head to the shelter.

Kent mainly talks about what's happening in school-particularly what subjects he likes. Jack can see how important education is to Kent. Kent gets it. Jack gives Kent a little advice about math. He tells him that if you don't understand a certain topic, either do a google search or go to the public library. Going to the public library to look up related topics to math is great. Kent nods and seems to appreciate this advice.

Then Kent talks about studying for the SSAT and how he feels pressured to do very well. They talk about random things, and they are back at the shelter.

Jack reads out loud to a little boy and then plays a card game before going to sleep. The night goes by fast and it's time for another day at work. It's a rather cool morning despite the sun being out in a cloudless sky. Jack will warm up soon because moving boards expends a lot of energy. On the train, he wonders if he'll ever have enough money to live comfortably again. Right now, he is making the best of a bad situation. He is still technically homeless. Oh well. I'll do this work until I can get on my feet.

Jack is a good employee. So, when he's at the jobsite, he is all business. Since marine construction can be dangerous, he is always alert. In fact, he rarely lets his mind wander while at work.

Jack moves boards practically all morning. His hands are sore from doing this repeatedly but doesn't complain. Complaining will do him no good. The other workers will just laugh and tell him: If you can't handle it quit. He has seen this happen to other workers.

After lunch, Jack is laying sod down. Not as strenuous as moving boards, he is quite content with the change. The boss is pleased with Jack's work and tells him to keep up the good work. This energizes Jack, so he works even harder. The workday flies by and now it's time to go back to the shelter.

Jack's back is sore from bending over to put sod down. He figures his back will heal in a little bit of time. After taking a shower, he writes this poem:

> They say no pain no gain, like it's good to strain, I bet they've never done marine construction, back aches are a function, of grueling manual labor, I favor, the office job setting to that, but some money is better than begging for money, plus, now I have a warm place and mainly good food, and of milk and honey, so I can't complain too much, and when my writings sell, I'll enjoy a life of luxury, it's meant to be,

Then, Jack plays Monopoly. Jack loves this board game. Even though he rarely wins since living in the shelter. But he always has a good time, so it's worth playing. The game is over and of course, Jack doesn't win.

Now he reads Oliver Twist to a middle-aged man. The man has only seen the movie. Jack reads the book for a good hour until his throat becomes sore. The man has tears in his eyes.

Then the man says, "This was the last book my mom read to me before she passed away. I was ten."

Not knowing what to say, Jack looks down and nods slowly.

"Thank you. Thank you. You don't know how much this means to me."

This makes Jack feel good inside. He has tears in his eyes. It is almost bedtime and Jack reads his own poetry. He can't get out of his mind how much reading out loud helps others. He is choked up over what the middle-aged man said. Now he really doesn't want to move to public housing soon.

He gets angry as he envisions James in his mind's eye. James telling him what to do with that stupid smirk on his face. Jack bawls up his fists but realizes it's not worth it. Hurting James won't solve anything- he'll just get into trouble. Yet he really wants to knock James out. Jack takes some deep breaths and thinks about what he wants to do tomorrow. He closes his eyes as the lights go out.

The next few days are routine. He's working and going to the gym. Jack checks his email every now and then to keep up with what Curtis is doing. Jack isn't sure if he'll try to stay with Curtis when James makes him leave the shelter for public housing.

Having made so many friends here, Jack feels like these people are good family. In fact, almost everyone in the shelter is on friendly terms with him. Well Jack has a few more months to make this decision.

Tonight is a special night because Kent has a basketball game. It appears half the people from the shelter are attending. Jack is also there cheering. Kent is much better than everyone else.

On the opening tip, Kent goes coast-to-coast to score the first points of the game. The game is not competitive. Kent scored 25 points by the end of the first half. While in the arena, Jack looks around attempting to spot scouts here for Kent. Kent has told Jack that there is interest in him even at such a young age.

Jack spots a man with a clipboard jotting something down. Then there is another man with a cap studying the game intensely. After the game, a few scouts talk to Kent's parents. They say the usual platitudes: stay focused, keep up the good work. He isn't even in high school, and he has the scouts interested Jack thinks.

Jack has been Kent's unofficial weightlifting coach. However, Jack knows Kent will need a professional strength and conditioning coach to take his game to an even higher level. Back at the shelter, Kent is so excited. It seems like his dreams are coming true. He wants to be a top scholar and athlete.

The only thing that could hold him back is a particular test to be admitted into the elite private schools. This standardized test, the SSAT, is notoriously difficult. Even Kent wonders how he'll perform on it. His parents cannot afford a tutor. So, Kent partly entrusts his future to Jack. Jack is so happy to help Kent that he can barely sleep tonight. He is thinking how he wants Kent to study- math and English 2 hours a day. He finally calms down and sleeps with a wide smile across his face.

Jack wakes up and heads to the public library. He goes straight to the section containing test prep and checks out 3 books. Once back at the shelter, he skims through the first book to get a general idea about the test. Then, Jack grabs a notebook and comes up with an 8-week study plan for Kent. It's a rigorous plan, but Kent can do it, Jack thinks. Kent needs a high score to gain admission into the elite private schools.

Right now, Kent is sleeping. He is probably tired from last night's basketball game. Jack doesn't want to disturb him, so he tries to write poetry. But for some reason, Jack suffers from Writer's Block. So, he reads the newspaper. Jack isn't reading but skimming because he doesn't care about the articles. He's passing time until Kent wakes up and is ready to study. Finally, after sleeping half the day, Kent is fully awake. To Jack's delight, Kent is ready to study.

Jack tells him, "The first order of business is to see where you stand. Let's observe your score to pick out any weaknesses. I'll time you to make sure you work fast enough."

So, on a beautiful day, instead of enjoying the outdoors, Kent is taking a practice exam. He works efficiently with time to spare. After time is up, Jack grades the diagnostic exam. Jack is surprised at the results.

"Great job, Kent! You pretty much got the highest score possible. You don't have to study for this test unless you want to."

"I want to make sure I can get into those elite private schools. So, I will study anyway."

Jack shares his study plan with Kent. Kent takes his time mastering every aspect of the study plan. Jack loves Kent's attitude and is glad he takes his education seriously. Jack, somewhat bored at the shelter, goes to the gym.

Chapter 17

IT'S FAIRLY CROWDED TODAY and there is a wait at every exercise machine that Jack wants to use. He isn't annoyed because he isn't in a rush- there is nothing he wants to do back at the shelter. Jack bench presses and puts up a personal best. He wishes Kent was around as a witness. Since Kent would understand how great this personal best really is.

Jack swims a little bit and then goes to his favorite thing in the gym- the sauna. The sauna feels so good after exercising. And thankfully, he's the only one in there so he can relax. While in the sauna, Jack doesn't think about anything and just enjoys the heat. As his skin prunes, Jack is reminded that he can't stay in here much longer. He could dehydrate.

So, he gets out, takes a shower, and heads to the shelter. It's loud there as everyone is playing some type of game. Some people are playing board games and others are playing video games. Jack used to play video games in arcades. But now there aren't many of those around.

After learning the controls, he is confident that he will dominate. Unfortunately, this is all in his mind. Jack loses every game and then he plays a board game. He has success and wins a couple games. Jack really believes one man is cheating. He can't prove it, but it's odd that in a game of chance, the man always finished in the top 3. The man plays games almost every day. So, Jack thinks he has figured out all the tricks. Tired of the board game, Jack plays a few card games just to pass the time. By now Kent is back from the movies.

Kent goes right up to Jack and explains every scene he can remember from the movie. Jack loves this because he rarely goes to the movies. Plus, Kent seems happy to explain all the details of the film.

Jack is the type of person that thinks books are always better than movies. He's been disappointed in the movies so that's why he usually just reads books. However, Jack wants to go to plays because it's something he has never done before. In fact, he wants to travel to New York City to see a play on Broadway. When will he do this or how? Jack has no idea.

Of course he doesn't have the money right now. When I get back on my feet, I'll go there. Tired of doing nothing, Jack gets on the computer to send an email to Curtis to stay in touch.

Jack is surprised that Curtis has sent him a message. Curtis writes that he is doing well and is very happy "like he was never homeless." Curtis has made room for Jack at his house. Yet, Jack is reluctant to go there. It seems like a good idea to live with your best friend. But Jack is thinking about the quote "the grass is greener on the other side."

I mean it could be fun living there, but there always seems to be unforeseen consequences for every action. What if some-one has a bad attitude? Plus, James doesn't annoy me quite like he used to. I'll just tell Curtis I'm fine and that we should keep in touch anyway.

After writing Curtis an email, Jack reads part of a novel. It's the latest book he bought from the bookstore. Jack likes buying books sometimes instead of borrowing them from the public library. Because he doesn't have to worry if something happens to the books. This book is an action/adventure novel-Jack's favorite genre to read.

Jack reads the book until it's time for dinner. While at dinner, Jack can't help thinking about the novel. So, he is ready to get back to the shelter to read more. At the table, Shirley is talking about the current sales at the mall. And how everyone should update their wardrobe while everything is cheap.

Jack wears the same pants almost every week and his pants are starting to look like it. But Jack doesn't dress to impress anyone. He wears clothes that are practical. However, being ragged is a whole other thing. I may go to the mall next weekend.

The nearest mall is very nice. It's a couple of stories high and loaded with great stores. Unfortunately, Jack can't afford much there. But he enjoys window-shopping at the mall. Jack has been to the mall countless times with Kent. Kent plays basketball so much that he needs new shoes at least every 3 months. This would be expensive if it were not for Kent's coaches. They know he is extremely poor, so they chip in so that the shoes are affordable.

And Kent loves shoes by the Jordan brand. Without assistance, the latest pair would cost 150 dollars before tax. Shoes were expensive when Jack was Kent's age. But 100 dollars for a pair of sneakers was unusual. Now 100 dollars seems to be the average price for a decent pair of shoes.

Jack has strawberry cheesecake for dessert and then listens more to what Shirley is saying. Now she talks about the latest news stories. She is well-informed and loves to read newspapers. She doesn't read as many books as Jack, but she reads the newspapers every morning. Every now and then Jack will keep up with the news. He sees the news as a conversation piece. As Jack zones back into the present, another person is talking about the news.

He is talking about some strange new virus threatening a country in Asia. This proves my point, Jack thinks. There is always something negative happening and I just don't want to hear about it. Now it's time to head back to the shelter. It's mild outside as Kent explains how he plans to study in the next few hours.

As soon as they are in the shelter, Kent cracks open a history book. He understands the importance of education. He has watched his parents struggle and vows to never live like them when he's older. Kent reads a few chapters ahead of where his teacher left off. Jack taught him this study technique. Jack can't believe how great Kent's work ethic is. Jack knows Kent will succeed in anything because he doesn't give up. Jack, even with an advanced degree, has never worked as hard as Kent. He's copying Kent as much as he can.

Jack works on his novel until the lights are turned off. Jack is thinking about his book as he lies in the dark. Jack drifts off to sleep. Before he knows it, his alarm rings. Indicating that it is time to get ready for work.

Jack is dragging. The morning came too fast today. While on the train, Jack tries to get a few more minutes of sleep. But it is hard to get any rest because the ride is bumpy.

Jack is not sleepy when he arrives at work. He performs well. His boss teaches him how to operate an excavator. This is a machine that can be used to dig holes. The boss instructs Jack for an hour. Then the boss lets him dig. Jack finds operating the machine challenging at first. The controls that move the excavator are sensitive.

By lunch time, Jack gets the hang of it. The boss lets him put dirt behind a newly made wall of wood to stabilize the wall. This process is called backfilling, and the crew does this often.

In the afternoon, Jack back fills with the best of them. He backfills for the rest of the workday. The boss is proud of him and says so. Jack is happy. Because he was going to quit because none of the crew showed him how to do anything. He's able to figure things out on his own, but sometimes everyone needs help. Jack is glad that no one in the crew seems jealous that the boss is instructing him.

After work, Jack stops at a convenience store to purchase painkillers. His hands ache from using the levers to operate the excavator. Even his forearms are sore. Fortunately, after an hour of taking medicine, he feels fine. Which is great because he plans to go to the gym with Kent later. Jack usually looks forward to this.

Kent looks dejected as he enters the shelter. Kent throws his backpack on the floor and sits on the couch- holding his head. Jack approaches him immediately.

"What's wrong buddy?"

"My English teacher said my research paper was late. She's giving me an E on it. Meaning, I'll have a B for the class."

Jack is dumbfounded. To him a B is not bad. In fact, a B is great. Kent's parents must be pushing him too hard. To get this upset over a B is ridiculous. He wants to talk to Kent's parents. But then again, Kent is not his kid. Jack doesn't know what to do or say.

They sit silently for a few minutes and Jack still doesn't know what to do or say. He wants to say the right thing. So, after realizing that, he must console the boy.

Jack says, "Kent, don't get so upset. Everything will be fine. It's not like one B is such a bad thing. Just see if you can get extra credit somehow."

Kent replies, "You know, I never thought about that. I'll ask my English teacher tomorrow about extra credit."

A smile comes across Kent's face and Jack knows he'll be ok. In a matter of minutes, Kent seems happy, and he is ready to go to the gym. The weightroom is crowded so Jack decides to play basketball. He is the last one picked. After a few minutes of running, Jack is fatigued. But he manages to get his second wind. Jack hustles on the court- snagging rebounds and taking charges.

Kent is impressed with Jack's tenacity. Although, he isn't that skilled. On the other hand, Kent uses his speed to get steals and transition lay-ups. Kent can run all day and not even look tired. Jack doesn't know if he is too old to be Kent's type of shape. After a couple games, he is ready to lift weights. Jack waves to Kent and goes to the weight room.

Still breathing heavily from playing basketball, Jack can't exercise right yet. He takes deep breaths for 10 minutes. Then Jack exercises his legs. Squatting medium weight feels good, so Jack does more leg exercises. Then Jack works his abs for a while and then Kent enters the weight room.

Jack asks, "Aren't your legs sore?"

"Not really. I'm in great shape. You should do more cardio. You'll be fitter."

Jack nods his head in agreement. But at his age, a lot of running hurts too much. Maybe I should swim more. Kent continues to lift weights for 30 minutes without a problem. Then as usual, they relax in the sauna and then the jacuzzi. Kent seems to be in a good mood. It's like he has forgotten about his grade situation. Jack is happy about this. He realizes that this might be the first time Kent has ever failed at something.

He'll fail again at some point, and I hope this prepares him for the future. Jack wonders if he should ask Kent about getting a lower grade than he expects. Maybe another day Jack ponders. The hot water in the jacuzzi is so comfortable that Kent almost falls asleep. He's lucky, Jack thinks. He has never had a serious injury. He already ices his knees as a precaution. He's got all his bases covered, Jack thinks.

When they get back to the shelter, Jack's stomach begins to rumble. He reads a good novel to pass the time. Kent does his homework and studies for the SSAT just in case. He is so excited to study, Jack thinks. He is 14 years old with such a laser focus.

As it's time to walk to the soup kitchen for dinner, Kent seems disappointed that he must part from his studies. He seems anxious just to read. Jack wonders if Kent's attitude is good or bad. Well, he does have hobbies.

It's "Philly Night" again at the soup kitchen. The chefs cook up Philly cheesesteaks for everyone. Jack isn't sure if he should eat so much. Considering how bad red meat is for the body. He looks at his other options: cereal or salad. Jack decides to eat a cheesesteak. It's good. The bread is fresh, and the meat is cooked just right. I should save a cheesesteak for tomorrow.

The chefs also cook boardwalk fries. I must work this off at the gym tomorrow. Jack isn't usually greedy, but he eats until his stomach feels like it may bust. Walking back to the shelter is a struggle.

At the shelter, Jack blocks out the discomfort by reading The Cat In The Hat to a child. Jack isn't sure who enjoys the book more- he or the child. Jack tries his hand at rhyming like Dr. Seuss:

> They say two is better than one, except maybe
> for tongues, or even thumbs, then again, it's
> good to have a backup, if one thing acts up,

> sometimes it feels like luck, when two people
> do the same thing, and only one gets messed
> up, both could have poor diets, one stays
> thin, the other becomes obese, where every
> meal is a feast,

I may share this poem with Kent. Kent enjoys good poetry every now and then. Jack finishes up a rhyme before it's lights out.

Before he knows it, it will be time for work in the morning. As he stretches out on the cot, he can feel that his muscles are sore, but it won't be long before he'll be in a deep sleep.

Jack sleeps soundly throughout the night. He only wakes up when his alarm clock goes off. Jack gets up, ready for work and jumps on the train to go to work. The train ride is not peaceful. One guy has his music blasting, and some people are talking loudly. Jack tries to take a quick nap, but it's impossible.

So, he looks out of the window to observe the scenery. The view is wonderful. The houses are big and colorful. Jack hasn't seen anything like this before. He notices the exotic cars in driveways: Jaguars, Benzes, and even a Ferrari. As a kid, Jack collected pictures of exotic cars. Always telling himself that one day he'll own one. He chuckles at this- obviously thinking of how he had it when he used to live in a carboard box. Jack is just happy about a hot meal. He snaps out of his thoughts by the announcement of his train stop.

Jack gets to work on time, and it looks as though it is time to drive boards into the water. Because the tide is out. The boards will create a barrier between water and the land of a house on the shoreline. Carrying boars to the barrier can be challenging for those that do lift weights. Even though Jack is in shape, his lower back is sore. It still gets sore even though Jack does exercises to specifically strengthen this muscle. Overall, Jack can't complain too much. It's money in his pocket. And that's better than playing Bingo and card games in the shelter all day.

So, Jack changes his train of thought and focuses on his job. By lunchtime everybody is ready for the subs that one of the crew members buys. Jack grabs a very greasy sub and chows down. It doesn't take him long to eat the sub. Jack wants more to eat. So, he drinks a lot of water to try and fill him up. This doesn't work and 2 hours later he is hungry. What to do, what to do? I'll tough it out and wait until the workday is over. But Jack can't help thinking about food as he works.

Finally, the workday is over. Jack rushes to a convenience store and grabs 2 candy bars. He eats both and he is full. However, eating all this candy hurts his stomach. Jack has trouble keeping it down on the train. Fortunately, by the time he makes it to the shelter, his stomach feels fine. I may go to the gym with Kent later.

While waiting for Kent to come home, Jack cracks open a great novel and immerses himself in it. Time goes by rather quickly and Jack sees Kent walking through the door of the shelter. Kent seems to be in a good mood and tells Jack how his day went. Jack listens intently like Kent is his son. Kent got an A on a math test and learned a lot in science class.

Kent explains how a neuron works. Well, that's the basics, Jack thinks. As all the technical elements and principles of neurons flood Jack's mind. Wow, it's been a long time since I thought about neuroscience. Then Jack zones back into what Kent is saying nods his head. They chat for a little bit and go to the gym.

After a long day at school, Kent still has plenty of energy to exercise. Jack and Kent lift weights together and then swim. Not a particularly strong swimmer, Kent sticks to the basics and doggie paddles most of the time. Jack wades around in a pool because weightlifting has sapped most of his energy.

Jack tries to swim, but his body is worn down. He watches Kent doggie paddle. Jack believes Kent can succeed at any professional sport. He's so athletic. If he keeps training like this for a few more years, the sky is the limit.

After swimming, Kent and Jack go to the sauna as usual and then the jacuzzi. Man, I feel so relaxed. Jack almost falls asleep as the warm water gets his blood flowing. Kent doesn't seem to enjoy being in the jacuzzi. Jack notices him looking preoccupied. Jack wants to know what is bothering Kent but decides to ask him later.

On the way back to the shelter, Jack says, "Hey Kent, what's wrong?"

"Well, I don't know what to do. Should I work on academics or athletics?"

Jack thinks for a while and says, "It doesn't matter. Both paths are good. I mean, I know it's hard deciding which one so do both. Keep training physically and studying your course work. The boarding school you want to attend has great academics and a great basketball program. You don't have to choose."

Kent nods and says, "Thanks."

This word makes Jack feel good all over. Kent is really like a son to Jack. Jack wants to talk to his son, but he knows he will never see him soon. Because of his ex-wife. She hates Jack. When Jack left his job, Beth changed. She called him stupid and insulted him every day. Jack believes she is part of the reason he became dispirited and homeless.

Thinking about how she treated him- he balls up his fists

and starts breathing heavily. Jack gets a hold of himself. He realizes she is far away and can't influence what happens to him at the shelter.

Jack plays Connect-4 and then chats with Shirley. She's reading a chic magazine while listening to Jack talk about Kent. She puts the magazine down when Jack talks about Kent's future.

She says, "It's good that he has a mentor. You are helping this kid see clear."

To hear another person agree with what he does gives Jack confidence.

"Kent will turn out fine. I'm sure of it," Shirley adds.

Then Jack cracks open a novel to read to an old woman. She is very thankful. Her kindness reminds Jack of why he reads to others. He writes this poem:

> Kind words turn anger into joy, leave a troubled man happy, as a child with a toy, or even just a child with a stick, fascinated playing with it, no shortage on the fun uses, some may be clueless, to loving the simple things, not even diamond rings, or living fit for a king, can soothe the heart, like a genuine compliment, you'll stand tall, like the Washington Monument,

It's time for bed. Jack sleeps well and wakes up a few minutes before his alarm sounds. He sits up in his cot, contemplating different things in his life. He's getting tired of doing marine construction. He must get up so early in the morning. However, Jack remembers reading to others doesn't generate much money. In fact, he doesn't have many options as far as employment. Then he wonders if he should tell Curtis his problems.

So that he could live in Toronto. I'll make up my mind eventually. As he boards the train to work, Jack realizes he would miss most of the people in the shelter. Other than James, everyone else has been friendly and just all-around fun.

James hasn't announced the exact date when they will be relocating to public housing. Jack isn't sure why he dislikes public housing. But it's just something about it. Work is uneventful and the day goes by slowly.

On the way back home, Jack wonders if his writings will ever sell. He feels like he has an ace up his sleeve. But so far, he hasn't shared his novel with his friends. And he hasn't submitted any part of it to a literary agent or publisher. What are you afraid of Curtis used to say. Jack could never answer this question. He would just say when I'm ready.

Having been writing seriously ever since he lived in his cardboard palace, Jack has quite the collection. He's written over a thousand poems and four short stories. Maybe I'll go to a publisher in a few weeks. But doubt still lingers in his mind. Am I talented enough to ever be profitable? Oh well, I might as well try.

A few minutes after arriving at the shelter, Jack goes straight to his writings. He picks out some of his greatest poems and heads to a computer. He submits these poems to a literary agent electronically. The website states that an agent will get back to him in a few weeks. Jack is so excited that he runs around the block. He runs quickly but is not out of breath. All the weightlifting and swimming has increased his stamina. He pants slightly once back at the shelter.

Kent is home from school and immediately asks, "Hey Jack, what's going on?"

"I submitted some of my writings to a literary agent. Hopefully I can make some great money."

"Good for you."

Tears come to Jack's eyes as he thinks about all he has been through. Ever since he became homeless, Jack feels like a drain on society and worthless. Now he has a purpose. Reading newspapers and books to homeless people feels good, but Jack never felt great about himself until now. Jack and Kent go to the gym.

As usual, Kent plays basketball while Jack swims. Jack swims a few laps in the pool and is not tired. His stamina is really improving. A month ago, he could only swim one lap. However, he starts to feel tired and gets out of the pool.

Now that his muscles are loose, Jack lifts weights. Being in a good mood has made Jack stronger. He reaches personal bests in the bench press and squat. Kent enters the weight room a few minutes later. Kent is in such good shape that he played full-court basketball, and he can lift weights without signs of fatigue.

Jack sees himself as Kent's mentor. He makes sure that Kent achieves his dreams while not taking life too seriously. Kent can be too serious sometimes. Especially about sports. He occasionally has outbursts of anger when he loses. Jack is glad that Kent seems calm lately. After lifting weights, they get into the sauna. Kent falls asleep for a little bit and snores.

Jack elbows him and Kent wakes up saying, "Man, all this exercise might be draining my energy."

Jack is shocked. Because Kent is usually full of energy all day long. Then they get into the jacuzzi until their skin prunes. Then it's back to the shelter.

At the shelter, Jack reads to a young homeless man.

Until James says to everyone, "I have a special announcement. It's about public housing. All of you will end up in public housing within a week. The shelter will only be used by the mentally challenged. Public housing is only a block away. So, you all will not be far from the soup kitchen."
Jack is happy about still using the soup kitchen. He isn't a good cook. Plus, going there is very convenient.

James continues, "Moving into public housing will help you all immensely. It will be like living on your own. I may stop by every now and then to make sure everything is fine."

James always makes Jack's blood boil. His smugness is too much. Jack restrains himself from running up to James and knocking him out. Now everyone in the shelter is talking about this announcement. Some are happy about moving into public housing. They look forward to more privacy. And how good it will feel to have something they can call their own.

Shirley is elated about moving. She explains to Jack that privacy is something she hasn't experienced in a long time. She never lived as hard as Jack. Remember, Jack lived on the street in a cardboard box. He had plenty of privacy. He was alone too much for a normal person. In fact, he believes he is mentally scarred from this type of hard living. He's never told anyone about this- but when he is alone for over an hour, he becomes frightened. Maybe this is post-traumatic stress, Jack thinks. Hopefully, it will go away one day. Jack takes his mind off his problems by playing cards.

Poker isn't Jack's strong suit. Glad I'm not playing for money. After a couple of games, Jack gets the hang of the game and wins a few hands. They play Poker until it is time for bed. The game has its intended effect. Jack is very relaxed and has a clear mind. However, Jack doesn't sleep well.

He dreams of being in his cardboard palace during a bad thunderstorm. The wind is blowing hard. The box is almost destroyed. Jack keeps waking up. He wants to do some reading to help put him to sleep. But it is lights out at the shelter. So, he's wide-awake hoping to fall asleep soon. Jack counts sheep. Yet he can't sleep. Jack watches the clock as the minutes turn into hours. Now it's 3:00 AM. Now he's able to sleep. He is knocked out completely until his alarm rings. It's time for work. On the train, Jack is surprisingly alert and isn't drowsy at all.

In fact, he can't believe how clearheaded he is after only 3 hours of sleep. At work, Jack drills holes in poles and then puts rods in them. To strengthen a wall made to keep water from overtaking waterfront properties. This procedure is called putting tiebacks in. Tiebacks reinforce the bulkhead. Drilling takes a lot of effort and can wear your muscles out over time. Jack drills the poles all morning.

During a coffee break, his hands are trembling from the impact of holding the drill for so long. Fortunately, his hands stop shaking after the break. Then it's time for him to drill more holes.

Jack doesn't take another break until lunch. After work is when Jack really feels it. While on the train, his lower back is sore, and his hands are numb. Also, Jacks legs are tired from standing while drilling most of the day.

I can't wait to swim at the gym. Swimming gets rid of Jack's soreness for the most part. Once off the train, now Jack's chest hurts. How can this be? Then he remembers having to push on the drill very hard to get it started in the lumber. Jack limps for a bit, but after a few steps he back to his normal stride.

Once he arrives at the shelter, he opens his poetry book and writes:

> Hard work pays off, at least that's what they say, well, I've got to work hard, I need the pay, it's better than living on the street, so I shouldn't complain, even if I feel a little pain, it isn't that big of a strain,

Chapter 18

THEN, HE CLOSES HIS poetry book and takes a nap. As usual, Jack plans to go the gym when Kent gets here. Maybe from not sleeping well last night, Jack is completely unconscious a few minutes after he closes his eyes. He doesn't wake up until he feels a light tapping on his side.

It's Kent saying, "Hey, are you ready to hit the gym?"

It takes a second for this to register then Jack replies, "Yeah, of course."

Once at the gym, Jack gets in the swimming pool and instantly feels better. He swims half a lap to get his blood flowing. Then he runs underwater to strengthen his legs. After that, Jack lifts weights and works his entire body. He starts with which ever body part hurts the most. So, he exercises his lower back. The muscle is tight at first, but after a few repetitions, it feels normal again. His lower back feels better than normal. Jack moves on to work his chest and arms.

After the weight work, Jack thinks he can play basketball with the young bucks like Kent. Although Jack looks in shape from lifting weights, he is short, so he is the last guy picked. Everyone on the court is under 30 except Jack. He has a lot to prove.

On the first possession, Jack drains a three from the corner and a smile comes across his face. Then he steals the ball and makes an easy lay-up. The other players can see that he is not scrub. As the game progresses, Jack is slowing down.

His running stamina is terrible. Even though he swims a lot. While tired, his opponents take advantage. They run plays designed for whoever Jack is guarding. Jack must quit because his side is hurting. After the game, Kent checks on him to make sure Jack isn't going through anything serious.

Jack doesn't try to act tough and says," I'm leaving basketball alone. I'm too old to do this anymore. My chest doesn't hurt; I just don't have any energy to run or jump right now."

Kent plays a few more games of basketball as Jack watches from the sideline. Then they go into the sauna. It is like Jack can feel his life force coming back. He is rejuvenated and his muscles no longer ache. Kent can see by Jack's face that he is better now. And once they go into the jacuzzi, Jack looks strong.

Jack says to Kent, "I'm fine now. I can't run up and down that hardwood like I used to."

Jack also notices that his lower back no longer hurts, and he can't believe how quickly the pain went away.

Back at the shelter, nothing is going on. Some people are socializing while others are playing board games. Kent does homework in a quiet corner. He must be a little tired, Jack thinks. What determination! And Kent is also dedicated to athletics. He wakes up every weekday at the same time and runs a few blocks to improve his stamina. Then he goes back to the shelter to do countless sit-ups and bodyweight squats. And since Jack told him to include push-ups in his routine, he does a lot of them too.

The only thing that worries Jack is that Kent seems too serious at times. He is still a kid, yet he is so focused that he carries himself like an adult. Kent rarely does anything just for fun. Everything to him has an ultimate purpose. Even playing basketball at the gym appears like a chore. Kent rarely smiles even after hitting a big shot or making a deft move. I guess it's just his competitive spirit.

Jack wants to take a field trip with the youngsters at the shelter. Maybe I'll take them to play laser tag. Jack wants to coordinate this event with their parents and run it by James to maybe get a bulk discount. Jack debates whether to participate in playing laser tag. He used to take one of his nephews to play laser tag many years ago. In fact, he probably loves the game more than his nephew or any kid for that matter. Maybe I'm too old for laser tag. Well, I may at least try.

Now Jack is convinced to plan such an event. Jack thinks about taking the kids to an amusement park. That may cost too much. James probably doesn't have enough funding to aid in this adventure. Even though Jack doesn't pay for housing, he spends money eating out a lot. This may not seem expensive, but Jack's pay is very small. He doesn't like to talk about it. He recalls days working at his old job. He was living like a young movie star.

He lived in a three-story apartment equipped with a sauna and a jacuzzi. Things change. That's the attitude that keeps Jack from wallowing in self-pity. Really, he has a positive attitude right now despite everything that has happened. Now Jack thinks on the bright side of living in public housing.

Fortunately, he will still have a free place to stay and most of the people currently at the shelter will be his neighbors. Plus, he won't have to share a bathroom with many people. Jack plans to buy a computer and a tv for his soon to be living quarters. Nowadays computers are necessary just to keep up with things, Jack thinks.

Now, Jack is reading a play by Shakespeare to a few

adolescents. At first, they aren't paying attention. But Jack is reading out loud so passionately that they are attracted to the play. Jack reads Shakespeare in his spare time but doesn't write plays himself. He's never written one play. After reading the first act, the adolescents clap.

They shout, "More!"

So, Jack continues reading. Knowing people enjoy what he enjoys pumps him up. Jack reads the entire play out loud. The adolescents want to hear more.

But Jack says, "My voice is getting raspy. Maybe someone else could read."

No one wants to. They are scared to read in front of each other. So, Jack decides to read part of another play by Shakespeare. His throat is sore. He must stop reading after the first act. Jack drinks water but his throat still hurts. He doesn't talk until tomorrow and goes to sleep before the lights go out.

The dreaded alarm goes off and it is time for work. Jack looks out of the window at the shelter and is pleased. It's raining. You can't do marine construction when it rains. Jack expects a short workday. He goes to work. It's a nasty day all-around. The wind is blowing, and the rain is coming down at an alarming rate. The boss tells everyone to go home and enjoy the day.

So, Jack heads back to the shelter and gets on a computer. He checks his email and responds to a message from Curtis. Jack tells him that he will stay put in Vancouver. Then he surfs the internet to pass the time. Jack reads a novel for an hour and then writes this poem:

> Tired of watching tv, reading books, writ-
> ing hooks, so I look to do something fun
> in the city, nah, not really, I'm so bored,

> everything feels like a chore, I'd rather just mope around, negative thoughts abound, no positive though can be found, I think I'm tired of life right now, forget that, there's got be something to do in the city, okay, let's go out, no need for anymore self-pity,

Maybe I should buy some shoes. Jack is thinking of not quitting basketball after all. He currently wears non-basketball shoes. Jack walks to a shoe store. All the basketball shoes are expensive. Jack is not willing to spend that much money. The running shoes look nice, but don't offer any ankle support. Jack leaves the store disappointed and doesn't know what to do next. All his friends are working Kent is in school right now. Jack ponders going to the gym, but he'll wait until Kent comes home to do that.

So, Jack walks around the city. He walks all the way to the coast. No one is swimming in the sea. Jack gets close to the water and now he knows why. Although a relatively clean city, the water looks horrible. Some type of scum keeps washing up on the coastline.

There is a basketball court nearby, but no one is playing on it yet. Sometimes Kent plays on this court on the weekends. In a way Jack loves playing basketball. Even though it hurts his body. Plus, he isn't good. Jack walks along the coast for a few more minutes. Then he heads back to the shelter.

Jack is so bored. He reads a book for a while then sits around doing nothing. He thinks about his son Brent. He deletes an email that he was about to send to Brent. The frustration of wanting to get in contact with his son makes him angry. To calm down, he reads news on the internet. Nothing positive in the headlines, but Jack continues to read the news.

Bored on the computer, Jack looks at the time. Only a few more hours until Kent comes home.

Jack is really looking forward to going to the gym. It's always the highlight of his day. Jack engrosses himself in a book to pass the time. He reads until his eyes hurt and his vision is blurry. Then Jack closes his eyes to relax, and he drifts of to sleep.

He has a terrifying dream about a man killing him in his cardboard palace. He wakes up immediately. This dream is odd because Jack was never threatened with death during his time on the street. Yes, he was beaten up sometimes, but no one ever flashed a gun or a knife. Yet, I'll never go back to living like that, Jack thinks.

Jack wonders about living in public housing. Will it really be an improvement from living in the shelter? The neighborhood in which he will live in is considered rough. And this worries Jack. Even while growing up, Jack lived in a good neighborhood with no real crime. People tell stories of blatant drug use in the public housing area. But there is no turning back. Thinking positively, I'll be closer to work and the houses look good. Plus, the houses are very clean.

Despite being in a rough neighborhood, the city hires people to clean these houses often. The houses even have yards. Jack is wondering if he wants to buy a dog. He had plenty of pets while growing up. Including two dogs. Jack has always loved animals. He hasn't had a dog in a long time. While remembering some of his pets, Kent walks through the door. Kent is ecstatic.

"Hey Jack, guess what? Some college scouts want me to attend their schools in some years. And I'm not in high school yet. Well, I'm ready to go to one of the top schools now. I'll continue studying for good grades to reach the next level."

Jack just smiles. He knows everything will work out for Kent because he isn't afraid of hard work. Kent studies for a little bit and then they go to the gym. Kent doesn't play basketball, so he lifts weights while talking to Jack.

Kent is so locked in. Nothing seems to distract him from the purpose of getting an education. While doing arm curls, Kent talks about attending a certain prep school in New Jersey. Jack wants him to shut up. Kent is so arrogant right now. Not wanting to hurt his feelings, Jack lets Kent run his mouth.

Kent finished a set of arm curls. After drinking water, he does more arm curls. Kent wants to get stronger because he believes this will help him on the basketball court. He especially loves lower body work to increase his vertical leap. But right now, Kent is concentrating on his upper body. Next, Jack and Kent bench press. Both do the same number of reps. Then they get into the sauna. Kent is exhausted.

"I told you not to overdo it," Jack says.

Kent just shrugs his shoulders and closes his eyes. They get in the jacuzzi, and Kent begins to feel better. Once they get back to the shelter, Kent is up and running. He immediately hits the books to prepare for school tomorrow.

Jack reads to an old man. Instead of a novel, this man wants Jack to read a sports magazine. It's an American magazine and the old man seems to enjoy it. Jack jokes to himself that the man is old enough to listen to Joe Louis on the radio. After reading to him, Jack starts to think about work. So, to distract himself, Jack plays Solitaire on the computer.

Jack quickly gets tired of this and plays chess on the computer. Game after game Jack keeps losing. Frustrated yet determined, Jack keeps playing chess. And he still loses. Jack gets up from the computer in disgust. He lies down early before "lights out."

Chapter 19

THE ALARM CLOCK SOUNDS, and Jack hops up from his cot. He is ready for the day. He doesn't take a nap on his way to work. He's not groggy and feels like working today. And there is a lot to do. After putting in a small bulkhead, the crew clean up the trash around it. There is a significant amount of trash- including extra wood and some boxes. Jack is the hardest worker today. He puts most of the trash in the truck himself.

Nick, the boss, has promised to teach Jack how to do everything within the next couple of months. Jack is excited about this because he will get paid more as he gains more skills. For the rest of the day, the crew are cleaning up different jobsites. And Jack's lower back is very stiff.

He stretches after work, but he's in pain. On the way home, Jack buys painkillers at a drugstore. The pain subsides by the time he reaches the shelter. However, Jack doesn't think he can go to the gym later with Kent. Jack lies down on his cot, trying to keep every muscle still. The lower back is used in practically every movement. So, Jack lies on his back with his eyes closed. As soon as he is somewhat comfortable, he drifts off to sleep. Kent arrives at the shelter from school.

"Are you ok?" Kent asks.

"Not really. I'm not sure about going to the gym. My lower back is killing me. It needs rest. Maybe I'll be ok by tomorrow."

Jack is concerned. He does physical work, and a sore back can hurt production. I won't tell my boss about this injury. A couple hours later, Jack is still on his cot. He gets up and feels worse than before. His entire body is stiff. He is hobbling whenever he walks.

After a few minutes, he gets it together and reads to an old woman. Jack is shocked at how many people can't read. Most people would think that in a developed country, practically everyone could at least read a newspaper. But it's just not the case. Especially among the elderly. How have they made it so long without the essential skill of reading?

Jack also feels sorry for the woman because she suffers from memory loss. As soon as Jack reads an article, she forgets what he has read. She asks him time and again to reread articles. Jack is getting frustrated, but he calms down and realizes she can't help herself. I'll try to do some good.

He reads the entire newspaper to her, and she is thrilled. Until she asks Jack to read the newspaper. Jack loses his patience and walks away from the old woman.

Jack's back is no longer hurting so he goes for a short stroll. When he returns to the shelter, the old woman is still sitting in the same seat looking lost. Jack has a soft spot for her because he remembers how his grandmother was. It was sad watching her forget what someone said to her. The woman does not recognize him as he walks by.

Jack finds a quiet spot in the shelter and reads a good novel.

Jack reads for some time until Kent says, "How is you back now?"

"It's a little sore, but I may go to the gym tomorrow. How was your workout?"

"Excellent! I dunked on a couple of guys and hit a personal

best doing pullups. Hopefully, I can do as well on other exercises tomorrow. I'm in great shape now, but I'm ready to go to the next level."

Jack nods his head in approval and adds, "I always knew you could. You are so motivated. I think you can do anything you put your mind to."

Kent smiles and then they talk about the latest novels that they want to read. Kent does his homework without any help as usual. He's only in middle school and he never slacks off from his schoolwork.

A little tired of doing intellectual activities, Jack sits in front of the tv and watches a few sitcoms. They are surprisingly funny and entertaining. They have Jack laughing his head off.

It's now time for bed and Jack can't believe how fast the evening hours went by. Oh well, I wish I had more time to read. But there is always tomorrow. Once on his cot, Jack drifts off to sleep as the lights are turned out. Dreaming about being on the beach, Jack is rudely awakened by his alarm clock thinking not again.

Jack wants to hit the snooze button, but a job is a job. Jack is moving slowly this morning and barely manages to catch the train before it pulls out of the station. It's a mostly cloudy day and Jack hopes it rains. If it rains, the crew will not work. Unfortunately, overcast does not mean precipitation, and Jack is disappointed.

In the morning, the crew works on building a pier. It's to be long- 500 feet to be exact. Since Jack is a new employee, he fetches the tools, nails, and bolts. He gives them to the rest of the crew as they put the pier together. Jack is amazed how they can make something from nothing.

Jack gets his wish of rain in the afternoon. However, it only drizzles and the crew work on. Jack's back feels a lot better today. He can bend over without any significant pain. I can't wait to go to the gym. The drizzle slacks off- which is good because the unfinished pier was getting slippery. Walking up and down the pier, is a good way to learn things. The boss is pleased with Jack's work.

He tells him, "Keep it up. You may have my job one day."

Jack just nods and feels good inside. In fact, he can't wait to move up to receive better pay. And he wants more respect. Sometimes he is treated like a rookie at training camp. This gets under his skin. Jack has never been teased on a job like this. He's really getting bullied but tries to keep his cool.

Although he is ready to knock some of them out, he wonders if fighting will gain respect. They are almost as annoying as James- almost. They have nicknames for him. Jack doesn't stand up for himself because he isn't sure how the crew will react. If I talk back, I might get fired. But how long can I take this?

Jack speaks up and says to the crew, "Stop making fun of me!"

They just chuckle, but after that the teasing is over with. Jack is so relieved. He did not have to use violence to make his point. The clouds have gone, and it is a beautiful, sunny day. There's only about an hour left in the workday. The boss lets everyone off early. Jack is as happy as a little kid with a new toy. What to do with the time.

Once at the shelter, Jack is thinking of what to do. Bored, Jack looks at the calendar to see when it is time to move into public housing. Jack sweats a little bit when he realizes time is really ticking down. He is so against moving, but complaining to James won't help one bit. Because the decision is out of James's hands.

The City Council has already decided the move for some of the city's homeless shelters. I guess I could write to the City Council, but I doubt this will do anything. To take his mind off this hopeless situation, Jack writes some poems. One poem is as follows:

> Feeling so hopeless being homeless, like society has disowned us, no respect as we walk down the street, some mean people point to the garbage cans, when we ask for something to eat, without money, life seems incomplete, they treat us badly like they are so elite, tears won't help me find a home, I suck it up, the streets I used to roam, they say get a job, since being homeless, love from average people I've never known,

Jack wonders if submitting this piece to the City Council would change anything. Oh well. I'll keep writing- pouring out my pain. Then Jack takes a short nap. Jack likes to nap whenever he uses a significant amount of brainpower. He seems refreshed after a nap. Jack looks at the clock. It won't be long now until Kent comes home from school.

Then they will go to the gym. Jack is ready to lift weights now. To clear his head, Jack goes for a stroll downtown. Unlike a tourist, there isn't much he hasn't seen downtown. However, he is still amazed about how great downtown is. For example, the McDonald's doesn't look like a typical fast-food restaurant. The restaurant has leather seats and even some pillows. Plus, the entire downtown area is very clean with little trash on the sidewalks.

Jack does a bit of window-shopping and stops in a Starbucks for a drink. The coffee is strong. But Jack downs it quickly. Scientists say that drinking coffee before a workout is beneficial. Unfortunately, Starbucks is too expensive for Jack to go there regularly. Strolling through the city's center, Jack stops in a music store.

The store has a wide collection of music. So, Jack listens to some samples. He sees an album of Chinese reggae and can't help but check it out. The songs sound good even though Jack doesn't understand the lyrics. He bobs his head to the rhythms for a few minutes and then listens to rock music. Jack leaves the music store. Then he does more window-shopping in expensive stores that only carry designer clothes.

Jack must admit that the apparel looks great. But can't picture himself spending a lot of money on clothes. Even when he made great money at Panacea Pharmaceuticals, he never paid $200 for a shirt. Oh well. Jack shrugs his shoulders and walks down the boulevard.

Jack observes some guys rapping on the corner:

D.
Dave

I'm D, from Van city, rhyming is a passion, I can flow all night, tongue everlasting, record labels tryna sign me soon, blowing up like a bomb, boom, something like spring, I'm in full bloom, nectar-sweet style, original, so I'ma be on top for a while, forget the critics, their opinions stink like a pile, of, get'em E,

E.
Edward

Coolest in the group, hottest in the booth, a stand-up guy, causing problems, can't cover me with a roof, I'm the big hurt, you're a minor scrape, is the truth, I'm very wise without a single wisdom tooth, they were pulled out, like a pitcher giving up homers, I'm a loaner, not a loner, I'm a business owner, lending out my rap services, some careers will be over, if my connection surfaces, your turn Shawn,

S.
Shawn

The Devil couldn't hold me, escaped from Hell like Spawn, I'm a big buck not a fawn like Bambi, can't we all get along, right our wrongs, I express peace through songs, my instrument, just my voice, hopefully soon, I'll own a Rolls Royce, I've got plans, to reach a higher level, change my life, but I'm no rebel, for an average life, I just can't settle,

Not half bad. Jack doesn't say anything to them. They seem to be having a lot of fun. Jack walks in the mall for a few minutes until he sees the time. Kent will be home soon, so Jack heads back to the shelter. He takes a shortcut down a road that natives to Vancouver say to avoid at all costs. There is graffiti everywhere. Jack also sees extremely thin people.

These people ask Jack for money. This causes Jack to have a flashback. He recalls begging for money- looking disheveled with long fingernails and unkempt hair. Now of course, living in the shelter, no one would figure he's technically homeless. He is well-groomed with clothes that aren't decades old.

Feeling sorry for these people, Jack gives one of them 10 dollars. He wonders if she will use this money to support a drug habit or to get something to eat. Some people currently at the shelter are receiving help for a substance abuse problem. He would ask these homeless people to come to the shelter, but there isn't enough room. As Jack arrives at the shelter, Kent is walking in. Kent looks like he had a hoe hum day.

Jack says to him, "Hey Kent, how was your day?"

"Fine. I did well on a history test, and I took a math test today. I think I did well."

They relax for a little bit and then they head to the gym. Jack's legs are weak from his long walk earlier in the day. He squats massive weight, but he really feels it when he is done. Kent is fresh and is as strong as an ox. He squats more than Jack now. Kent plays basketball almost every day. Plus, he's a lot younger.

Jack is nowhere near being weak, but his best days are behind him. He has a few grey hairs, and his hairline recedes some. Midlife hasn't bothered him at all. "We all get old" is his mantra so he just keeps it moving.

Kent plays basketball as Jack swims. All the sore muscles from weightlifting don't ache as Jack enjoys moving in the pool. He stays in the shallow end- practicing his stroke. Then he swims a few laps. Now, he is dog-tired.

Even though Jack swims regularly, doing a lot of laps raises his heart rate almost to the point of exhaustion. After 10 minutes, his wind comes back, and he treads water for more exercise. This is a good regimen. By the time he was done in the pool, Kent finished up on the basketball court and they got into the sauna.

Kent can barely talk because he played ball so hard. He does this to test his fitness. Kent always says he'll swim more, but playing basketball is just too fun to pass up.

There is little competition on the court because Kent is in excellent shape. And he's better than all the guys he plays against. Despite most of them being of college age. They are athletic, but Kent is a once in a generation player to Jack and many others. Kent can already dunk and has a tricky crossover that works almost every time. Jack laughs when he sees him play because he is a flashy player. Kent plays to the crowd no matter the size. After going to the gym, Jack is back at the shelter talking to James.

Jack says, "James, I don't want to go into public housing. Can I stay in the shelter?"

James replies, "As aforementioned, the City Council has decided that unless you are mentally challenged, you must find another place to live. There are no buts about it. Plus, why wouldn't you want a place of your own? You'll have privacy and it will feel like you have your own house. All your friends will be with you. You can still read out loud to others. I think public housing will be perfect for you. You can move around and everything. And you'll have a real bed not some old stiff cot."

Jack thinks about what James is saying and he makes a lot of sense. Jack really can't object. I guess it is just about getting used to something new. Maybe I should look on the bright side.

"I guess you are right James. It's just that I'm so comfortable here. Even without much privacy, I must admit staying here has been enjoyable."

James nods and replies, "I understand. I've lived in a shelter a while back and the sense of community was very strong in that environment. See, I grew up extremely poor and when hard times came, I didn't have a choice because my home was taken from me."

This is the first time Jack sees James as human. Normally, he can't stand even thinking about James in a positive light. Because of James's attitude. Jack can't believe it. James seems cool right now. They engage in small talk until it's time for dinner.

The chefs at the soup kitchen cook Mexican food for tonight. Jack has never had authentic Mexican food. He has only had fast-food from Taco Bell. Jack eats a couple burritos, and he can't lie: the food is very tasty. In fact, Jack is now sold on this type of food. The food is so good hardly anyone talks at dinner. Shirley only says two words.

Back at the shelter, Jack reads to some homeless children. He reads nursery rhymes- which are intriguing even to adults. The kids love this type of stuff too. However, Jack realizes it is time to stop when a few kids start napping. Jack can't believe they can sleep through the great nursery rhymes of Dr. Seuss. So, he dismisses them and reads nursery rhymes for himself. This entertains him until "lights out."

Jack sleeps well and only wakes up when his alarm sounds. He reads more nursery rhymes until he leaves the shelter for work. It's a day with no clouds in the sky. This doesn't always make for a good workday. Because Jack has no sunglasses and the glare from the sun can be intense. Sometimes it is hard to see where to put the nails in the bulkhead. Although this has become less troublesome since Jack has gotten better at his job.

The train ride to work is rather uneventful so Jack is daydreaming. He imagines being a big celebrity from writing nursery rhymes. He has a big mansion with lots of exotic cars.

Jack has a smile on his face while thinking about these things. He wonders if he should rhyme more. He usually rhymes just to pass the time. He thinks of some rhymes off the top of his head but doesn't come up with anything great. Now Jack is at work.

The boss pulls him aside and asks, "How long do you plan on working here?"

Jack isn't sure what to say. Although this job is decent, Jack has been thinking of other employment to make money. He hasn't submitted any applications, but he's thinking about doing so. He wonders if he should tell his boss the truth. Since saying a few more months could create a negative work environment.

So, Jack says, "Maybe 3-4 years."

The boss stares intensely at Jack as if he is peering into his soul.

Nick nods his head and replies, "I keep asking you this because you are such a good worker."

Jack is surprised since most of the crew are always criticizing him.

"I maybe even work here longer."

Nick then says, "Ok. I'll teach you all that I know."

Nick walks over to the chainsaw. Jack has never operated a chainsaw before. He owned a house, but always hired people to do everything. Including cutting the grass. The boss shows Jack the most basic thing: how to start a saw. This is simple. After a few tries for himself, Jack has mastered this skill. Then it is on to cutting wood. This may seem easy, but if you put the saw's blade too far in the wood, you can damage the saw's motor. Meaning, the strained motor will no longer function. Cutting through huge poles puts a large amount of strain on the chainsaw.

Jack cuts in a pole and the sawblade becomes stuck in the wood. But after the 4th cut, he gets the hang of it. As to not confuse Jack with too much information, that's all Nick teaches him today.

So, Jack is back working with the crew. The rest of the workday is uneventful and it's time to go back to the shelter via train. Jack is excited to learn something new and progress at his job. But I would read to people all day if the pay were better.

But I want a higher standard of living. I'll think about this later. I'll enjoy the train ride home. It's a beautiful sight: looking at British Columbia. People would pay to see this. Jack hasn't seen anything quite like this. While admiring the scenery, Jack thinks about his ex-wife.

She was beautiful and seemed right in every way. Until he married her. She was demanding and had to have everything her way. Those were the main reasons that contributed to the breakup. But jack must admit, it wasn't all her fault. He was a dedicated if not obsessed worker. He came home late almost every weeknight. She didn't understand why he had to work so hard.

Also, Jack's idea to quit his job and put money in real estate was the last straw. When he lost most of his money in this venture, they split. Blackballed, Jack couldn't find a job in Neuroscience in North America. A friend in Vancouver was supposed to help him. Jack moved there, but things fell through, and he ended up on the street. Jack is still staring at the scenery when he hears his stop called.

At the shelter, he writes this poem about hard living:

> A cold world it can be, especially, with little money, begging for food, you must forget about pride, and just try to survive, on the

streets, not an easy feat, fast food most of the
time, or food in the trash I dine, on, the hard
life, God what did I do wrong,

Jack clears his mind. He feels good now. He's ready for Kent to tell him how his school day went.

Kent walks in the shelter and says, "I got in!"

The special high school, Welch's Academy, has accepted him. Initially, Jack is happy that Kent will live his dream out. But the school is in the United States, so Jack will not see him much. Kent may come home on some holidays, but he'll basically be at Welch's all year round. Jack wonders who he'll go to the gym with since Kent will be gone. Oh well. I must deal with it. So, after going to the gym, Jack, Kent, and Kent's parents dine out. It's a celebration for Kent's achievement. His mom cries as she explains how much Kent means to her.

"I'm so proud of you too," Kent's dad says before bursting into tears.

Then Kent cries. Jack doesn't remember seeing Kent this happy. Jack feels like a proud parent.

"Congratulations Kent. I knew you could do it. You'll make the NBA. I'm sure of it. Your discipline must be up there with Navy Seals. Hopefully, I'll see you on an NBA court soon," Jack says.

Kent is no longer sobbing. He eats a tender sirloin steak. The steak sauce adds to the taste. The sirloin is big, but Kent finished it off with little trouble.

Jack can't believe that his best friend will be gone in a short time. He basically taught Kent how to lift weights. Kent is a better basketball player because of using weights.

Jack orders BBQ ribs. They are so tender that the meat falls off the bone. Jack loves ribs so much that he could eat them every night. The conversation at the table is about whether Kent is ready for a new environment. He'll be fine, Jack thinks. Kent is a very tough and motivated person. In fact, Kent is the most disciplined person Jack has ever known. That is strange for someone so young. With an attitude like that he can't fail, Jack thinks. Like most parents, Kent's parents are worried with him being so far from home. Jack assures them that there is nothing to worry about. But of course, they still worry. With live chat, they will be able to communicate with him daily. After dinner, Kent tells Jack a few things at the shelter.

Kent says, "Even though I look fine, I'm not sure if I can do this. You know studying all day while training at basketball good enough to be successful."

Jack can't believe how nervous Kent seems.

Jack replies, "I guess being somewhat unsure is natural, but you are smart and athletic. Plus, if it doesn't work out, you can always come back here and train at home. There shouldn't be any pressure on you in my opinion. Just do your best and everything will be fine."

Kent nods his head, but his body language is all wrong. This isn't good, Jack keeps telling himself. Jack thinks about what he can do to help Kent. But other than words of encouragement, he isn't sure. Jack has trouble falling asleep as he continues to wonder how to help Kent. Jack falls asleep about an hour later than usual. His alarm sounds as usual on a weekday.

Chapter 20

JACK IS MOVING SLOW this morning but manages to catch the train before it pulls off. Together the crew is putting together a dock. Jack puts on gloves and helps guide poles to build a foundation for the dock. The boss uses a machine to drive poles in the ground. Then it's time to frame the dock. Jack observes how to use a level to make sure the dock isn't set on a crooked frame.

Jack is tired from carrying boards to the dock all morning. He drinks Gatorade at lunch time, but his energy remains low. Because it looks like it may rain, the boss shortens the lunch break. As to finish building most of the dock before precipitation. Surprisingly, no one is rushing. Everyone is working hard but working efficiently.

Jack finds the pace doable but worries that later he won't be able to keep up. Because his legs are tired from all that walking in the morning. He tries to proceed with no problem, but the boss can see that Jack is laboring.

Nick says, "Why don't you go home and get some rest."

Jack wants to say he is fine, but the pain has spread to his lower back.

He replies, "Ok. I'll leave now."

Nick nods and Jack is on his way back to the shelter. With all this pain, he is barely able to walk to the train. He plops down in the nearest seat. The pain is excruciating. He plans to buy painkillers from a drugstore on the way to the shelter.

He pops some pills and hopes to be relieved as soon as the medicine enters his bloodstream. Jack feels better by the time he arrives at the shelter. Are the painkillers working now or is it all in my mind? Jack wonders this for a second and then doesn't care. All he knows is that he can walk without much pain. Plus, I may feel fine by time it is time to go to the gym.

Jack sits in one of his favorite chairs and relaxes. He doesn't think about anything. His mind is clear, and time goes by rather quickly. By the time he is out of this mental state, a few hours have passed, and he is feeling refreshed.

At least mentally. As soon as he stands up from the chair, the tightness in his back is still present. He winces but fights through the pain to check his email. He has 5 messages and 2 are spam. The only important message is from Curtis. Curtis writes that he is doing well. He wants to know definitively if Jack is staying put in Vancouver.

Jack thinks carefully about his next step. He concludes that living in public housing is better than living in a crowded house with people you don't know. I mean Curtis is friendly, but Jack isn't sure if he'll get along with so many people in the same house. Curtis has his granddaughters living with him.

Oh well. It's my decision and I'm standing by it. Jack replies to Curtis that he is thankful for Curtis's hospitality, but he'll make it out here. Jack hopes to stay in contact with Curtis because he is a great friend.

Jack remains on the internet to do random searching and keeping up with the news. Nothing special is happening and Jack is bored. He plays Solitaire to pass the time. What an old game. Jack does some reading and then reads to an old woman.

Reading out loud for some reason is entertaining to Jack and he loves it. Unfortunately, he is approached by James.

James says, "Are you ready to move?"

Jack wants to tell him the truth but says, "I guess."

James has a wry smile. Why does he have to be this way, Jack thinks. His blood pressure rises. James walks away, and Jack is glad because he barely holds his temper. Jack must calm himself down. It's like James criticizes everything he does. Jack wonders If he punches James, will he understand why he was hit? Jack concludes probably not. James would just press charges and still be annoying. Jack recalls having a bully in high school who reminds him of James. He kept picking on Jack for no real reason. The bullying only stopped when Jack went to college- far away from the bully.

Jack wanted to slug the bully so badly, but he prayed to the Lord and managed to get over it. Well, if I see him today maybe my rage would be reignited. Jack may never respect James, but Jack can't hit him just because he is nerve-wracking. Man does he test my patience. So, Jack gets back to reading to this elderly woman.

She falls asleep as Jack is halfway through reading the book. But Jack keeps reading until she begins to snore. Jack smiles and quietly leaves his chair. He sees people playing a card game. The game seems fun, so Jack participates until Kent arrives at the shelter.

Jack tells Kent, "My body seems to be breaking down on me. My back is sore along with one of my legs."

"So, I guess you aren't going to the gym?"

Jack smiles and says, "Well of course I'm going! I may not lift much, but some light exercise may do me some good."

Jack tries to be tough with a forced smile as he gets up from the chair. But the pain is acute. But true to his word, he goes to the gym. He works his arms and then spots Kent who is bench pressing. Jack jumps in the pool. He hopes the water will loosen up his muscles. This works.

After being in the water for 10 minutes, Jack swims in the shallow end of the pool and his lower back is not as stiff. I could run a mile, Jack thinks. Jack is now watching Kent play basketball. As usual, Kent is dominating the competition. He makes some fantastic passes and dunks a couple of times.

Jack has never seen someone so young be that explosive. He knows Kent could play in the NBA. To go from being homeless to being rich, Jack thinks. And Kent is into his studies. So, he'll know what to do with all that big money.

In the sauna, Jack tells Kent, "You can make the NBA if you stay healthy."

"Well, I hope so. I'm tired of hard living. Not having much money and living in a shelter."

Jack just nods. Jack did not grow up in a shelter. He has no idea how that feels. Kent has never lived in a place he can call his own. That's why Kent is so motivated. He sees sports and academics as ways to improve his standard of living. He tries his best at everything. This part of Kent's personality worries Jack. How will he react when he fails at something? Jack has been meaning to discuss this with Kent's parents.

Kent says, "I can't wait to get to Welch's Academy, so I can have a room to myself and privacy. All my life I've had to share something. Now I want to be a little selfish."

"I see your point. But you'll still share a bathroom according to the layout of the residential area."

"Yeah, but I can study in my room and not hear people talking and babies crying."

Sometimes Kent does homework at the public library because of this background noise at the shelter. Plus, Kent loves to read. He'll finish his homework and then browse in the library for hours. He reads whatever books catch his eyes. Jack has been to the library with Kent and Jack can't keep up with him. Kent is from one aisle to the other. And Kent is not skimming through books. He doesn't speed read, so he spends all day in the library at times.

Kent asks Jack rhetorical questions. Jack realizes Kent doesn't want him to talk but just wants to be heard. Kent continues to talk until they get back to the shelter. Jack reads to a little boy.

Wow. I'm tired of hearing Kent right now. I hope he isn't like this tomorrow. Jack only reads a few pages of the book. He is tired. He sits on his cot planning out what to do tomorrow. Sleep is setting in, and he can barely keep his thoughts straight. Jack wants to ask his boss something, but he can't remember and drifts off to sleep.

As usual, Jack's alarm sounds signaling time to get ready for work. He is dragging today and really wants to go back to sleep. But he gets up and heads out the door on time.

It's going to be a rough day at work. The crew must carry boards to make a wall to keep water from overtaking the property. Jack doesn't know how the older guys can carry boards. Jack is in shape, and he struggles sometimes. At least my lower back feels fine. Some in the crew tell him not to lift weights. Because this job depends on keeping a healthy body. Sometimes injuries occur when lifting weights. But there is no way Jack will only swim for exercise. Carrying boards hurts his hands because it's hard to grip the boards. Even though the boards are not extremely heavy.

Now Jack is at work enjoying coffee before getting to work. This helps to wake him up, even though he loves coffee because of the taste. Of course, he must add creamer and sugar to the coffee- all black coffee isn't that palatable. Time for work.

Jack grabs a board and starts stacking. It doesn't take long for fatigue to set in. Everyone slows down by the afternoon. Even Jack becomes winded. What a workout. His shoulders are burning along with his legs.

Yet Jack doesn't complain and gets the job done. On the train ride home, Jack notices that his back feels better from this workout of carrying boards. Then when he doesn't exercise his lower back. Even though Jack is sweating profusely, he is not tired one bit.

Jack has down time before Kent arrives at the shelter. Maybe I should buy a vehicle soon. Riding the train every day gets annoying. I want a quieter way of transportation. I'll save money for a vehicle. That will take a long time because I don't get paid much. I could work at this job all my life and still be broke. Kent arrives at the shelter now and all Jack thinks about is going to the gym. They talk to each other for a bit and then head to the gym.

Jack swims in the pool. Kent doesn't feel like playing basketball today. He also swims. Kent is a terrible swimmer. He can barely swim half a lap without losing his form. Some time ago, the lifeguard asked him if he was ok because he was swimming in such an awkward way. Sometimes Jack brings this episode up when they want a good laugh. Kent does some water aerobics in the shallow end of the pool while Jack swims laps in the pool.

"How come you aren't playing basketball today?"

"Well, there isn't any competition, and I'm tired of dominating the same people day in and day out. I'm ready to go to Welch's Academy for a real challenge. I haven't played against real competition in years."

Jack swims freestyle because he is skilled in that technique. He has tried doing the backstroke, but he gets water in his mouth and eyes. Mainly because he doesn't keep his back straight. His stamina has improved greatly. He can swim 20 laps in a row without stopping. Kent is amazed.

"I thought you swim to pass the time."

Now resting, Jack says to Kent, "You try."

"No way. I can barely doggie paddle in the shallow end. Let alone swim multiple laps in the pool."

Tired of swimming, they head back to the shelter. Well, it won't be long Jack thinks. Kent goes to Welch's Academy soon. He has never been away from home for an extended period. Soon he'll be thousands of miles away. A few years ago, Kent attended a basketball camp in Seattle, Washington. But that city is only 3 hours away by car from Vancouver. Any time Jack talks about him being away from home for so long, Kent says I'll be fine. Kent seems ready to accept the challenge.

At the shelter, Jack reads a short novel to a few children before dinner. These kids love the novel. They don't make any noise and they are not restless. Not one child complains that he or she is bored. Jack is such a great reader. I should've been a teacher. The time goes by fast and now it is time for dinner.

To Kent's and Jack's surprise, Kent has a going away party at the soup kitchen. Jack can't believe no one talked to him about this. He is not mad. He figures they didn't want him to give any hints to Kent. The chefs cook Kent's favorite: beef ravioli. Kent always talks about beef ravioli since he had the real thing a few years ago. At the party, people provide Kent with all the school supplies he needs. Plus, they give him a gift card to buy new clothes. He doesn't need a lot of new clothes. Welch's Academy has a uniform policy.

James hosts the party, and he isn't sarcastic- to everyone's surprise. Maybe he isn't that bad, Jack thinks. Kent is so shocked and grateful that he is unable to speak. He can't help but to shed tears. Seeing Kent like this chokes Jack up. He barely holds back tears.

After a few minutes, Kent stands up and says, "Thank you everyone. I'll do my best at Welch's Academy. I won't let you all down. Thanks again for the support."

Even the chefs tear up. Everyone claps. Then it is time to eat real beef ravioli. Wow, Jack thinks. It is better than I thought. Jack had previously had beef ravioli in a can. Everything tastes so right.

Jack eats six ravioli and is full. Kent, who usually eats in moderation, is stuffing his face. He needs to slow down, Jack thinks.

"Kent, relax a little bit,"

Kent looks up and says, "Oh."

Then Kent takes his time eating.

To stay with the theme of Italian cuisine, the dessert is the Italian specialty tiramisu. Kent absolutely loves this dessert. He eats two slices of it. Jack eats a slice too. Jack likes cannoli more, but the chefs did not prepare them.

After dinner, all Kent talks about is the generosity and support of everyone around him. He didn't know he was this loved. Jack nods as Kent talks. Jack knew how many people respected Kent. They saw his commitment to his studies throughout the years.

On the weekends, when other students were partying, Kent would be in the public library from open to close. He was studying all day because he knew what he wanted. I guess growing up extremely poor can motivate anyone. There is a fire inside of Kent. I wish I was like that at his age, Jack thinks.

Back at the shelter, Kent passes the time before "lights out" by a playing a video game. Kent is playing against people from around the world. It's an action/adventure shooting game. He has headphones on while using a fake gun. Kent plays every now and then, so he isn't good. He starts getting frustrated because his opponents are very good.

Jack tried to play this game a few months ago. Even though he didn't know much about online games. He sees these things as a distraction and a waste of time. He would rather read to others or read to himself. I guess I'm old school. He chuckles as he sees how immersed Kent is in the game. Jack writes these two poems as the day comes to an end:

> Pen and paper, two simple things, but together, with a creative mind, can bring insights, new ways of seeing the same things, challenges can be overcome, face certain fears, nowhere to run, you gotta take a stand, standing so strong, you can't be budged, by a battering ram, keep your lips tight, just like a clam, some actions don't need to be explained, stick to your plan, the only way to lose is to give up,

> The hand is quicker than the eye, the treasures go to the spry, sometimes to the ones that lie, being sly I try, to stay on the right side, but sometimes I feel like Mr. Hyde, even though I'm a doctor, like Jekyl, especially when heckled, then, I remind myself, I'm special, a genius, but when you are poor, that fact is meaningless, when you can barely

> shop at payless, so I read and write to relieve
> stress, I feel better now,

Well, tomorrow is the weekend. What should I do? I'll find something to do before the weekend is over. As the lights go out, Jack is ready to wake up in the morning for a day off. Without his alarm being set, Jack doesn't get up until 10:00 AM.

He is so refreshed that he jumps up from his cot and cleans himself up. Now he is thinking of how to spend the day. Going to the mall seems cool. Jack is not in the mood to shop around. He knows what Kent would do. He would go to the park and play basketball all day. Sometimes Jack goes with him just to watch. There are good players out there. Of course, Kent dominates even though some of the guys are at college-level ability.

People from the shelter are visiting public housing to get a feel for the neighborhood. I may go there later. Jack had been there before but didn't look around much. He's heard nothing but bad things about the area. They say: it's crime-infested, the water sometimes shuts off, and there is always a police presence. Like most people, Jack is concerned about a lot of crime. When he lived in his cardboard palace, Jack was able to stay in safe areas. At least compared to where he will reside. Sure, he was beaten up a few times, but no one used knives or guns on him.

And there weren't drug dealers around. Jack worries when thinking about his new home. He can't remain in the shelter, so he has no choice. Unless of course, he resorts back to his cardboard palace. However, he vowed to himself to never go back to living on the street. No matter what. To distract his mind from such a depressing subject, Jack decides to read to children. The distraction works and Jack is happy. After a couple hours of reading, Kent approaches him.

"Hey Jack, are you coming along? You know where I'm going."

Jack puts off seeing his new neighborhood to watch good basketball.

"Yeah, I'll go to the park," Jack replies.

This park is the biggest and most beautiful park in the city. It is next to the sea and is frequented by many locals and tourists alike. It is usually crowded. The beach is also crowded. Although the water is dark and Jack refuses to swim in it. There is room in the park to play soccer. Jack has played soccer there and is thinking of doing so now. Especially if he gets tired of watching basketball.

Jack and Kent arrive at the park early. No one is on the basketball court yet. They shoot around for a bit and then play one on one. Of course, they aren't going 100 percent. After about 20 minutes of light play, people begin to file in. Jack sits on a bench as Kent and other players organize pick-up basketball games. Jack watches them play for hours until he sees people playing volleyball. They let him play and Jack enjoys himself.

None of the volleyball players are good so the game gets interesting. Jack tries to spike the ball but doesn't jump high enough. However, he makes a great diving save later in the match. They play volleyball for a long time until they are tired. Then Jack sits back down on a bench to watch the man who rarely gets tired- Kent.

It's like Kent is a level above everyone else on the court. Sometimes he doesn't cross anyone up but runs by them. By now, the basketball court has drawn a lot of spectators. The crowd oohs and ahs as Kent dribbles up and down the court.

Of course, he is the star. Jack has been at the park so long he loses track of time. Wow! We've been here all day.

Not wanting to miss dinner at the soup kitchen, Jack yells, "Hey Kent, it's time to go!"

Still enjoying the game, Kent has a look of disgust on the court. But he leaves right away. He is extremely hungry too. All Kent talks about on the way to the soup kitchen are his basketball moves. He asks Jack if he saw when he did a hesitation step or when he dunked on a certain opponent. Yet Kent is not arrogant. He's excited that he can do so many wonderful things on the court.

While at the soup kitchen, Kent explains to Shirley and others how much fun he had playing basketball today. These people are unathletic, so they don't grasp the significance of a well-timed block or steal. But this doesn't matter to Kent who wants someone to listen to him, Jack thinks.

Jack eats like a pig. Tonight is taco night. He eats until he can't eat another mouthful. He has eaten too much and now his stomach hurts. Everyone is talking about going to the movies to see the latest action film.

The film has received plenty of press attention and Jack can't wait to see it. One of his favorite action heroes is in the movie. Jack asks the others what time they want to go to the movie theater. Shirley says right away, and Kent doesn't care about the time. We will go at 8:00 PM Jack tells everyone.

Then Jack looks at his wallet and says goodbye to twenty dollars. Jack plans to buy a drink and popcorn at the theater, so all his finances in his wallet will be drained. However, he rarely goes to the movies, so he believes the price is worth it. Especially since all his friends are also interested in the film. The movie theater is state of the art. The seats recline and the screen is extremely large. There are no bad seats in the theater.

The film is excellent. Although the theater is crowded, no one makes any noise. Everyone is on their best behavior. Also, the film's plot is first-rate. It's impossible to guess what happens next. Just as Jack likes it. During the movie, Jack looks around the theater, and everyone's eyes are glued to the screen. After the film, no one complains.

Shirley says, "Wow! I can't believe how good this movie is."

Jack nods. The screenwriters hit a homerun with this one. Jack watches the credits to catch the names of the screenwriters. I'll look them up on the computer. Jack is one of those people who believes books are better than the movies. If the film is this good, imagine how wonderful the book is?

Jack read the reviews before seeing the movie and all the critics gave it thumbs up. Jack rarely reads what critics write before viewing a movie. Because a poorly rated review makes you reconsider seeing the movie. It's almost lights out at the shelter when Jack and friends arrive there. So, they move as quietly as possible. Jack is tired and goes right to sleep.

The next thing he remembers is a group of people in the morning heading to church. They are singing hymns, and some are praying. Jack hasn't been to church in quite some time. Even though he was raised Christian. His mom and would tell him to go back to the Lord and attend church regularly. He would say ok, but he was never serious about going back. However, he knows the Bible well and used to read it all the time while living on the streets. It was calming even amid poverty and occasional violence.

Watching these devout Christians getting ready for church leads Jack to pray immediately. And Jack sings a few hymns to himself. He starts with Blessed Assurance. Jack feels the spirit around him and decides to read the Bible. Before he realizes it, Jack has read the Bible for an hour. He is contemplating going back to church. But he doesn't have any church clothes. At least that is his excuse. There are non-denominational churches that don't have a dress code. Oh well, I'll go to church another time.

He cracks open a novel to pass the time. It's a great novel by an old European author. Jack loves old literature. In college, Jack was considering double-majoring in Neuroscience and European Literature. Tolstoy is his favorite European author. With nothing to do, Jack plans to finish reading this novel for the rest of the day. After reading for hours, Jack must stop. His vision is blurry from all this reading.

He takes a walk around the city. Jack is wowed by the city's beauty every time he's downtown. So big yet so clean. Jack stops by an outdoor food market and orders an Italian sub.

Jack didn't come here with Kent because he wants to relax by himself. The onions are so strong that Jack must breathe through his mouth. He knows everyone will be able to smell him for the rest of the day. Oh well. This is a good sub. Jack orders chips to go along with the large sub. Jack is being greedy. He knows the sub is too much to eat in one sitting. However, he keeps eating way past being full. Jack can barely walk. He waddles his way back to the shelter.

Most of the people are eating lunch at the soup kitchen. Jack enjoys peace and quiet. He does some uninterrupted writing. He writes this poem:

> I've been to many cities, but none as pretty as Vancouver, no trash on the streets, like someone used a hoover, a bit overcrowded, but which big city isn't, but it's still amazing, the water by the beach is a little suspect, is it algae, or some type of scum, from pollution, yet people seem not to mind jumping in, I'll

> stick to swimming at the aquatic center, at
> least it, doesn't get too cold in there in the
> winter,

Then Jack reads the news. An article about weightlifting caught his eye. The article looks at how weight training during old age is beneficial. It strengthens bones and muscles. Also, weight training increases coordination. Which can prevent falls so common among the elderly.

Jack reads another article about lifting weights. It's about a 70-year-old man in great shape from weight training. His physique is better than most weightlifters'- including Jack's. His secrets are exercising consistently and eating the right foods. Sometimes this elder man competes in 5k races. He is a true athlete. The next article explains how running for 5 minutes a day is beneficial. Jack reads a few more articles until he gets tired of reading.

Now Jack is playing chess against the computer. He celebrates beating the computer for the first time. Jack plays every now and then. But it's a fluke. He plays five more games and doesn't come close to winning a single game. Frustrated, Jack gets up from the computer and writes two poems on chess:

> The game they claim will make one smarter,
> so I play the game and study it harder, yet I'm
> still not great at it, confused every time I lose,
> which is almost every time, so I'll just stick to
> composing rhymes, where I feel one of a kind,
> the best poet there is line for line,
>
> Playing chess they claim makes you smarter,
> it forces your brain to work harder, than any

other game, it's like steroids for your brain,
improves everything, processing speed to
concentration, the benefits are seemingly
amazing, chess to me is frustrating, so many
different things to keep track of, to become
good is a labor of love, constantly playing
and memorizing strategies, thinking about
movies mathematically, you must know all
64 squares, and to be aware, of a multitude
of attacks, really a never ending brainstorm,

Jack is proud of composing these two poems. Writing for him is effortless. Unlike playing chess. I may stick to connect-4 and checkers. By now most of the people are back from lunch at the soup kitchen. The noise level at the shelter increases dramatically- which is fine by him. It was getting boring at the shelter with no signs of life. To pass the time Jack plays connect-4 with some of the kids at the shelter. These kids are smart because Jack doesn't beat them every time. But he usually wins with no problem.

One kid, Devon, is great at the game. Jack cannot beat him all day. This is frustrating- losing to a 12-year-old. Embarrassed, Jack tells everyone he just isn't on his game. But really, Devon is exceptional at playing connect-4. He plays almost every day. Yet Jack can only see that a 12-year-old kid beat an adult.

Some of the adults poke fun at Jack until he says, "Well you play me!"

And of course, they don't. They know Jack would beat them all easily. After losing to Devon for the 4th straight time, Jack throws his hands up and then reads a novel. Now Kent plays connect-4.

Kent believes he'll destroy Devon because he is a genius. But no. Devon beats him too. After losing six in a row, Kent throws his hands up and decides to read some Shakespeare.

"It's just a game," Kent tells everyone.

Devon wins at connect-4 all day. A 12-year-old is the master of this game.

Kent reads Hamlet for the hundredth time. He knows the play by heart. That's why Kent does so well in English classes. He has already read all the books that his English classes cover. Kent doesn't just read books for school. He's an avid reader. His parents always stress the importance of learning. He takes this to heart. Plus, his mind is like a sponge: soaking up the world's greatest books and plays. Even though Jack is older than him, Kent is more well-read.

Kent can recite plenty of quotes from famous authors. He loves to learn. But Kent remains humble. He rarely shows off his knowledge of literature. He gets excited about certain books. He's not condescending at all. That's another reason why Jack is so proud of Kent.

Jack is proud of Kent for many things. While growing up, Jack was never this humble. Jack used to test people's knowledge. He was never suspended from school, but his parents were upset with him. Kent has never been to the principal's office for anything. He's never even been to detention in all his years in school. And since Jack has known Kent, Kent's knowledge has increased ten-fold. They constantly debate which book is better and talk about the underlying themes in literature.

Jack used to suggest books for Kent to read. But as aforementioned, Kent is now more well-read than Jack. Kent tells Jack which books he should check out. Jack's been reading novels by Indian authors because of Kent's suggestions. Jack is currently reading a book on Gandhi. Jack started reading the book a few days ago and he just can't put it down. He's already halfway through reading it. Jack is glad Kent suggested this book. Every book that Kent recommends is good.

Being poor, Jack rarely buys books, but he goes to the public library often. He vows to buy new books once he can save up some money. After reading for an hour, Jack takes a break and relaxes. Devon is still playing connect-4 and remains unbeaten. No one is even a challenge.

Jack wants to try his luck again, but he hates losing. There is no way he'll play Devon again for a long time. How can a 12-year-old be so crafty, Jack thinks. The game may not be as complicated as chess, but still no adults have beaten him. No one has come close, including Kent.

Oh well, I'll get on the computer to pass the time. Jack checks his email and then listens to music. He clicks on a classical music channel. A song by Bach is playing. Sounds good, Jack thinks. He's been listening to classical music for years. But he can't quite get into it. He appreciates the skill necessary to play this style of music. But he has no interest in listening to this music for long.

After about ten minutes, Jack switches to a jazz channel. He is tapping his feet to the rhythm. Jack doesn't know much about jazz composers. But he knows good music when he hears it.

It's now time for dinner so Jack goes to the soup kitchen with everyone else. Dinner is uneventful. When they go back to the shelter, Jack resumes listening to music. He continues to vibe until "lights out."

Chapter 21

JACK WAKES UP IN the morning on Sunday. He debates whether to go to church. You know what, I'm going to church this morning. He finds a good shirt and pants and links up with Shirley. She is one of the faithful. Jack can't remember the last time she missed a church service. The church is 2 blocks away. Shirley and Jack walk to church.

The church is non-denominational, so it is very welcoming. There are even people of different religions here. They love hearing the positivity of Christianity. Shirley has told Jack that the preacher doesn't talk about "Fire and Brimstone." He concentrates on how forgiving and merciful God is.

The congregation sings a few songs and then the preacher dives right into the sermon. The preacher talks about how God is with you no matter what. A tear forms in Jack's eye as he recalls living in that cardboard box on the streets. He remembers being beaten and dealing with the weather. Digging in trashcans a lot of days and eating fast-food when he could. I'm never going back to that, Jack vows.

Jack tries to hold back any more tears, but he can't. They stream down his face. Shirley holds his hand. She probably believes the sermon is causing this reaction, Jack thinks. He is now sobbing uncontrollably. So, he goes to the bathroom to calm down. Looking in the mirror, he's able to compose himself. He's no longer sobbing but the tears are still streaming.

Jack didn't know he was scarred this deep. He knows that the shelter is a nurturing environment. But he realizes he suffers from post-traumatic stress. Just like soldiers in a warzone. Ok, I'm ok. Jack is not quite as distraught as earlier. He leaves the bathroom.

Jack finds his seat and does his best to sit still for the rest of the service. His body is in the church, but his mind is on the situations he went through while living on the streets. I thought I had these images under control. No one can tell he is bothered. He smiles when Shirley looks at him.

Jack says to her, "It's such a nice day. Let's stroll through the park."

"But Jack, the park is not nearby. By the time we get there, part of the day will be gone."

He didn't think about that. She's right though. The park is not downtown.

"Well, let's go window shopping." Jack says.

"Sure."

They are now in the financial district. They enter a store selling designer clothing. Jack shakes his head at the prices. $300 for a pair of jeans. That's enough for a shopping spree in a typical clothing store. Shirley is excited. She goes from clothes rack to clothes rack studying each outfit. Jack is ready to leave the store. There are other stores he wants to visit.

Next, they go into a music store. Jack listens to classical music while Shirley listens to rock music. Jack likes rock music but doesn't feel like hearing it today. They stay in the store for quite a while. Jack wants to go back to the shelter now. But Shirley sees a few more stores she wants to go in.

They go into a shoe store. Jack isn't interested in shoes.

Especially since he only lifts weights and swims in the pool. He doesn't need any shoes. However, he spots some attractive shoes that are reasonably priced. He tries them on. They are comfortable. Jack checks his wallet but decides not to buy these shoes right now.

Shirley tries on 4 pairs of shoes. Even though she knows she isn't buying a thing. She tries on running shoes. Jack finds this amusing since she doesn't enjoy walking let alone running. Now they go back to the shelter.

Once at the shelter, Jack reads the Bible. His mind drifts to being in church as a young boy. A specific sermon pops in his head. The pastor preaches about not telling everyone your dream. Because people will discourage you. You could possibly lose confidence in yourself. How true that is, Jack thinks.

His parents and ex-wife called him stupid. For wanting to pursue real estate investing instead of remaining in his field of expertise. Even though he was unsuccessful, knowing you took your own path is worth more than I could imagine, Jack thinks. I may be poor economically, but I feel great psychologically. Where was I? Oh yeah, the book of Mattew. Jack meditates on some of the scriptures. Jack is in a happy place now. He has no worries. Then he watches tv until "lights out." I have work tomorrow.

Once his alarm sounds, Jack gets right up and is off to work. He's not sleepy so he doesn't nap on the train. Instead, he is wide awake. Unsure of the near future when he must move into public housing. It's just not right. Why change a good thing? He has constantly complained to James who tells him to deal with it. It's out of my hands is James's favorite response. But Jack can't let it go.

He wrote letters to the top official who oversees homeless shelters all over the city. The official responded after the third letter. He wrote that it is best for everyone if most people are in public housing. Because the transition from dependence to independence will be easier if the people get a feel for regular life. And hopefully, after public housing, the people can branch out and live on their own soon. This letter angers Jack. He wants to remain in a stable environment. He doesn't know how he'll do in a different environment. Jack thinks about writing another letter but realizes this man won't change his mind. I must tough it out.

The commute seems faster today. And before Jack knows it, it's time to get off the train and do construction work. Today, the crew is cleaning up a jobsite. They are picking up unused wood pieces and other waste. It's an easy job- putting waste in the back of the dump truck. The crew does this all day. Everyone chips in except the boss. He is on his cell phone handling business. While working, Jack is thinking about what to say to Kent. He leaves for boarding school tomorrow night.

Jack has a few things to say that are planned out. He wished him the best and wants him to still concentrate on his studies. He'll think of more to say later. Well, work goes by quickly and Jack finds himself on the train heading back to the shelter.

Arriving at the shelter, Jack goes straight to the computer to get on the internet. He wants to search online to pass the time. Jack plays games on the computer. Kent is back from his last day of school. It's obvious Kent is excited about leaving the shelter.

The first thing he says to Jack is, "It's almost that time."

Jack nods. Jack has never attended a boarding school. So, he isn't sure what to say to Kent about boarding schools. Kent goes on talking about how wonderful this school will be. And how he's setting himself up for success for the rest of his life. Jack listens and is so happy for his good friend.

Then Jack interjects, "Will you miss us?"

Kent stares at him and says, "Very much so. Everyone has been so helpful and friendly. I will miss hanging out with you. Going to the gym and talking with you have been fun. We can keep in contact by email, but I don't know how busy I'll be. I think I'll be very busy. In addition to the rigorous coursework, I'll be playing sports all year long. The school has a good track team."

Jack says, "I know everything will be fine and fun. What an experience! I wish I were going to school there. I'd be excited too!"

"Yeah, I can't wait. I want to see how my basketball skills match up against some of the best young ballplayers."

Jack adds, "I know you'll represent Vancouver well. I know you are the best player anywhere for your age. You just have to stay healthy."

Kent already knows these things because Jack has told him time and time again. And his parents have always made him feel that he can do anything. And it helps to have a vertical leap over 40 inches.

In elementary school Kent played kickball often. But he didn't play just for fun. He would test his speed after games by running the bases repeatedly. He would do leg exercises in his room. After doing this for a year, Kent was the only one in his elementary school with a true six-pack.

He didn't not work his upper body, so he didn't look bulky. But since exercising with Jack, he looks like an NFL player. Yet he maintains cat-like quickness. Even when playing basketball, he would rather use his speed than his strength.

Jack asks Kent, "Want to go to the gym?"

"Of course."

The workers at the gym congratulate Kent. They know this is the last time he'll go to this gym in a while. Kent has tears in his eyes. He sees how much he will be missed. Kent plays basketball. Jack watches him play ball instead of swimming. As usual, Kent impresses. He crosses over one defender and then dunks on two guys at the same time. Jack has to applaud. Beautiful work. A few plays later, Kent steals the ball and throws a perfectly timed no look pass. It's clear that he is the best player on the court. After six games, Kent is ready to lift weights.

While lifting Kent says, "Welch's Academy has a great weight room with personal trainers. I should be more athletic after one semester."

Kent has gotten stronger every month since weight training with Jack. A testament to Kent's work ethic. It can't be genetic, Jack thinks. Kent's parents are not in great shape. In fact, Kent' dad has never touched a weight. Kent is a hard worker who rarely gives up on anything. Now Jack and Kent are bench pressing.

Kent puts up a personal best of 375 lbs. That's amazing for a 14-year-old. Jack can't believe how strong Kent has gotten. Even though Kent works hard, it is still something how motivated he is to reach his goals. Jack congratulates Kent and then they get in the sauna to relax.

The sauna feels hotter than usual. Which is a good thing because both guys are a little sore from lifting weights. The heat seems to work wonders, Jack thinks. As he moves his arms back and forth. They no longer feel tight. Kent looks like he is about to go to sleep. He worked out hard. He lifted every weight in sight. He worked his entire body and is totally drained. However, once they leave the sauna, maybe from the recuperative powers of the sauna and Kent being so young, he now has more energy than Jack.

They get into the jacuzzi, and Kent says, "I'm feeling like I could lift all over again!"

"Really?"

"Yeah really. I could run 5 miles!"

Jack replies, "Well, I'd like to see that."

"I'll bet you something then," Kent says.

"Ok, what?"

"If I can run 5 miles without stopping you have to buy me dinner tonight."

Jack thinks carefully and replies, "No doubt. But if you can't run 5 miles you have to do my laundry tonight."

"Deal."

"Run around the track in the gym and I'll make sure you run 5 miles."

"All right," Kent replies.

Kent does a bit of stretching and then he starts running. Kent is running, but his stride isn't good. In fact, he looks like he's about to pass out. Well, looks like I'm going to win, Jack thinks.

After the first mile, Kent looks like an Olympian. His running form is flawless. His knees are high, and he is breathing easier than in the first mile. Now Jack is worried. And for good reason. I shouldn't have made that bet. Kent glares at Jack as he runs by him- showing off. After running 5 miles, Kent says, "Well, I don't know where I want to eat yet."

Kent isn't out of breath. He played basketball; he lifted weights; and he now ran 5 miles. Yet he doesn't look tired at all. Was he pretending to be fatigued in the sauna, Jack thinks.

They go back to the shelter and freshen up a bit.

Kent says, "I think I want a nice juicy steak. Let's go to a steakhouse."

Imagining a steak makes Jack's mouth water. This dinner is going to run me 50 dollars. But hey, it's a one-time thing.

"Fine," Jack responds.

They take public transit to a great steakhouse. Kent really wants me to go broke, Jack thinks. As Kent orders a 24 oz T-bone steak. There is no way he can eat all that, Jack thinks. He must take a doggie bag, Jack thinks. Jack orders a big steak too. It's a 12 oz sirloin. His favorite. For some reason, it doesn't take the chefs long to prepare the steaks. As the server serves the food, Jack gets even hungrier as he smells the aroma from the meat and onions. Then they dig in. While Jack puts steak sauce on the meat, Kent is already cutting through the T-bone. He's eating like he never ate before.

Jack says, "Slow down. Don't choke on your food."

Kent looks up and replies, "Yeah. I guess I am eating like a barbarian. It's just so good."

"Mine is too," Jack responds.

There is no real conversation going on. The gym workout must have made them very hungry. All they focus on is the next bite. At least Kent is taking his time now. Even though he has a 24 oz steak, he finished eating it at the same time as Jack finished his steak. Yes, he ate the entire T-bone. Jack can't believe it.

As they leave the restaurant, it's obvious that Kent ate too much. He is holding his stomach while walking slowly. Jack finds this funny and teases him.

"Hey, are you ready to run another five miles?" Jack says while pointing at Kent's stomach.

Kent looks at him with a wry smile. Kent looks sick. I hope he doesn't vomit or anything.

Kent says, "I do feel sick. But the feeling will go away soon. I think I was just being greedy."

That's obvious, Jack thinks. But he doesn't say this to Kent. He doesn't want to criticize him too much. Because Kent can be very sensitive.

Once at the shelter, Kent takes a nap. Jack looks at the clock. It is almost 8:00 PM- 2 hours until lights out. So, Jack decides to immerse himself for the rest of the night in a wonderful novel. He tries to read it until lights out, but his eyes become tired. So, he puts the book down and relaxes. His mind is clear. He is not worried about anything. It feels good having a full stomach and a relaxed mind.

As Jack's eyes get back to normal, he resumes reading the novel. So caught up in the storyline, he reads the entire book just before lights out. And then he closes his eyes. He is ready for work in the morning.

Today, the boss has something to show Jack. Nick shows him the books. The books indicate how much money the company makes and how much money the company spends. Jack is rather clueless on how a business is run.

Jack says, "So, what do these numbers mean?" pointing to the liability side of the ledger.

Nick calmly explains everything about the business in 15 minutes. Until Jack understands the numbers. Well Jack pretends to understand everything. Really most of the things go over his head. But Jack figures he'll understand it later. Especially if he mentally reviews what the boss said.

After this tutorial, Jack and the crew get to work building a 500 ft pier. A daunting task, but Jack is confident that he'll do as good a job as any other crew member.

They buy the bolts necessary from a hardware store. Then they drive poles in the ground in the water for the foundation of the pier. Jack observes a crew member guiding the poles as the boss is driving them in with a special machine. Lining up the poles takes precision. Half the day goes by, and they still haven't driven enough poles to start the next phase in building the pier.

Nick treats the crew to lunch by taking them out to the local seafood restaurant. Jack loves seafood. At the restaurant, he orders raw oysters, steamed clams, fried fish and greens. Wow, Jack thinks as he savors the taste of oysters with hot sauce. There is nothing like fresh oysters to start off a good meal. Jack doesn't eat too many because he is saving room for the main course.

The boss, Nick, doesn't care about saving room. He eats 7 to 8 oysters before his entrée. Nick orders lobster and shrimp. Jack wishes that this is his meal, but he doesn't want to choose one of the most expensive meals on the menu.

The fried fish is excellent. Dipping the fish in tartar sauce, Jack forgets all about lobster and shrimp. The greens top it off. They are collard greens doused in a bit of vinegar. It's obvious why the restaurant has been in business for so long. The chefs are amazing. Jack finishes his meal with sweet potato pie. He doesn't know how the boss expects us to get back to work after such a big meal. Well, they do get back to work and Jack can barely move.

They resume driving poles. This takes the rest of the day. Meaning, real work begins tomorrow. Driving poles takes little energy because the machine does all the work.

After work, Jack goes back to the shelter and checks his email. Curtis has a message for him. He is doing fine and wants Jack to visit him. In a way Jack wants to see him. But he doesn't have the money right now. Jack responds to the message explaining that maybe in 3 months he'll visit Curtis and his family.

Jack emails his son, Brent. Jack doesn't expect a response. But he'll keep trying. Until one day, Brent realizes how important it is to have a relationship with his dad. Jack hasn't been in contact with his ex-wife for a long time. He holds her responsible for being homeless. After the divorce, he had little money so that precipitated into him being homeless. He tries to forget about her, but his anger runs deep. So deep that he is a bit scared of what he'll do if he ever sees her again.

To take his mind off Beth, he plays chess. He takes his time and thinks through every move. However, his efforts are not enough to defeat the computer. Frustrated, Jack gets off the computer and writes these poems:

> They say anger is a great motivator, but I write out of love and joy, hate is not a major, factor, sometimes I want to go after, those not treating me fairly, most of these people I barely, know, maybe if I could see more sides of them, I would not concentrate on their flaws, seeing the best out of others takes all, of my compassion, this takes some masking, but some experts believe lasting joy results from having, a short-term memory on being wronged,
>
> The only way to lose is to give up, living on the streets, though I never felt stuck, I knew bad luck, is not forever, things will get better, that's what I tell myself, and I'm not afraid to ask for help, going into the shelter, was a good move, it soothes my soul, to have support, and of course, a place to stay,

Writing these poems puts Jack in a good mood. So, he decides to try beating the computer in chess again. He performs well but loses again. Proud of coming close to winning, he celebrates by drinking fruit punch. He watches tv and sleeps in his cot right as lights out is announced.

When Jack wakes up in the morning, he gets ready for work and realizes Kent is really gone. Jack drops a few tears. He's closer to Kent than his own son. While on the train to work, Jack thinks of the great times he has had with Kent. Most of the memories deal with sports and exercise.

Jack recalls the first time he saw Kent play basketball. And how Kent kept getting better. And Jack remembers when he first went to the gym with Kent. Kent could barely bench press his own weight. Look how far he has come, Jack thinks. Jack is no personal trainer, but his little bit of expertise in weightlifting has helped make Kent stronger and probably faster.

Jack laughs when he recalls how he could never convince Kent to swim consistently. Although swimming is great exercise, Kent avoided it like the plague for some reason. Well, he's an excellent basketball player so he knows something, Jack thinks.

Jack is now at work setting boards to create a wall. This wall holds the water off the land. This is called building a bulkhead. The crew hasn't finished the long pier yet. Some of the raw materials haven't come through. So, they are working on two jobsites at the same time. This is common. It's not confusing to the crew because they've done it so much. Running boards take the most out of you because each board weighs 75 lbs. Every man handles the boards, so everyone is tired by the afternoon. And today is no different.

By lunch time, everyone's muscles are extremely fatigued and, in some cases, sore. Even though Jack lifts weights, the constant lifting of the boards can be exhausting. Fortunately, they have a long lunch break to recover. They eat a lot of protein for lunch.

The crew eats twice as much as a normal group of people. This hunger is all from running boards. No matter how well they recover and refuel, the crew cannot set as many boards in the afternoon as they did in the morning. It's physically impossible. Jack tries to be as efficient, but his body is stronger than his mind. His will pushes him to carry more boards, but his hands are tired of gripping boards. But the pain does not last long.

While on his way home, his muscles are no longer fatigued. Lifting weights every day may be the cause of this adaptation. Even though Kent is gone, Jack plans on going to the gym. He can't wait to train. Jack can exercise longer than before because he doesn't have to wait for Kent to come home from school.

Jack changes his clothes at the shelter and goes to the gym. He does his typical training program: swimming and weightlifting. He exercises so much that his muscles rarely get sore from his workouts. However, he still gets tired. After swimming a lot of laps, his heart rate is high. It takes some time for it to normalize.

Jack wants to run but his knees ache every now and then. Plus, swimming also loosens his muscles. Which minimizes the chance of pulling a muscle. So, now it is time to lift weights.

Jack works his abs because the experts say strong abs support the lower back. Jack does sit-ups while holding a weight to make the exercise more difficult. He keeps training even when he feels the burn. The experts also say training to failure makes you stronger. So, Jack is working his abs very hard. He can barely walk when he finishes his ab workout.

Jack takes a much-needed break and drinks from the water fountain. Jack is careful not to drink too much- to not get a cramp when he goes back exerting himself. He wonders if he should do more ab work. Since his abs are no longer sore. I don't want to overdo it. Jack calls it a day and hits the sauna.

While there, his mind is totally focused on his workout. He mentally reviews all the exercises he performed and then relaxes. Usually, he'd be talking with Kent about anything. I must adjust to going to the gym by myself. It will take some getting used to. He did lose his second-best friend since Curtis left. Oh well.

As soon as his skin prunes, Jack hops in the jacuzzi. The warm water feels great, and Jack wants to stay in it all day. He's thinking of doing this, since he doesn't have much planned later in the day. But his skin looks bad from being in the warm water too long so, he exits the jacuzzi.

Back at the shelter, Jack chats with Shirley before they head to the soup kitchen for dinner. Tonight, the chefs prepare Mediterranean food. Jack eats a pasta-like dish called orzo. Along with stuffed grape leaves and shrimp kabob. Everything is delicious. So delicious that Jack goes back for seconds and thirds. Although Jack eats a lot because he expends so much energy at the gym, even eating this much is abnormal. Glad it is a short walk to the shelter.

Tomorrow, Jack will be in public housing. Oh well, at least I'll still be close to the soup kitchen. Even though the house isn't as close to the kitchen as the shelter. Jack is trying to look on the bright side of moving aka being kicked out of the shelter. I'll have more privacy and it should be quiet when I sleep at night. But I must buy a computer. Internet access is free for those in public housing. He's contemplating whether to buy a cheap computer or one of high quality. Right now, Jack uses a computer to search the web and to check his email. He's thinking of putting his writings on a computer.

Jack wants a used computer for the price, but he doesn't trust used things. He's saved enough money to buy a great, high-quality computer. His last computer was of high quality and it lasted 12 years. It became outmoded, even though it still processed information fine.

While living in his cardboard palace, Jack wanted to transfer his writing from paper to the computer. Mainly because he almost lost his papers in a bad storm. The rain poured down. He was able to wrap his notebooks in plastic bags until the threat of water damage subsided.

That scared Jack- who thinks of his works as sacred. No one has read them yet. Because Jack is preparing to reveal them once his works are published. He would only let Curtis and Kent read a few poems.

Everyone saw Jack working diligently until it was lights out time. Oh yeah, Jack thinks. I can write all night in public housing if I want to. Jack is joyful thinking of having more time to work on his writings. Maybe I'll like public housing more than living in the shelter.

He has a little yard that he can enjoy when the weather is fair. Now Jack can't wait to move in. Which is a good thing since he is moving in tomorrow. Jack does some writing before the final lights go out. I'm still going to miss this place. Jack writes a poem about the shelter:

> When times were hard, this was a great place
> to stay, people here helped me along the way,
> now that I'm straight, I look back on their
> generosity, praising them is my reciprocity,
> it's amazing what a few kind words can do,

> you guys picked me up when I was blue, I didn't know how living in a shelter would be, but now I'm glad to have met you guys, you made me see, friends are forever,

Not bad, Jack thinks. I could've had a better rhyme scheme. Just in time Jack thinks as the lights are turned out and it's time to sleep. So excited about moving, Jack does not sleep well. He keeps imagining being in his house already relaxing. Jack finally dozes off, but he must get up in a few hours for work. He is unusually alert. Because he is still pumped up about moving in his house later today. The workday is uneventful. Jack is bored since he is ready to enjoy his new abode.

At the shelter, Jack gathers his belongings and heads to his house. It's move-in day for those that used to live in the shelter. So, there are volunteers to help everyone get situated. After about 2 hours, Jack is comfortable in his house and is happy. Despite being a public house, the home is clean and looks modern. The heating and air-conditioning system is new along with the stove and oven. Jack doesn't care about the stove and oven. He'll be eating most of his meals at the soup kitchen. But I may cook down the road. The living room is spacious, but without a tv, the home is too quiet. Jack plans to buy a tv soon along with a nice computer.

In the meantime, Jack writes pages for his novel and these two poems:

> In a place without a computer or tv, it's so quiet, maybe I should buy a pet, I have cabin fever already, because I'm used to being around a steady, flow of people and interacting with them, but in this realm, I can

> actually hear myself think for a change, and see a little greenery out my window pane, maybe I'll grow a small garden in my backyard, buy a picnic table, play some cards,
>
> It's so quiet I can hear myself think, I wish my best friends were here, no email, I sometimes enjoy being alone, but without good company, any house is not a home, from a cardboard palace, to a king's, living solitary is my biggest fear, so I understand why some join the wrong crowd, and become proud of doing negative things, approval can bring, no better feeling, than respect from your peers, I used to live off of that, back when I was studying for my PhD, I was first in the study hall, and last to leave, willing to flip pages of textbooks, even if papercuts caused my fingers to bleed, this hard-driving attitude I received, from my parents, military-like discipline,

Jack writes and writes until his hand is tired. He figures this is a good time to stop writing. Jack goes to his kitchen and gulps down a bottle of water. That's almost all that is in his fridge since he doesn't need food. The water is so cold that it hurts his teeth. Jack toughs it out. Then he sits down and lets his mind wander.

He thinks about the weight room and how much stronger he's gotten over the past few months. Then Jack thinks of how long he'll work in construction. It doesn't pay that well, but it is a job. He can live comfortably since the government pays his rent. Plus, he doesn't have to buy food. Because the soup kitchen serves 3 meals a day. He looks at his alarm clock and it's time for bed. He must work tomorrow so he needs his rest. It's so peaceful at night. Unlike at the shelter. Jack gets up for work and he is so refreshed.

Chapter 22

JACK JUMPS OUT OF bed because he feels so good. As usual, he takes public transportation to work. While on the train, he doesn't take a nap but observes the surroundings. There are the tall projects near the train. In the distance, there are the big houses with luxury cars in the driveways. Two different tales in the same city. It's a nice day for outside work- the temperature is fair and there are no clouds in the sky.

Jack is now at work ready to begin the day. The crew is still working on a long pier. Jack lays out boards to be cut and hands bolts to other crew members to frame the pier. Then he cuts boards the right length to be nailed onto the pier. These boards are what people will walk on. Jack cuts all the boards without making an error. This takes the entire workday. And Jack's arm is sore from using the table saw for 8 hours.

Jack isn't sure if he'll go to the gym. He is exhausted. As he gets closer to home, he just wants to stretch out. I'm supposed to buy a tv and computer today. So, Jack cleans up and fights the urge to relax. Jack heads to an electronics store and looks for a high-quality tv and laptop. The store is crowded. It's difficult for Jack to move around. After about 30 minutes of shopping, Jack heads home. He sets up his tv. He is very tired. He goes to bed without watching tv or using the computer.

Jack wakes up for work and is refreshed. His arm is not

sore one bit. He's up early and searches the internet on his new laptop. He's passing the time. He leaves for work, and he talks to Shirley. They engage in small talk.

While riding the train to work, Jack thinks about his finances. He's been saving most of what he makes from construction. Yet, he is far from being financially secure. Really, he is still poor despite not having to pay for room and board. He buys some snacks although he frequents the soup kitchen. Maybe I should look for better jobs. Jack likes his current job, but the pay isn't enough.

Jack really wants his writings to sell. So, he can retire from normal work and write poems and novels for a living. But I don't know if I'll ever make money from these things. Nothing is certain. Jack spaces out until he hears his train stop being called.

The crew is still working on the long pier. So, Jack must use his arm to nail down boards. The pier is near completion when the nails are in the boards. Jack nails the boards down. He takes plenty of breaks, but his arm is back hurting. Oh well. I've got to tough it out, Jack thinks. His wrist is now bothering him. The boss sees him favoring that wrist. Nick walks to his truck and retries a wrist supporter.

"Here you go," Nick says handing Jack the wrist supporter.

Jack puts it on, and it makes a difference. The pain eases off and then Jack feels no pain in his wrist. One thing is bothering Jack: there are screws and a screw gun.

Yet he is hammering nails. Yes, using a screw gun takes more concentration. But it saves time and is easier to use physically. He wants to say something to the boss, but he doesn't want to come off as a jerk. It just doesn't make sense. Oh well. I'll focus on my job. I can't do anything about the situation. Now, it is time for lunch.

Jack buys lunch this go around. Usually Jack buys sub for himself, but he's in a good mood. He orders fried chicken from the local store. The crew demolishes the chicken within 10 minutes. They talk for a bit and it's back to work.

The boss decides to give Jack an easy task. Jack puts in bolts to further stabilize the pier. Doing this takes strength, but it's not as repetitive as nailing boards down. So, his arm will not hurt from putting in bolts. Jack drills into the poles holding the pier up to put bolts in them. Then he puts nuts on the bolts. This keeps the bolts in place to stabilize the frame. Other crew members assist Jack because he is still a beginner at using the drill.

Sometimes the drill bit becomes dull, and the drill will not go through the wood. Jack must change the drill bit right away. But now he believes he has the hang of it.

After work, all Jack hears is the rumbling of the generator supplying the drill with power. He hears this ear hallucination on the train. He can't hear the train's sound one bit. But by the time Jack is home the hallucination ceases and Jack gets ready for the gym.

He watches a little news then heads out the door to go to the gym. Jack doesn't feel like swimming, so he goes straight to the weight room. Since his arm has been sore from previous days, Jack will work his abs and legs today.

Jack does sit ups and leg lifts until his ab muscles are fatigued. Then he takes a break and then does the entire ab workout again. By now he feels the burn and then he exercises his legs. Jack does some squats. He cuts his workout short and gets in the sauna.

Now his arm starts feeling better. All his muscles are loose. I feel like a million bucks. Jack gets in the jacuzzi to relax his muscles even more. Now I feel like a billion bucks. I could run a marathon. Rejuvenated, Jack jogs home.

He checks his email and sees that Kent leaves him a message:

> "Hey Jack, I'm doing great. I'm already the best player on the basketball team. My studies are challenging, but interesting. I've been studying a lot. The library is fantastic. My teachers are well informed in their subjects. I don't know when I'll be back home, but I'll keep in touch. How have you been?"

Jack smiles because he is so happy for Kent. Even if he doesn't make the NBA, he'll be able to get an excellent job. Because he is on track to being accepted into an elite university. Whether in Canada or the U.S., Kent can't go wrong.

Jack replies:

> "Glad to hear you are staying focused. Keep up the good work. Everything is fine here. I am now in public housing. I'm adjusting to it and right now, I love the privacy. I'm doing well and I wish you the best. Write back soon. Later."

Jack wishes he has the money to visit Kent. I hope his games are on the internet. Even though Kent is in high school, Jack knows he'll hear about him through other media. He is that good. Plus, Kent is still growing and maturing physically.

Jack remembers Kent's dad saying his son is an amazing athlete. Initially, Jack thought it was a parent's pride. But after watching Kent play basketball, Jack knew he was something special. Now that Kent is getting special training at Welch's

Academy, there is no doubt he is far beyond being an elite player. Jack looks at other email messages and they are all spam. Now it is time to head to the soup kitchen for dinner.

He meets up with Shirley and she talks about how her day went. Some people at her job are annoying her because they don't come to work all the time. She hasn't told her boss about them yet, because she knows how hard it is to find a job. Plus, these workers all have families. She asks Jack for advice, but he doesn't know what to tell her. Jack is certain that Shirley will come up with a good solution. He sees her as being smart.

His mindset shifts to food. He is so hungry and happy because the soup kitchen usually serves good meals. I wonder what is on the menu tonight. Jack is not disappointed.

The chefs cook Chinese food. Jack has a taste for shrimp fried rice and sweet and sour chicken. It's been a while since Jack has had good Chinese food. He can tell the food is going to taste great because the aroma is intoxicating. Jack starts off with Lo Mein. Then he eats shrimp fried rice. He does not pace himself well. He is full and unable to eat any of the sweet and sour chicken.

He wants to try some, but there is no room in his stomach. Jack sips freshly made green tea before talking with people at his table. They talk about how everyone is adjusting to public housing. Most seem content with the move because of the newfound privacy. Jack doesn't say much. He is thinking about what he wants to write about back home.

He is composing a poem in his mind right now. Jack writes this poem down as soon as he gets back home:

> Playing sports is supposed to be fun, especially for those at a young age, instead, a lot of kids are made, to play sports by pushy

> parents, who don't allow their kids to choose,
> what to get involved in, some parents tell
> their ten-year-olds, that failure embarrasses
> the family, and themselves, well that's a lot
> on a child not even twelve,

Then Jack watches sports on tv before calling it a night. Jack wakes up and goes to work. He is groggy. He did not sleep well. He dreamed of being seriously injured while working at his construction job. Yes, it is potentially dangerous work, but he hasn't seen anyone injured since he's been working this job. Yet, when he tells himself this, he can't get these negative thoughts out of his mind. He tries hard to think of other things like weightlifting and playing sports. But to no avail.

By the time Jack gets to work, these thoughts are making him sick. Although at this current jobsite nothing can go wrong. Sure, a nail could fly up and hit him, but he wears safety goggles. If he falls off the pier, he'll land in shallow water. Plus, the current isn't strong. He wonders if he should talk to someone about this.

It's like he is having a panic attack. Fortunately, by mid-morning these harrowing thoughts begin to ease up. So much so that he can concentrate on the task at hand. He is back nailing boards down.

Jack doesn't talk much and focuses on not making any mistakes. This is challenging as the day goes on because his arm is getting tired. With the wrist supporter his hand is fine, but he's thinking of buying an elbow sleeve and a shoulder sleeve. None of the other crew members have any type of support. How can they do this? Jack must take a break.

The boss doesn't seem to care if you take a break. If it isn't for a long period of time. So, Jack drinks water quickly.

Then he stretches to relieve the soreness in his arm, elbow, and shoulder.

Unfortunately, all this stretching isn't helpful. So, Jack grins and bears it for the rest of the workday. After the workday, Jack goes to the drugstore and buys an elbow and shoulder supporter. Jack isn't sure if using these supporters will work, but he must try something. Although simple inventions, these supporters are expensive. But Jack doesn't care. If they work. Jack goes home, relaxes for a bit and heads to the gym.

He tests his sleeves out as he exercises his upper body. The support is amazing. And weightlifting makes his arm feel much better. He works his arms with moderate weight. He also benches moderate weight. Instead of being sore and fatigued, his arm is more limber.

Then Jack swims. But this makes his arm hurt so he only swims for five minutes. Then he enters the sauna. Now his arm feels great. Jack is debating whether to go to the doctor just in case. I'll be fine, Jack keeps telling himself.

Jack leaves the gym without getting into the jacuzzi. And he watches tv until dinner time. It's not much on so Jack reads a novel he checked out from the public library. It's interesting, but Jack's mind is elsewhere. He's having trouble concentrating because he is hungry. He's happy when it is time to go to the soup kitchen for dinner. While at the soup kitchen, James addresses everyone.

"Hi, everyone, I have great news. We have great news. We have additional funding from the government. We will provide you with an allowance every week. I know some of you guys have jobs, so think of the extra money as a bonus. It's not much, but it is enough, so you won't have to eat here for every meal. You will be able to go out to restaurants and not worry about having enough money for other things."

Even though the food at the soup kitchen is great, going out to eat every now and then for a change in scenery is great. Jack has been keeping track of the money he makes from work. It's not a lot of money. He wants to make enough money that he can take trips to watch Kent's basketball games. Plus, Jack wants to buy a decent car. Preferably one not over 3 years old. He's been looking for a car online. He would rather drive to work since using public transport is frustrating. Waiting for trains and buses to go anywhere has Jack ready for personal transportation.

I'll be able to take vacations and enjoy this great city. Jack hasn't done much sightseeing because he was trying to survive. He estimates that he'll have enough money for a car in a few months.

Chapter 23

JACK IS NOW BACK home watching tv. He's sleepy but decides to watch one more show. Then Jack goes online to pass the time and to read the news. Nothing unusual is going on. Typical stories about crime and unrest around the world. Jack wants to do some writing, but he is tired. I'll do it tomorrow.

It's warm in the house. Jack drinks ice water and sleeps. He wakes up early to work on his novel for about an hour. Jack is pumped up for the day. Maybe I should do this every day. He even writes this poem:

> Just putting in work every day, I just know
> I'll get higher pay, from my novel someday,
> sooner than later, I can't let my confidence
> waver, I'll make it big, I can't wait to savor, a
> life of abundance, no longer concerned with
> how I spend each cent, pockets full of money
> not lint, getting so much coin, they'll think
> I print, money,

Jack started writing when he was living on the street. This was to relieve his anger. And to keep him from doing anything negative because he had an outlet for his frustration. Tears form in Jack's eyes when he recalls how hard life was. He would read his poems on the street to get a few dollars from passersby. One time he received 100 dollars from a man that loved one of his poems so much.

Jack used to dream of being discovered on the street. And then being signed to a deal because of his poems. Unfortunately, most people either ignored him or said, "Get a real job!" Jack wanted to fight those that insulted him. But he knew getting mad would not help his situation. Although being extremely poor, he has never been to jail. He won't do anything to jeopardize his freedom. Jack snaps back into the present and gets ready for work. He's running late, so he skips brushing his hair and other things to get ready for the day.

Everyone is still working on the pier. Jack is nailing down boards. He is almost done. He finishes nailing in 2 hours. It's now time to make all the boards even on the pier. Doing so makes the pier look good. This is time-consuming because no wood pieces can fall in the water. That would be considered pollution. Another man must catch every cut-off board. Like most things on this job, the work isn't too difficult. But you must pay attention. The saw has a guard, but it is very dangerous using it. At least my arm gets a rest from hammering nails in the boards.

The man catching the wood cut-offs uses a crab net. This slows the job down because the crab net is small. So, he must empty the net often. By the end of the workday, Jack still has the other side of the pier to do. Jack brushes sawdust off his clothes but he remains dirty. Public transit despises dirty people on the train and the bus. So, Nick, the boss, gives him a ride home.

Nick has a nice truck with leather seats and other luxury features. This is way more comfortable than public transit, Jack thinks. Jack and the boss engage in small talk until they reach Jack's home. Jack says thank you and takes a shower immediately. His knees are sore from being on them while cutting boards. Still a faithful weightlifter, Jack drinks a bottle of water and heads to the gym.

After lifting weights for a good hour, Jack's knees feel better, and he swims in the pool. He swims a few laps and then gets into the all-healing power of the sauna. The heat feels so good for everything. Jack is refreshed. He could lift more weights. However, Jack doesn't want to overdo it. He hops in the jacuzzi. He stays in it for a short time and then he is back home.

As usual, exercise makes him hungry. So, he walks with others to the soup kitchen. Their stipend kicks in in a few days. Everyone is talking about what restaurant to go to. Jack already knows he wants to go to a seafood restaurant. He hasn't had non-soup kitchen seafood regularly. Before Nick treated the crew, Jack last had seafood while living on the streets. He found a half-eaten lobster tail in a trashcan. It was tasty.

After eating from trashcans, Jack would always brush his teeth and use mouthwash. Jack believed using mouthwash would kill bacteria living in trashcans. Jack shudders when he recalls that hard life. He lives like a king compared to that. But he refuses to forget his struggles. He promises himself to help homeless people if he ever makes it rich as a professional writer. But right now, I must worry about me.

Of course, he donates money to charity when they ring their bells. But nothing major. He remembers some kind souls given him money whenever he read his poems. Without them, he would've fed himself solely by digging in trashcans. There was the option of stealing, but Jack never did that. He always found a way to fill his stomach without that.

Jack never had any friends while living on the streets. Sure, he recognized some faces, but they were more like competitors. There was only so much food available. So, the homeless people were like wild animals. Carving up territory to roam. Jack never experienced a lot of violence among those on the street. However, at the shelter, he had heard stories of hand-to-hand combat breaking out over sandwiches.

Snapping back into the present, Jack is now walking home from the soup kitchen. Some people are going to the movies. Jack is heading home to work on his writings. He writes this poem:

> When people become desperate, especially addicts, you gotta be careful, they are controlled by their habit, of using drugs, even alcohol, I saw two drunks fight, they used broken bottles, which can cut through you like knives, luckily and thankfully, they both became too tired, to even stab each other, then when the conflict was done, they hugged it out like brothers, a drugged-out bum is similar to an animal with rabies, neither is in a stable state mentally, look into their glossed-over eyes, they can't think logically, it's best just to get out of their way,

Jack is so motivated that he writes until bedtime. His hand is sore from writing so much that he sleeps with his wrist supporter all night. Jack sleeps well. He gets up early in the morning to work on his writings some more. He composes this poem:

> A sore hand is a minor inconvenience, to one day live like a prince, right now it's another day, another few cents, I convince myself that hard work pays off, if that is true, I've worked enough for my fortune, to last a century or two, a true legacy, but mentally, I have my doubts, without, having a lot of money physically, in my clutches, so for now, my transportation are the trains and buses,

Then it's time for construction work. The crew finishes putting the long pier together. So, now it's off to a new jobsite. That is one thing about this work- you never do the same thing for long, Jack thinks. Now it's time to put together boat lifts. This is tricky. So, never having put one together, Jack is watching carefully how to do this. After seeing the third lift put up, he is ready to put one up for himself. Jack takes his time and is successful on the first try.

Hardly anyone does this the first time. Proud of himself, Jack puts together another boat lift. However, this time he makes a mistake, and the lift falls apart.

A crew member says, "It happens."

Then the crew members put the lift together properly. Slightly embarrassed, Jack watches other crew members assemble the boat lifts. He takes mental notes and sees where he went wrong. Jack didn't put a bolt in a particular spot and that's all it took. Jack does put a lot of pressure on himself and figures he'll get it right next time. It's a learning experience. No one tries to embarrass him or anything like that.

This is encouraging to Jack who initially thought he would be made fun of. And be held to this failure as long as he works with these people. Jack doesn't lose confidence and plans to buy everyone lunch tomorrow.

On the way home, Jack has put his mistake out of his mind and is looking forward to watching tv. Or maybe even visiting Shirley. He has become close to her since Kent's departure. She's cool and smart, Jack thinks. For someone who doesn't read newspapers, she knows a lot about a lot. Well, she watches a lot of tv and not just dramas. Whereas Jack watches tv for escapism. He's not trying to learn anything.

After getting cleaned up, he heads over to Shirley's house. To no surprise, she is watching a tv program on surgery. Jack isn't interested and almost falls asleep. But Shirley is on the edge of her seat.

Once the tv show is over, Shirley asks, "How was your day?"

"It was terrible. I put together something that fell apart."

Shirley laughs. But not in a mocking way. More like you will get them next time type of way. Then Shirley explains her day cleaning houses. Her boss is thinking of giving her a raise. Of course, Shirley doesn't get paid much so every little bit helps.

"Yeah Jack, I'll be a manager soon. I can sit back and command," Shirley says with a smile.

Jack replies, "I'm still the low man on the totem pole. I do a lot of the grunt work."

I wish I could sit back, Jack thinks. She doesn't know how good she has it. Well then again, she didn't have an easy, early life. Her dad was a gardener in Washington D.C. He died from lung cancer because he was a chain smoker.

"I haven't had an easy job my whole life. Even when I was 8, I helped by dad fix cars. I never owned one myself, but I know a lot about them."

"Good. So, when I buy a car, you can help me to

understand some things. I don't even know how to change the oil." Jack says.

Shirley replies, "Oh that's easy. I'll help you save money from professional mechanics."

Jack nods. He's all about saving whatever money he can. Right now, he has a little money in the bank. He wants to invest his money despite his failure in real estate. Clearly, he knows nothing about investing. But Jack realizes investing is a great way to increase his money.

He asks Shirley, "What do you do with your money?"

"Well right now, I haven't been able to save much money. I'm saving up money for my niece to go to college. She is young and I'm always thinking about her future."

That's just like Shirley, Jack thinks. Always looking out for others. Jack and Shirley talk some more and then Jack goes to the gym.

Shirley always says she'll got to the gym. But right now, she is watching tv at her house. Jack is motivated to exercise because he knows a strong body makes him feel better. When living on the street, he would have aches that seemed to come from under use of his muscles. Mainly, due to conserving energy since he wasn't sure where his next meal was coming from. Now, living the high life- he can go all out and isn't worried about survival. And today at the gym, he plans to go all out. I'm swimming 50 laps today, Jack thinks.

He is shivering at first because the water in the pool is cold. I'm not giving up. Swimming will warm me up and it must improve my fitness. After swimming 30 laps, Jack's muscles begin to hurt, but he powers through. Completely out of breath, Jack makes it to 50 laps. I'm about to pass out.

I can barely move. Jack thinks as he stumbles out of the pool and walks to the water fountain. Taking sips of water,

Jack still feels bad. My heart is pounding. Am I going to die? Jack sits down on a bench and his heart continues to beat rapidly. After about 10 minutes, Jack is fine.

All his muscles relax, and he stand up straight now. Regaining his balance, Jack walks to the weight room and wonders what should I lift? My commonsense tells me no, but my energy level is now high. I'll do a light workout. Jack finishes his weightlifting session with no problems. He skips the sauna and the jacuzzi. I'm dead-tired. But thank God my heart rate is back to normal.

Jack loves to work out. It takes his mind off any stress. Jack is thinking about the mistake he made with the boat lift. Maybe I should do some reading. I'll read when I get back home.

Once at home, Jack cleans up and then opens a book. He's reading the latest mystery novel for about a half hour. Then he begins to think about work again. I'm tired of this. What can I do? Now Jack imagines a boat lift falling apart when a family is near the lift- crushing them. Jack hasn't felt this bad since living on the street.

He used to envision garbage trucks crushing him in his cardboard palace. Mistaken him for just trash. Oh well, I'm tired of worrying. Maybe I should drink a beer. But I don't want to be a wino. He recalls the many people on the street addicted to alcohol. I guess that could be why they are so poor, Jack thinks. Or maybe they just need an escape.

Jack's escape was to write- especially poetry. He would strain his eyes at night because the only illumination at first was from streetlights. Writing poetry didn't always work as an escape. So, Jack would force himself to sleep. What to do now? I guess I'll write this poem:

> Long days and longer nights, life really is a fight, when homelessness is one's plight, unfortunate events led to this life, it's hard with nothing but strife, nasty food from the trash, or buying unhealthy fast food, going to a real restaurant I would have a blast, except that I smell and then I'm asked, to leave the establishment, when I speak they tell me I need a mint, wow, where has the fun in life went, I yearn for the days to pay rent, to have some more privacy, a long life not likely, unclean and looking sightly, makes me say why me,

A tear forms in Jack's eye as he recalls the worst time of his existence. I thought writing would make me feel better. Instead, I feel angry and even more frustrated. I need to write something positive. Jack brainstorms for a while but can't think of anything to write. Well, it's time for dinner.

Jack looks in his wallet. I want to go out tonight. He walks to Shirley's house. She is busy getting ready for work. She must do some late-night cleaning.

Jack asks, "Do you want to go out to eat?"

"Sure. I'll take the bus to work after dinner. I must go to a rich family's house. They are having a get-together tomorrow morning. They want to make a good impression."

"When will you be back?"

"By about 1:00 AM. It's a big house. But I'm getting paid well, so I can't complain too much. I'm making in one night what I usually make in a couple of days' work."

For dinner, they go to a steakhouse. Jack orders a big ribeye with potatoes. Shirley orders sirloin.

"Man, I was hungry. Exercise leaves me famished," Jack says.

"Well, cleaning is like exercise, and I've been exercising all day."

"Maybe I should do cleaning to get in better shape. You finished eating way before I did."

"Yeah. You only exercise for what, an hour? I'm working all day, and now into the night. But my dad would say at least you have work."

"No doubt in that," Jack responds.

She has no idea how good she has it when compared to living on the street, Jack thinks. It's time for dessert, and Jack orders cheesecake. The cake is so firm yet soft, Jack thinks.

"How's your dessert?"

Shirley replies, "Not that great. My cheesecake is too hard, and the ice cream isn't fresh."

"Wow, everything tastes good to me."

"That's because you've never had great cheesecake. My mom worked in a restaurant as a cook and made desserts from scratch. In fact, she won awards for her desserts. But she was never paid well. Anyway, she would bring her latest creations home for us to try them. This went on for a while until my dad realized eating these desserts was making us fat. So, she started bringing home salads and light snacks."

"So, you know how to cook well?" Jack asks.

"Of course. But cooking takes time, and I'd rather go to the soup kitchen. As you know, the cooks there are skilled. They cook as well as my mother used to."

Once back home, Jack has a couple hours before his bed-time. Should I read a book or book or watch tv, he ponders. Then it hits him- if I want to be a great writer, I must put the time in. It's time to write, Jack thinks. But what should I write about? This problem hits Jack a lot- how to be original in every writing session.

Having no guidance on what to write, Jack scribbles down whatever comes to his mind. This seems like it fits, Jack thinks as he describes a particular scene with one of his main characters. This scene, only 3 pages long, takes him about 2 hours to get right. Perfect! Jack says out loud before calling it a night and then drifts off to sleep.

Wow, I have a few hours before I go to work. I'll do some writing to pass the time. As his alarm clock goes off, Jack is getting ready for work. I'm a little early, but I might as well head to the jobsite. Should I add another plot twist or cliffhanger, Jack thinks on the train to work. Maybe I should go with the flow. Whatever pops in my head is what I'll write down. Deep in thought as his stop is called, he rushes off the train before the doors slam shut.

I must pay attention at work. Sometimes working at a construction site can be dangerous. Especially around the chainsaws. I'm ready to put together boat lifts. I've gone over how to do them many times in my mind, Jack thinks.

Jack tells the boss, "I can do boat lifts again."

Totally shocked by Jack's boldness, Nick responds, "Oh yeah? You know every time you mess up you cost me money. I'm not being mean, but I'd rather you just assist the other crew members right now."

What could Jack do but nod and put on a fake smile. But how else can I truly learn without hands-on experience, Jack thinks. Oh well. There is no need to argue. I should give him a piece of my mind, but right now I really need this job. A couple hours into the workday, Jack thinks he has mastered how to put together boat lifts.

He says to a crew member, "Can I try to at least hook up something?"

"No way! The boss is the boss. He may change his mind tomorrow. He's not a mean guy. He hates losing money. Which makes sense if you think about it. I mean we get paid no matter what. But sometimes he incurs a loss when things don't go well. It's not about boat lifts. These are small jobs. But what happens if you mess up a dock or a long pier? Exactly. We may have to do half of it over again. Don't be so hard on him. He is looking out for you. How many homeless people do you see out here? That's right. Just you."

Jack replies, "What is that supposed to mean? That there is only one homeless person on staff? I work as hard as anyone else. Yeah, you have been on the job longer, but I contribute. Homeless or not. I'll be on your level soon, but the boss is getting on my nerves. You talk about big jobs- I worked on big jobs too. I rarely make mistakes. Just because I lived on the street doesn't mean I'm stupid. I don't know what the other guys think, but I'm very productive. I just need a little more experience."

"Whatever you say boss," The crew member says.

Calm down Jack. Everything will be ok, he tells himself. Jack wants to learn how to do everything because he needs this paycheck. Jack punches a pole out of frustration. So, for the rest of the day, Jack watches boat lift after boat lift being put together. How can I make my day more interesting? I'll sing some of my favorite songs- quietly of course. Finally, the workday is over, and I can leave the jobsite before I slap someone.

Before leaving the jobsite, Nick calls Jack over to his truck.

"Listen, I know you are upset, but you can't punch things and do what you want. I'm giving you tomorrow off to think about your actions. If you keep this up, you'll be gone for good."

Wanting to protest, Jack opens his mouth but says nothing. The boss isn't listening to me anyway. As Jack walks away from the truck, He wonders will I at least get paid for tomorrow? I'm not upset. I understand Nick's reason for being mad. Look on the bright side, - I have tomorrow off. Unlike most workers, Jack sees this as an opportunity.

I'll go the library and study all day. I need to do some research for my novel. I don't want to get so happy. It's still not good not to work. Jack can't help but plan out his whole day for tomorrow. I wonder if Shirley will be working all day tomorrow.

The train ride home takes forever since Jack is so ready to get home and relax. Oh no, Jack thinks. As he checks his mailbox. A letter from James. Should I open this? I might as well.

Scanning the letter, Jack says out loud, "What? They want me to have a roommate?"

I should punch this wall. This roommate didn't stay in the shelter. I don't know who he is. I hope he isn't loud. I need my peace and quiet so I can study. I should get on the phone and chat with James right now. Punching in the numbers to the phone, Jack calms down so he won't yell at James.

James answers, "Hello?"

"Hey James, this is Jack. Why do I have a roommate?"

"Well, this guy was like you- living on the street. We rescued him and decided you two would be a perfect fit. I know you love your privacy, but you'll get along with him. His name is David, and he is fun to be around. You guys will be best of friends. He'll be arriving later today. So, treat him well."

Wow. They didn't ask me what I wanted. Oh well. I'll still

treat David with respect. I'll look on the bright side and accept him for who he is. I'll watch tv until I go to the gym. There is nothing on. He keeps flipping through the channels to pass the time. Then Jack heads to the gym.

At the gym, Jack jumps in the pool immediately and swims some laps. All this exercise has taken my anger away. I'm tired now. Should I lift weights? Not today. I'll get in the jacuzzi and then go back home. After taking a shower, Jack walks to Shirley's house to tell her about his new roommate. She is busy ironing clothes when Jack knocks on the door. She opens the door.

Jack enters her house and says, "Guess what?"

"Let me guess, you have a roommate."

"How'd you know?"

"I know because I'm getting a roommate too."

"What do you think of this?" Jack inquires.

"Well, I don't care. At least they'll be off the street and in a house. I was never on the street like you, but I understand how rough it is. I'm sure you'll get along with your roommate just fine."

I guess she is right, Jack thinks.

Jack and Shirley hang out until it is time to go to the soup kitchen for dinner.

I'm not that hungry, Jack thinks. The chefs serve an English meal: fish and chips and Shepherds's pie. The food is good, but all Jack can think about is what David will be like. He is probably in my house already.

"Are you full?" Shirley asks Jack sarcastically after his third Sheperd's pie.

Noticing the sarcasm in her voice, he says, "Well, you ate a lot too. How many chips do you need? And you know, potatoes put weight on everybody."

She responds, "Yeah, ok! But really, you are going to be fat if you keep eating like so."

Maybe if I nod and smile, she'll leave me alone. Shirley gets back to eating fish and chips. Jack is right- she stops talking about the weight thing.

Jack zones out. He imagines owing an indoor swimming pool. He's swimming laps and then relaxing on the patio. A smile comes across his face as he gets into his daydream.

"Jack! Jack!" Shirley calls him, but he doesn't hear her until she shakes his arm.

"What? What?"

"Jack, were you listening?"

"To what?"

"You know, the government will raise the minimum wage."

Back into reality, Jack responds, "Oh yeah? It's about time. However, that doesn't do anything for me. I already get paid more than minimum wage. But I'm happy for other people."

Jack is glad that some people will make more money. It's sad when you can barely make it by. If he didn't have this house through the government, he could never afford it. He would have to work multiple jobs to tread water. I don't know how people with children do it, Jack thinks. Well, dinner is over. It's time to meet David, Jack thinks.

Jack opens the door to his house and there is David watching tv.

David stands up and says, "Jack, how are you?"

Jack wonders how long David has been off the street. His clothes look old, and his hair is unkempt. His shoes have holes in them, and he smells a little bit.

"I'm fine David. How are you?"

David huffs and says, "Better now that I have a real home.

Shelters. Well, you know about them. James told me everything about you. Including the fact that you love your privacy. Trust me, I won't be in your way, and I don't like loud noise. So, you'll be able to write without interruption."

"Thank you. That is what I was worried about. Make yourself at home. Do you have a job?"

"Yes. I work for a nonprofit that provides free prosthetics to the poor. The company is called Helping Hands."

How can I hate him, Jack thinks. Jack nods not knowing what to say next.

David continues, "I'll be gone from 8 am to 6 pm working. So, I doubt you'll see much of me during the week. On the weekends, however, I like to relax. On a different note, I plan to buy a computer tomorrow. Because I need to use the internet mostly for leisure."

Jack says, "Well you can use my computer whenever you want to right now. I write the old school way- pen and paper."

I hope he is not a mooch. Usually when someone asks for something right away, that's a bad sign, Jack thinks. But I shouldn't jump to conclusions. I'll keep an open mind.

It's time for Jack to go to sleep and David is watching tv. David doesn't have the volume high. Maybe he will be considerate, Jack thinks. Well, I'll finish up on this poem and call it a night:

> There is nothing like the art of writing, putting down my thoughts is so relaxing, I let the pen flow, strike the page with more energy than lightning, my brainstorms generate strong winds of change, that range from treating the homeless better, to whether school education is as cracked up as it is

> supposed to be, can we improve the learning experience, from elementary to university, instead of looking down on those who have failed miserably, I should come up with my own remedy,

Let me make sure my alarm is set.

Then Jack goes to his bedroom door and says, "See you tomorrow, David."

"All right Jack, have a good rest."

When will he go to bed, Jack wonders. Oh well, I know I need rest now.

Beep. Beep. My alarm is going off. I'm ready to start my day. I'll go to the soup kitchen for breakfast. I'll eat light since I ate so much English food last night. After eating cereal and cheese toast, Jack takes public transit to work.

While on the train, Jack realizes he is off today. Man, I almost forgot. I'll get off at the next station and head back home. What am I going to do all day, Jack wonders. I don't want to spend any money. So, the only thing I can do is read at the public library. But I can't read all day. That gets boring.

10 minutes pass and I still don't know what to do with my time. Well, I'm home now. I bet David is asleep. Jack opens the front door and David is reading a newspaper.

"Hey Jack, I thought you had to work?"

"Well, I remembered that I'm off today. I'm surprised you are up so early."

"I can't stay in the bed long. I like to get moving in the mornings. I always read the paper. Then I head to the soup kitchen and then I take public transit to work."

"Anything good in the paper?"

"Not really. Same ole same ole. Except there is a United

Nations meeting here in a few days. The public is invited to attend. I may go to this event."

Wow. This guy is sharp. I judged him all wrong.

"Since you aren't working, what are you doing today?" David asks.

"I figured I would spend a significant amount of time at the public library. I may go to the art galleries and museums downtown. I used to go to the library with one of my friends. But he went away to school. However, we never visited the museums downtown. I always like to learn something," Jack replies.

"Sounds cool. How's the food in the soup kitchen?"

"Excellent. It's close to 5-star quality."

David looks impressed.

"Before coming here, I ate at a soup kitchen, and the food was horrible. I would describe the food as fuel for my body. I ate it because I needed to stay alive. Now, I have another reason to be glad to move out here. It seems like you are living the good life."

Jack smiles and says," Well, it's better that where I was before. But I need my own transportation before I can profess to living the good life. Also, feel free to chat with the people around here. They are friendly and will help you with whatever you need."

"Thank you. I'll head to the soup kitchen now," David says as he puts the newspaper down.

I might as well check my email. A message from Kent:

> "Hey Jack, how's it going? I'm doing well here. I'm excelling in the classroom. I haven't got a B yet- all As. I'm training for basketball. I swim to improve my stamina. The gym is a world class facility. I have my first

> game in a few months, and I can't wait. I'm stronger and probably faster than ever. I don't know when I'll be home. I may be home for Christmas. Gotta go. They keep me busy here. Bye. Write back soon."

Jack smiles. I knew he would make it.

Jack replies, "Glad to hear you are doing so well. I'm doing great here, but I miss not going to the gym with you. Well, talk to you later."

Jack goes to the public library and takes a beeline to the latest novels. I'm looking for anything that catches my eye. Spotting an action/adventure novel, Jack reads the first two pages. I'll read this book later. I'm not ready to go home yet. I'll check out the magazine section. Men's Health magazine looks interesting.

After getting a few pointers on weightlifting, Jack sits down and reads some of the action/adventure novel. What a good book! The suspense has me hooked already. I'll check it out and read the rest of the novel at home. Since I'm out, what else do I want to do?

I want to buy clothes in a way, but I don't want to spend a lot of money. So, I'm not going to the mall. I'll stop in the coffee shop and read there. Most people are at work, so the shop is not crowded. Jack orders a latte. It's good, but it isn't much better than coffee from the convenience store, Jack thinks. Oh well. Time to sip coffee and read the novel.

I can drink and read all day since I have nothing to do. Engrossed in the novel, time flies by. I need to stretch after a couple of hours of reading. Should I eat here in the coffee shop or go somewhere less expensive? Let me open my wallet and check my finances.

Oh well, I can afford to eat here today. Wow, this turkey sandwich is outrageous, but Jack happily buys it. He also buys apple juice. He reads the novel while he eats. This novel has a great story. I wish I could write like that.

Maybe I should rewrite my novel to have the cliff hangers that this book contains. How can I do this? I'll close this book and brainstorm. This is confusing, Jack thinks. As he reviews his entire novel mentally. Well, not the entire novel, but the main parts. I'm not sure what to do next. Since no one ever taught me how to brainstorm for a novel.

I guess I'll think of something. 20 minutes pass and I still don't know what I should do next. Either brainstorm or write down major ideas of what I want to write next. I'll brainstorm and then get back to reading this action/adventure novel.

I must stop reading. My eyes are tired, and I can barely focus on the pages. Jack has time to pass, so he heads home to work on his own novel. From sitting down so much, Jack figures his legs need exercise. I'll walk home. Taking in the sights, Jack realizes Vancouver is one of the prettiest cities he's ever seen. It's a bit overcrowded, but still very nice.

He can smell the aroma coming from the fine restaurants downtown. I don't want to sit inside my house writing just yet. So, I'll continue walking around the city. I'll check out the roads I rarely use. Ok. I'll walk to the historic part of the city. The cobblestones are hard to walk on. I would've stubbed my toe if I were careless. Then Jack walks home.

Chapter 24

Now that I'm home, I might as well watch television. It is the middle of the day and there is nothing good on tv. I'll work on my novel now. My hand is tired from all this writing. I'll take a break. I'll close my eyes for a second. I'm a little sleepy. I need to write more, but this chair is so comfortable. No, I won't sleep. I'll open my eyes and write a poem. Then I'll get back to working on my novel. I'll grab a pen:

> When it comes to rhyming, I have perfect timing, I make money, do what I say, just like Simon, I'm not the best, well I'm lying, to the top I go, at least I'm trying, it's easy for me no sighing, no whining, just providing, income to myself and the downtrodden, those homeless and sobbing, wanting, something better, rejected by society, family, whomever,

Tears are welling up. I still have a bunch of negative emotions about being homeless. What a powerless feeling. I'll work on my novel more to inspire others. And to make enough money to help the cause. Jack works on his novel until it is time to go the gym.

At the gym, Jack goes to the weight room. I guess I'll

bench press for a little bit of time. I'll move up in weight. Ouch! That last rep hurt. My chest feels like it is about to explode. I'm done lifting for the day. I'm going home. After stretching his chest, Jack feels better and is relieved that the pain subsides.

Then at the soup kitchen, the pain returns. Maybe I should consult a medical doctor. Luckily, everyone in this country has health insurance. In the United States, I'd be out of luck. But I'll give it another day. And if I'm still in pain, I'll go to the doctor.

Conversation at the soup kitchen centers around David. Who is either a great storyteller or a great liar. David is charismatic, but what he says sounds too good. For example, he claims to have been a drug addict. However, he has no track marks on his arms and his teeth are perfectly white. Also, he seems to be in great health and has a physique that rivals Jack's. And Jac lifts weights multiple times a week. How can he be in such great shape while being homeless? Did he do pushups every day, Jack ponders. But everyone seems to like David.

"This food is excellent. Way better than what I'm used to. At the other soup kitchen, we were lucky to eat meat once a day," David says.

Then Jack becomes more suspicious when David says, "And James helped me out a lot."

Since when has James been known to help others without helping himself? Even though James is right that public housing is better than living in the shelter. But he received a raise for coordinating the shift from the shelter to public housing. At least that is the rumor. James is so irritating that hearing his name raises my blood pressure, Jack thinks. What did David just say? These chicken and dumplings are so good, Jack can barely concentrate on anything else.

How will I deal with this chatterbox back at the house? Maybe I just need to tell David when he gets on my nerves in a non-rude way. That's all that Jack can think about at the soup kitchen. In the meantime, Jack has dessert- cheesecake to be exact. I must agree with David that the food here is great. Not even a 5-star restaurant could do much better.

Back at the house, Jack works on his novel. David is surprisingly quiet, Jack thinks. He is passing the time by looking in a paper selling televisions. David did not stop by the electronics store today. But he plans to purchase a tv very soon. He's an intense person. He is 100 percent consumed in whatever he does. Even when looking at the paper, you can see he is immersed in that activity, Jack thinks.

"Hey Jack, do you mind if I watch tv? I know you are writing so I don't want anything to distract you," David says.

"Oh yeah. I'll write in my bedroom," Jack responds.

David watches a comedy sitcom as Jack walks to his room. I hope he won't be too loud. Jack gets his wish. As he prepares to sleep, he can't hear the tv at all. It looks as though he'll be a good roommate, Jack thinks as he closes his eyes.

As usual, Jack's alarm wakes him up. Time to head to the soup kitchen for breakfast. Just cereal will do, and it will be time to go to work. There aren't many people in the soup kitchen because it is so early in the morning. And most of those served are unemployed, so they have no reason to get up early. I remember being like them. Feeling hopeless and worthless. Like you are a drain on society. Jack wishes he could hire them since most of them seem eager to work. They would work hard and be passionate in whatever they do. Well, enough deep thinking. Time to catch the train to work.

Jack is so well rested that he doesn't take a nap on the

train. Really, he is a bit nervous. I hope I keep this job. It gives me something to do. Plus, I'm saving up money for a car. Once at work, Jack avoids the boss thinking this is the best thing to do. This seems to be working because everything seems fine until lunchtime.

The boss approaches him and says, "Jack, are you calm now? You won't lose your job, but don't mess up again."

He gives Jack a stern look and then walks away without Jack having a chance to respond. I'm a little confused. Nick seems so nice most of the time. Now it's like he's a different person. I'll make sure not to make the same mistakes. Well, back to work.

Now it's just about doing the small things to the pier to make it look nice. Jack cuts off overhanging boards. The crew runs a rope through the outside poles to act as handrails. This is so easy, so the crew move to another jobsite.

Now the crew is working on a deck/patio that is by the water. Still considered a novice, the measurements are taken by more experienced crew members. While Jack takes mental notes. Maybe I should buy a notebook for these mental notes. On second thought, I'll figure this out. I can always ask for help on the next job. The workday flies by and it's time to go home.

I'm exhausted mentally from taking all these mental notes. I'll take a notebook to work tomorrow. When I get home, I'll write my mental notes down.

Jack naps on the train. It's a short nap, but since he is tired, he dreams. I'm at a jobsite doing my best on a deck. I'm making my proper cuts. Then the boss comes over and fires me!

Jack wakes up immediately after hearing the words that all employees dread, "You are fired!"

Yeah. I better take notes to get everything straight. I'll

calm down once I write some things down. Once at home, Jack drinks some water and then pulls out a notebook. After 20 minutes, he is sure that he wrote down all his mental notes. Now I can relax.

Let's see what is on tv. There is not much on. I'll work on my novel. Well, I wrote a few pages, and my hand is tired. Time to go to the gym anyway. I'll check my email before I exercise. A message from Kent:

> "Hey Jack! I'm still lifting weights. I'm very strong now. I'm the strongest on the team. I'm even stronger that the power forwards and centers. I also have the highest vertical leap. I'm glad I trained with you. It really laid the foundation for my incredible athletic ability. Hopefully you can see one of my games in person. Well, I've got to get back to studying. Later."

I'm tearing up thinking of those memories when Kent first began lifting. He could barely bench press his bodyweight. Now he can outlift the big guys. He will make it to the NBA. I'll write back later.

The gym isn't crowded. So, Jack is happy that he can get to all his exercise equipment. Pumped up from hearing from Kent, he sets personal bests. He is very sore now. I think I overdid it. Oh well. I'm sure I'll feel better later. I'm in fantastic shape.

David comes home with a brand new tv in his arms.

David sets the tv up in his bedroom and says to Jack, "I'll have a computer tomorrow."

I'm glad. He was on my computer too much. Jack nods

and smiles at David as David kicks his shoes off. He looks comfortable in front of his new tv. The tv is beautiful with a clear screen and built-in surround system. How can a man that was recently homeless afford such a nice, expensive tv, Jack thinks. On the way to the soup kitchen, David can't stop talking about his tv.

"You should see the features it has Jack. Maybe you should upgrade. I got it at a low price."

"Yeah, sure," Jack says.

Jack can barely keep his eyes open at the soup kitchen. His workout at the gym has worn him down. All he can think about is his comfortable bed. Shirley mentions the struggles at her job. She is having trouble staying calm cleaning this one house. The owners have bad attitudes.

"I'm so ready to slap both at the same time. With the same hand," She chuckles.

Everyone at the table laughs. Jack fake laughs. I'm too tired to pay attention right now. When they get back to the house, Jack goes straight to bed.

He wakes up in the middle of the night. I'm thirsty. I have water in the kitchen. After drinking some water, he hears David talking to someone on the phone.

David says, "Yeah, I can get that. I'll have it soon. I'll pay you when I can. I know what will happen if I don't pay."

I knew David was up to something. You don't buy a tv that great coming from the streets. Jack wants to confront David right away, but then he becomes fearful. I'm not sure of his connections. It's best if I keep this conversation to myself and let situations play out. Jack walks quickly to his bedroom so as not to alert David. These problems are what I don't need. I can't go back to sleep with this weighing on me. I'll write a poem or two until I calm down:

> Now I want him gone, I'm no James Bond, or cop or lawman, this is not in my plans, I just want to live peacefully, I could get jammed up easily, I don't care how much money I can make, why get involved in crime, I know what's at stake, just as my life was getting some balance, no malice, I just won't deal, I could get killed, I bet he'll say the tv fell off a truck, you think I survived on the streets by dumb luck, what's next, will he have a new truck, shucks, my heartrate won't go down, when I know I could be underground, depending on who he owns money to, how can I get out of this, I have no clue,

I'll write another poem tomorrow. I'm calm now. I can sleep. The alarm goes off. Signaling that it's time for another workday. Jack gets dressed and heads out of the door. Man, this situation still weighs heavily on my mind.

I've got to keep a clear head. Construction work can be dangerous. Especially if I'm not 100 percent focused. The excavator almost hit me with the swinging arm when I spaced out. I'll be fine. I'll feel ok by the time I hop on the train. It's a clear, beautiful day. Meaning, the workday will not be cut short by inclement weather.

I want to go back home and sleep. That is the only time I don't think about this situation. Oh well, I guess I'll just have to deal with it.

Once at work, Jack's mind is as clear as day. Even the boss can't bother him today. Now the crew is backfilling. Meaning, they are putting dirt behind a wall of wood. So, the water won't erode the property line. Everyone uses their shovels to make sure the dirt is packed neatly behind the wall. This is a simple job and Jack contributes easily. This is quite enjoyable. The crew moves at a slow pace- no one is rushing. They talk about a variety of subjects. One being about their jobs before working here.

"Yeah Jack, I used to drive trucks throughout British Columbia. But my ole lady didn't see me much even though I made great money. I did this for many years- saving up for you know, retirement. The years go by fast so it's important to save as much money as you can. This job doesn't pay as much as driving trucks. But I'm home every night," Mike says.

Jack replies, "Well, I've been homeless for too long. So, I'm holding on to what I have. Whether that be at this job or whatever. I don't know how long I'll work here because I'm on the boss's bad side. Also, I hope my writing career will take off. I should be well off in a few years."

"What are you writing about?" Mike asks.

"Well, I don't want to talk about it. You'll have to read my book when it is in stores. I want it to sell to lift myself out of poverty. Life is a lot better now that I have a house. But it will get better with a substantial amount of money. Everyone says, 'Money can't buy happiness', but I sure wished I had some money when I was living on the street."

"I hear that!" The crew says collectively.

Jack wants to tell them about David's suspicious activities. But he is frightened that if more people know about it, Jack could become a target. I'll play like I know nothing. All this small talk makes the day roll right along. Wow, it is already lunch time.

I want fast food, but I want to stay in shape. I guess I'll eat a salad. Jack orders a huge salad from the closest fast-food restaurant. It tastes so good, and it does have some meat. But will it hold me all day? This type of construction work burns a lot of calories.

One of the crew members, Leroy, laughs at Jack's salad and says, "You need more meat. You'll be hungry and tired soon if you only eat that.!"

"I'll be ok," Jack replies.

Eating food high in calories would put weight on me. Swimming practically every day has kept my bodyfat low. But I can do better. I remember the boss saying this job is like exercising. Observe all the moving and digging. If the work is that strenuous, how come everyone out here has potbellies. Jack chuckles at their plumpness. Not in a condescending manner, but at the fact that the boss is incorrect. Lunch is now over, and it is back to work.

My hands are sore from shoveling. I'm ready to go home and relax. I'm not exhausted; I'm ready for the workday to end. I would compose a poem now, but my concentration needs to be on this job. Since it can be dangerous.

Leroy sings, "I like that old school rock and roll."

Well, he tries to sing it. Everyone laughs at him and then they join in. What in the world? I've heard the song before, but I don't know the lyrics. I'm not sure if Leroy is singing this song because he likes it. Or is he poking fun at the original song.

There are plenty of rock and roll songs that sound better than that song. Next Leroy sings, "Tuiti Fruiti" by Little Richard. Now that's a good song. Too bad everyone is butchering it. I know I can't sing, so I'll stay quiet. Everyone has a good laugh and then they sing more songs.

Now it's time to go home. What a fun day at work. And I didn't get chewed out by the boss. I wish all workdays could be like this. Anyway, I can't wait to get to the gym. Jack changes clothes and heads to the gym. Unfortunately, his workout is constantly interrupted by the David situation. Man, I can't get this off my mind. What can I do? After his workout Jack goes home.

Chapter 25

DAVID ARRIVES WITH A new computer. As expected, it's an expensive kind. The computer is equipped with a huge monitor, scanner, and printer.

Hesitant to ask where it came from, Jack says, "Nice computer, David. It is way more advanced than mine."

"Thanks, Jack. I bought it from one of my friends who works at an electronics store. He gave me a discount."

Nodding his head, Jack looks over the equipment closely. Yeah right. I bet it's stolen or something. Well, at least he hasn't gotten a phone call from the mystery man like yesterday. David hooks his computer up and sure enough gets a phone call. Upon answering the phone call, David closes his bedroom door.

When David comes out of his room, it's obvious that something is wrong. He looks scared and nervous. His hands are shaking. Now I know he is being threatened by the man on the phone. I can't help it. I must ask him what's going on.

"Hey David, what is happening? Don't lie to me. I know something fishy is going on. You seemed happy, but as soon as you got that phone call, your demeanor changed."

"Well Jack, I owe a lot of money. While on the street, I found $20,000 in a trashcan. I kept it. Then I gambled it in a casino. So, now I have no money. Unfortunately, why type of people put $20,000 in a trashcan? Yes, organized crime. Now they want $30,000 and there is no way I can pay them back. At least they don't know any of my extended family. They only threatened me. However, they said if I don't have the money in 2 weeks, bad things will happen. What am I to do?"

I knew I shouldn't have asked him anything. I could get hurt now that I know these things.

"I'll help you pay it back some kind of way. Or can't you go to the police?"

"They say if I go to the cops they'll blow my head off. They have already threatened to break my legs."

My heart is racing. Why did I have to be so nosy?

"I'll try to help you, but I don't know what I can do. I don't have a lot of money. I don't even have $10,000 saved up. There must be another way. Can't you run away and go into hiding?"

"Where would I go Jack? I don't have family that would take me in. We've got to figure something out," David says.

"I'm thinking that you should tell them you have no money, but you'll do something to make up for it."

"I'll call them now," David replies.

"Hello? Yeah, it's me. I don't have the money. Is there something I can do to make up for it? Huh? I must do what? I don't know. Ok, I'll be ready in two days," David says as he hangs up the phone.

Turning to Jack with a dejected look, David says, "They want me to drop some packages in specific trashcans around the city. I didn't ask what these packages contain. But I'm sure they are either money or drugs. They claim they'll leave me alone if I do this and all my gambling debts will be forgiven."

Jack has a sixth sense that it won't end there. David is probably going to be used by them for the rest of his life.

But David is so happy now. Well, he is beyond happy. He is ecstatic.

"You're a quick thinker Jack. I've gotta make it up to you."

"What you can do is not gamble anymore and leave these guys alone."

"I'm done with that stuff. But I want to make it up to you. Can I buy you dinner or something?"

"You know, you don't owe me anything. Just stay out of trouble!" Jack says.

David is all smiles and nods at Jack. It's time to eat. So, Jack goes to the soup kitchen with Shirley and friends. Jack is worried about David who decides to eat at a local café.

Where David really goes is anybody's guess. Sure enough, when Jack returns from eating dinner, David is nowhere to be found. Jack goes to bed. In the middle of the night, he hears the front door being opened. David stumbles in- obviously in pain.

Jack gets up and asks, "What happened?"

"I told them I'm done, but now they want $20,000 as soon as possible. Or I must keep dropping these packages off."

I wonder how David can get out of this situation. The only person I know that could help is my old friend, Curtis. But he is thousands of miles away. I don't know David well enough to set him up in a new location with Curits. But something must be done.

"Hey David, your best bet is to keep delivering packages and hope everything will be fine."

"All right Jack. I'll keep delivering them."

This situation is worrying me. I can't sleep. I might as well work on my novel. Let me get a pen and my writing notebook. I can't believe I wrote all night. I'm done with my first draft. Now I just need to edit it. I might as well do this now. I'm not tired. The alarm for work goes off and Jack is done editing. All I must do is another rewrite, and my manuscript will be ready.

Time for work. On the train, Jack still isn't tired. At least I'm not thinking about David's predicament. I'm focused on my novel. It is drizzling at the construction site. But it's not enough precipitation to halt work. However, it is easy to slip on the ground and especially the bulkhead because of the drizzle. The boss tells everyone to be extra careful. Jack watches his steps as he puts boards in sequence for the bulkhead.

I've heard stories of injuries, but I haven't seen any since I've been working here. I guess everyone is smart or maybe lucky. Jack's lack of sleep catches up to him in the afternoon. Whoa! I almost slipped off the bulkhead. I would've fallen in the water. I can swim, but getting wet may make me sick. I haven't taken a sick day yet.

I can't wait to get home. So, I can sleep. The workday goes by slowly and Jack is now home. After a shower, Jack heads for his bed. I'm skipping the gym today. I'll set my alarm to ring at dinner time.

Jack wakes up a few minutes before his alarm sounds. Well, time to eat. What? David isn't back yet. Then Jack sees a note on the kitchen table.

"Sorry Jack. I had to do this. I need the money. You are creative. You'll think of something."

Jack stops reading the note. What does he mean? My mind is fully alert now. Don't tell me- no! Jack runs to his bedroom. Yep! David took some of his writing notebooks. Bye novel. I didn't type it up and that's my only copy. He will try to sell my novel on his own to pay off his debt. What am I going to do? Should I go to the police? I'll think about what to do at dinner.

"Yeah guys, David stole some of my writings. I keep my

poems in a drawer. So, I have all my poems. I'm more disappointed than mad right now."

"You should go to the cops and tell them everything. It may be a long shot that they find David, but it's worth a try," Shirley says.

"Well, I'll go to the police station after dinner."

Even though he is sad, Jack must admit that this good food is soothing. Steak and potatoes taste so good right now.

At the police station, Jack talks to Officer Johnson.

"What can I do for you?" Officer Johnson says.

"This guy David. I mean I don't know his last name off the top of my head. He moved in with me. He took some of my writings and is nowhere to be found. He owes money to an organized crime syndicate and that's why he took my notebooks. He has underworld connections, so there is no telling where he is."

"I can't promise we will find him. But we will try our best. His pictures will be circulated throughout the world. But, if he keeps a low profile, it will be hard to get him."

"Thanks Officer. I know you will do your best, and that's all I can expect."

I might as well write my novel all over again. This time, I'm saving my novel on my computer. After a few hours, Jack outlines his novel and is sure that he remembers the major points of his book. Pleased with his work, Jack goes to sleep-ready for the next day. You must forgive and forget. I'm not sad anymore. Jack sleeps well and his alarm wakes him up.

I thought I calmed down a lot, but I could slap David. Work is uneventful. At home, Jack gets a call from Officer Johnson.

"Hey Jack, we found a location where David was. He posted a picture on Facebook. He was at the Space Needle in Seattle, Washington. Police are searching for him across the city. I'll call you when we find more information. Have a good day."

This doesn't make sense. Why would he risk getting caught now? Jack goes on Facebook. However, David's picture at the Space Needle has been removed. Seattle is only a 3-hour drive from Vancouver. I guess David can hide better in the U.S. That's why he crossed the border.

Sometimes David seems smart and other times he is very clumsy. He thinks he can outsmart everyone. That's probably why he is in trouble now. He thought he could outthink those in organized crime. There is no way he comes out of this unscathed.

Strangely, Jack still cares about David's well-being. Maybe I should post on Facebook for him to turn himself in. Maybe the police can protect him. No, he probably wouldn't listen anyway. I can't stop thinking about David stealing my novel.

I should rewrite my novel as much as I can and show it to the police. So, even if they can't find David, they may find my novel in print somewhere. I had over 600 pages written. It was almost finished.

Jack calls Officer Johnson and informs him of this. Jack figures it will take a week to write out his novel from memory. Then no one will be able to make money from my book even if David sells it. Well, if it is translated into another language that could be a problem. But David isn't that smart.

I need to go the gym to clear my mind. On his way to the gym, Jack swears he is being followed. A black Mercedes car seems to be near him when he is a few blocks near the gym. What could he want? I don't know anything. Jack isn't scared, but a bit concerned. I'll exercise and if he approaches me, I'll tell him the truth about anything. It's not like I'm close to David.

So, after a good workout, Jack is walking home when a young man wearing expensive clothes calls Jack by name.

"Yes," Jack replies.

"Do you have time to talk?"

"No."

"Well, you have time to talk," The man replies while flashing a gun on his hip.

"Let's get to business. You know who I am, and you know what I want," The man says calmly.

"I don't know where David is. He took off and he left a note."

"Yes, we have no idea where he is. But if he gets in contact with you, it's best to call us. Here is my number."

"I doubt he'll call me. I'm not really his friend," Jack says.

"That makes two of us. But he owes us a lot of money. You are not really involved yet. But if he calls you, contact us. And please, don't tell the police that you talked to us. You know why."

Jack, already sweaty from exercising, is drenched now thinking about what he should do. The man steps into the beautiful Benz and speeds off. I hope David never calls me. He's going to fool around and get killed. I can tell. I can't risk my life.

Back at the house, Jack has a message on his phone. This better not be David. To his relief, James is inquiring about David. I'll call him back now.

"Hey James. David took off with my writings and I haven't heard from him since. The police last confirmed his location in Seattle, Washington."

"That's strange," James says, "David called me the other

day to say that he found a place in the United States. He didn't tell me where, but he seemed happy and confident."

"I don't know why he is happy. He owes money to the mob and a member of this group visited me. He was very scary. He told me not to go to the police and he made threats."

"Really? David seems practically harmless."

"I already went to the police."

"That is probably the best thing you can do. I won't answer David's phone calls. I don't want any trouble either," James adds.

"Has anyone been following you? Because I noticed a black Benz has been trailing me almost everywhere I go," Jack says.

"No. I haven't noticed anyone. I also haven't been looking. No one has approached me," James says.

"Talk to you later," Jack says.

On the way to the soup kitchen, Jack spots that same Benz trailing him. He imagines the man hopping out of the car spraying him with lead. Maybe I watch too many movies. I need to calm down. Being followed like this means I can't stop by the police station to speak to Officer Johnson. I wonder if my phone is tapped by these organized criminals. But I must maintain contact with law enforcement. I can't be totally bullied by these organized criminals.

I have no idea what these guys will do with my writings if they get a hold of them. They may throw them away since they are evidence. However, my hands are tied. I can't go to them and ask for my writings if they catch David. Then, they would think these writings are worth something. I'll come up with a plan. Anyway, it's time to eat.

The soup kitchen serves Jamaican food tonight. I love this food. Although sometimes it is too spicey. Jack eats curry chicken with a side of rice. The conversation around the table revolves around James. He is instituting a curfew because neighbors are complaining about wild parties. Parties supposedly from the previously homeless. The police were called to investigate because someone said cocaine was present.

Shirley says, "How can us poor folks afford cocaine?"

Everyone at the table shakes their heads. I'm not surprised. You just never know what's going on. The other residents hate those in public housing. They see them as inferior and as decreasing the property value. Kids taunt the formerly homeless people. This hasn't happened to me yet. But I've heard stories of us being egged on the way home from work.

Recalling this gives Jack a flashback of being jumped in his cardboard palace. He was jumped for no good reason. He didn't have to go to the hospital, but he was sore for a couple of weeks. He still has a bruise on his back from being stomped repeatedly. Kids can be cruel.

Once back home, Jack tries to remember everything about his novel. Then he pulls out the outline he made a few days ago. He reconstructs his entire novel. It still needs work, but I'm pleased with my progress. I need to rest to be ready for work tomorrow.

After sleeping soundly, Jack wakes up more than ready for work. Excited that he is almost done with his novel- Jack must stay calm. This type of construction work can be dangerous. So being alert but relaxed is necessary. In fact, once at work, Jack is his normal self.

I'm not going to think about my novel while at work. I must stay focused. Today, the crew is making a long pier. Jack is handing boards to some of the crew to use as supports for the pier.

Most workers carry 2 boards at a time. Jack can carry 4

boards because he is strong from lifting weights every day. And he's not tired. Well, not at first. Wow, it's afternoon now and my forearms are getting tired from picking up these boards. I need a break.

The boss is not upset that Jack takes a break. Since he normally does the work of 2 and sometimes 3 men. My hands are also tired. The ligaments in my hand are aching. I'll feel better in a few minutes.

During this break, Jack begins to think about his novel. You know, I should move one scene after the climax instead of before. Whoa! I almost lost track of time. Now I'll get back to work. And for the rest of the workday Jack carries boards. I can barely use a pen. This could be a problem when I get home. I'll stretch my fingers out until the soreness goes away. There we go. Everything seems fine.

I'll skip the gym today and write until dinner. After writing for a while, I need a break. I'll search the internet and then check my email. Wow! A message from my great friend, Kent:

> "Hey Jack, I'm coming home since I have a short break from school. The headmaster is paying for my plane ticket. My parents told me about your hardships. I'm sorry that your writings were stolen. However, I know you'll bounce back because you are very creative. I'm doing well at school, and we'll talk more when I'm home. I may show you some new exercises that I've learned. See you soon."

It's like everyone knows what David did. Maybe he'll be caught soon. I want to slap him around for a bit. I want to call Officer Johnson, but I don't know how I can do this without these criminals finding out. I must think of something. Whoever these bad guys are- they have a lot of connections. They follow me in a Benz that is top of the line and costs over six figures.

And the clothes he wears are of the designer type. I'm sure they have a few people working for them in the precinct. They are scary men. As Jack gets back to writing, the phone rings. It's Officer Johnson. Should I answer the phone? No. I don't want to upset these criminals. They are the type that can get away with murder.

Chapter 26

I NEED TO RID myself of stress. I'll stop by the store now and buy more notebooks. At the store, Jack finds great deals. He buys new pens and notebooks for under five dollars. Back at the house, Jack writes a poem:

> Pressure from this life, can break a person's fight for survival, can lead one to the bottle, but I just take the pain straight up, and keep going, even in bad luck, situations change, but the iron willed stay the same, knowing good days will come back again,

I may write another poem later. I'll do some brainstorming. My mind is drawing a blank. Man, I wish I had my writings that David took. There must be something I can do. But what? I'll talk to the man following me to see what he knows. I'll chat with him on my way to the soup kitchen for dinner. As usual, Jack spots the Benz as soon as he leaves his house. I wonder what he'll say. Oh well, approaching him is worth a try.

Surprised, the criminal rolls down the window and says, "What do you want?"

Jack clears his throat and says, "I'll get right to the point. What do you know about David?"

"For one thing, he owes us a lot of money. He disappeared without a trace. But don't worry, we will find him."

"I hope so," Jack says.

Not telling the man that his novel could make the criminals a lot of money- Jack hopes they never find out. These organized criminals are all about a dollar. I'll act as though my writings are for my personal gratification. As if they have no monetary value.

"What's so special about your writings?"

"I've been working on them for a long time. They are very important to me."

"Well, I don't car what's important to you. David better have our money or he'll never be able to walk again.

"How much does he owe you?"

"Don't concern yourself with this. You may be his friend, but you don't know the bad he has done. He reneged on a job, and he isn't that smart. Although, he walks around like he is some type of genius or something. Why? I don't know. Hopefully for his sake, he can figure out how to have our money. Now don't play around. You know what's going to happen if he can't come up with a certain amount of money."

I can't ask any more questions. These guys are as bad as I thought.

"And if I find out you told anything to the cops, you know what will happen to you. And I will find out. So, don't say anything specific to anyone. And I believe you will make it out of this situation. Well, maybe."

"Maybe? I didn't do anything."

"Listen, I don't care. I don't care about David, and I don't care about you. I'll disappear when all this is over. I'll leave you alone forever. I just want what is owed to me. Nothing more nothing less. Leave the cops out of this. For your sake. Now go away."

The man rolls his window up and Jack walks to the soup kitchen. Jack is still being followed. This is a lose-lose situation. Either I do nothing, and David may get beaten up or worse. Or I ask for police protection. Then I'll be looking over my shoulder for the rest of my life. But I don't want to be a hero. How connected are these guys? How long can David stay on the run from these guys?

Jack continues to think things over at the soup kitchen. To be honest, I don't think David is going to make it much longer. He doesn't have much money. Where could he hide? He's good as gone. Jack holds back tears when he pictures David being tortured. It's probably going to happen. If I'm not careful, this could happen to me. I wonder if David emails me if these guys could tell? But why would he contact me? He stole my writings. He probably feels guilty. At least I would think so.

After dinner, Jack is home watching tv when Officer Johnson calls. Should I answer the phone? I'm tired of being pushed around by these goons. But they told me not to be in contact with the police.

So, Jack lets the phone ring. I can only imagine the worst. David being found I water with cement shoes. Or maybe found in an alley beaten to a pulp. I can't just sit around and let things happen. I'll call Officer Johnson. Jack dials his number.

"Officer Johnson, can I help you?"

"Yes, Officer this is Jack. Do you know anything new?"

"We have an update on David. Someone spotted him in San Francisco. Then he disappeared before we could pick him up. It's like he knows where we are. We think he is receiving help from someone. A normal person could not avoid us this long."

Should I tell him about being followed? No, I'll hold off on that information. Maybe the criminals won't find out about my phone call.

"Thanks Officer. Please keep me updated."

"We will. We are also looking for your writings. So far David has not been spotted with anything in his hands. When we catch him, our priority will be finding your writings. I'm sure we will recover something."

"Talk to you later Officer."

That's reassuring. At least they are tracking him effectively. He can only hide for so long. Jack goes to sleep thinking if there is any more he can do. I tried my best. I really tried. Time for bed.

Jack wakes up. My alarm clock is so annoying. Maybe I should buy another one. Heading out the door, he spots that black Benz. Obviously, they don't know I spoke to Officer Johnson or else they would've threatened me or something. At least that makes sense. The comfortable seats on the train are now no comfort. I can't relax and take a nap. I'm so amped up. Will I be able to concentrate at work? I'll figure something out.

At work, Jack attempts to stay busy. I'll work hard to get these worries off my mind. Out of the corner of his eye, Jack sees that black Benz. I'm being watched. The car isn't too close so none of the crew notice it. Jack tries not to stare at it to avoid drawing attention. If any in the crew knows organized criminals are following me, I doubt I'll be able to keep this job. Because they would be scared. If I lose this job, I don't know what I'll do. The money is decent. Plus, I enjoy working with my hands.

Suddenly, the Benz pulls off. Jack doesn't see the car for the rest of the morning. It's now afternoon and the crew are taking a short break. It's been backbreaking work. So, the boss hands out bananas. Bananas are known to prevent muscle cramps. I'm so hungry from carrying boards that I need two of them. Zoom!

The black Benz zooms close to where the crew is sitting. But it doesn't stop. Jack pretends that he has never seen the car before. The crew doesn't pay attention to it. Eventually, the crew will notice this car if it keeps coming close. And I'll have a lot of explaining to do.

The boss tells a joke, and everyone laughs. Not because he's the boss, but because the joke is funny. I must remember that one.

Jack doesn't see the car for the rest of the workday. I'm thirsty from all that work. I'll go to the convenience store for a drink. I'm only a block away from my house. But I don't want to wait until I get something from my fridge. This sports drink is refreshing. I'm now at my house and I already drank it all. I'm a little tired so I'll relax and look at some tv. Just as he's getting comfortable the phone rings.

"Hello Jack. We found David. He was in Los Angeles trying to sell your writings to a well-established agent. Not trusting David's story of how he came up with the script, he called a private investigator. Who contacted us once he realized David was wanted by us. The exact way, the private investigator and the police would like to keep secret. Further good news: Your writings are intact- every one of them. And after reading through your work, this literary agent wants to work with you. His name is Jacob Price, and he should be emailing you soon. I'll update you on any new developments. Have a good day."

Wow! My dream of being an author may come true. But I can't be too happy since David is in big trouble. I'll see if his charges can be dropped. But these organized criminals still want money. Peeking out his window, I don't see anyone tracking me. But they know where I am. So, I'm not safe either. The phone rings again.

"Hey Jack, it's Kent. I just flew into town, and I'll be at my parent's house soon. Can I stop by?"

"Sure. I have a lot to tell you."

A few hours pass and then Kent stops by. They exchange greetings and Jack talks about everything that happened with David.

"Well, at least you recovered your writings. That's one positive thing," Kent says.

"That's true. But I'm concerned about David. I'm not sure he'll last long. I have an idea. If I can sell my writings, maybe I could pay his "debt" to these guys, and everything will be fine. I know they said the money is due soon. But what if I promise to pay them more later? Like double what David owes?"

"Sound good. And then make sure David leaves them alone- for the rest of his life," Kent adds.

"I'll try to talk some sense into him. These events would scare me so much that I would never do anything wrong. I believe he has learned his lesson."

"Anyway Jack, I'll tell you about school."

Kent talks for a good hour about sports and academics. He seems to be doing well at everything. There is nothing negative in his tone. To Kent, sports are important, but education is even more so. Kent still has his eyes on the NBA. But he's also looking forward to getting into a great university and getting a degree. In which major, he is not sure.

"Well Jack, I've talked until I'm a bit hoarse. Do you have anything to drink?"

"I've got bottled water. That's about all I drink. I'm trying to get in even better shape. So, I'm careful about what I eat and drink. Of course, I still go to the gym and everything."

Kent nods and says, "I bet I'm way stronger than you are now. We lift weights 3 times a week with strength and conditioning coaches. I've added 50 pounds to my bench and 70 pounds to my back squat. We take protein powder every day. I can jump higher, and I haven't gained a pound. The coaches' techniques are amazing. We get stronger, but we don't put on weight unless we want to."

Jack didn't know gaining that much strength without putting on a pound was possible. The old school experts believed gaining weight was essential to increasing strength. Well, times have changed. I guess weightlifting techniques like technology have improved.

"I'm going to the gym tomorrow. I don't believe you are way stronger than me," Jack says with a smile.

"Yeah sure. I have some days off. Time to eat," Kent says.

So, they plan to go to the soup kitchen. Once out of his house, Jack looks around suspiciously. No sign of that black Benz. I know they'll be back tracking me. I wonder where the police are holding David. I could call Officer Johnson, but those guys may find out. Thinking about these things puts Jack in a bad mood.

Kent is smiling until he sees Jack's face and says, "Hey Jack, you can't let these guys worry you."

"I know, Kent. But they really work my nerves. I want to stand up to them, but it's no telling what they would do to me."

"Jack, relax. I'm sure if you can pay them, they'll just leave you alone."

"Maybe," Jack says under his breath.

Or they may ask for money every now and then. The good food at the soup kitchen has helped me to forget their tactics.

This chicken gyro is amazingly good. The meat is tender with a touch of avocado. It's Mediterranean night. So, Jack eats grape leaves stuffed with rice. The entire soup kitchen is quiet as everyone is enjoying the great food. Even Shirley is stuffing her face. But I've noticed Kent doesn't have much food on his plate.

"Kent, what's going on? You used to have a big appetite," Jack says.

"Yeah, I know. But I don't want to put on weight. I've cut back on my food intake substantially. Because if I keep eating until I'm full, I'll gain like 15 pounds. It would be all muscle, but I may lose some of my agility."

"But 15 pounds of muscle can't hurt you," Jack adds.

"You may be right, but I'm comfortable the way I am. This food is excellent. I miss this cuisine. Although the food at school is decent."

Jack nods his head while stuffing his face. I could eat another gyro. But I won't because eating too much will result in a sleepless night.

Chapter 27

Now it's time to go back home, relax, and then get ready for the workday. I guess I'll do more writing. I may write a poem or two. One of his poems is as follows:

> It seems like the working man can't get a break, work and more work, how much can I take, straining for low pay, so cold symptoms go away, I need money right away, my clothes are starting to fray, do what I must to stay afloat, while my boss goes on vacation on his boat, he lives like a king, he might as well have a moat, it's cold working out here, he says grab your coat,

After work, Officer Johnson informs Jack that David is now at the local police station. So, Jack heads to the station. David is pacing in a jail cell.

His eyes light up and tells Jack, "I'm sorry, man. I had to try something."

"I'm mad at you, but I understand your desperation. I'm afraid of these organized criminals too. So, I will try to sell my writings. If I make a profit, I'll pay them. I don't want the police involved anymore. I will have to go under police protection if I testify against them in court. They have a long reach like an NBA player."

Since Jack refuses to press charges, David is freed immediately. Jack and David head home. On the way home, David walks up to the black Benz. Jack is out of range, so he can't hear the conversation.

David comes in the house and says, "They don't want their money next week. But they put off that date for 6 months. Now they want 75 grand!"

This puts a lot of pressure on me. Because if my writings don't sell well, I'll never amass that much money. But I can't say no, or else David will be in serious trouble. I need to some work right now to perfect my novel. Will David ever learn?

Well, it's time to write some more. David is watching tv. Apparently unfazed by his arrest and treatment. He's just happy to be free. Jack has been writing all evening and now it's time for bed. Even though David was arrested, no charges were filed so he still has a job. I don't remember the location of his workplace. I need rest to be ready for tomorrow. So, hopefully I'll sleep well.

Jack's alarm wakes him up as usual. David is sleeping in. I want to wake him up now out of meanness. Because David is depending on him to save him. It's me writing to protect him. Even though I don't technically own this house, I consider it mine. Something must change. He needs to pull his own weight somehow. Oh well. I should calm down before I just slap him.

Now Jack is on the train heading to work. He's no longer upset with David. He realizes that he must talk some sense into David. Before David makes another grave mistake. What should I say? I can't talk to him like a child because he is a man. Talking to him like a child will not help. David wants to be rich so badly. It seems like he'll do anything for the promise of big money. I'll think of something.

Work is hard. These boards feel heavier than usual.

A crew member asks, "What's wrong Jack?"

"I haven't been to the gym in a few days. And we don't lift boards every week. I've got to get used to lifting them again."

Man, my lower back is sore. So are my hands from handling these boards. After dropping a board, Jack takes a break. He isn't breathing heavily, and after a 10-minute break, his muscles have recovered. He feels stronger than ever. He even carries two boards at one time.

By lunchtime, the crew had nearly finished putting all the boards in a row. As to act as a barrier between property and the water. Dirt is put behind the wall of boards and tiebacks to support the wall of boards. This doesn't take as much effort as carrying boards. The crew completes the entire job by the end of the workday. I'm so ready to get home to go to the gym with Kent.

I'll show him that I'm stronger than he is. I'm back home relaxing for a bit. I'm waiting for Kent to come over. I'll write a poem before we go to the gym.

> Only the strong survive, but only the smart thrive, in a world that can be so cold, I'll remain bold, going after my dreams, it seems easy now, to compose a poem or two, just sit back relax, let the feeling overcome you, I'm in the zone, I can write all day, Writer's Block stay away, this is my heyday,

Not a bad poem. I can do better though. Jack hears knocking on the door. He opens it to find Kent.

“Hey buddy, are you enjoying your days off?” Jack asks.

“Yes, very much so. Although back at school I have little free time. It’s rare that I’m doing nothing. Now I get to sit in front of the tv for a while,” Kent says with a smile.

“That’s what it is like for me practically every day. That’s part of the reason I write- to not get bored,” Jack says.

“Well, I’m never bored at school. By the time I’m done with classes and working out, it’s time to do homework. Then I’m off to sleep. But of course, it’s worth it. I can see how close I am to my goals of attending an excellent university and making the NBA.”

“I’m so glad everything is working out for you. I’m doing well, but this guy David is not right in the head. He’s strange, but I think he’s a good person. Anyway, let’s go to the gym to see who is the more powerful,” Jack says.

“Sure. I know I’m stronger. We even take whey protein at school to improve not only our strength but our stamina. There is no way you’re as strong as me. I mean no way,” Kent says emphatically.

At the gym, Jack and Kent decide which exercise to do first.

“Let me see your bench press,” Jack says.

Kent puts 350 pounds on the bar and does 3 reps.

“I told you I’m strong.”

“Yeah, yeah,” Jack responds.

Then Jack benches 350 pounds 5 times. Kent’s eyes are wide.

“I’ve never seen a man lift so much weight so many times! Yes, I’ve heard of guys, and I’ve seen guys do this on the internet.” Kent says.

But something is wrong. I’ve got to act tough in front of Kent, but I hurt my left pec muscle showing off. It’s not throbbing with pain, but it's obvious that the muscle is strained. Will this affect my work? My job requires physical labor. I guess I'll see how I feel tomorrow. I can't pretend anymore.

"Hey Kent, I hurt my chest. I'm done lifting weights right now."

"Why did you strain?" Kent says.

"Yeah, I've never put so much weight on to bench press. I thought I could lift it with no trouble. I work out with weight all the time. I hope I can keep my job in Marine Construction. I'm thinking about going to the doctor in a few days. However, it's probably just a muscle strain. I should be fine in a few hours," Jack says.

"I hope so. I know how important your job is. But look on the bright side, you've saved your money. Even if you are out of work for a while, you'll be ok," Kent says.

That last sentence gives Jack a flashback. Tears are welling up in my eyes as I recall that dreadful Cardboard Palace. There is no way I'm going back to that. Maybe I'll find a physically less-demanding job.

Back at the house, Jack is feeling a lot better. But his chest hurts whenever he moves his upper body in a certain way. David is home watching tv when he sees Jack wincing.

"What's wrong?"

"I hurt my chest lifting weights. But it feels like a muscle strain, so I should be fine soon. However, I've never had a muscle strain in my chest."

"I'm sure you'll be ok. You may have to take a few days off work," David suggests.

"No! I must work. I must show everybody that I'm a great worker."

"I think you better take some time off. There is no way you'll be able to lift boards or anything."

"You are right. I'll call my boss now and inform him of my injury."

Man, I hope Nick is understanding.

Jack dials his number and the boss answers, "Hello?"

"Hey this is Jack. I hurt my chest lifting weights and I need some time to heal."

"How much time do you need?" Nick asks.

"Maybe a couple weeks of rest. I know that I've made some mistakes. But I generally do a lot on the job, and I really need a break," Jack says.

"I hear you. But too bad. This is life. You're fired! You can't work so I'm supposed to keep paying you? You do ok work, but I'll find someone better. Oh yeah, good luck."

And Nick hangs up the phone.

What a prick! I guess I'll find another job soon. Yes, housing is free, but I want a lot of spending change. I'll think about what to do next. At least I'll have more time to write. They say to always look on the bright side.

"I just have to let it go," Jack says.

"What? You were a good worker. You never missed a day," Kent says.

"Well, that doesn't mean much now. I'm not too worried. I'll find a job somewhere soon."

At least my housing is free along with meals at the soup kitchen. I may make money reading to people again. I need to talk to James about getting this position back. I'll get paid less, but it is a relaxing job. It's the most relaxing job I've ever had. Plus, it is fun watching people enjoy listening to great literature. It's a win/win situation all the way around. I'll visit the shelter to see James after dinner.

The soup kitchen serves so called American food. Hot dogs and hamburgers are the meats. There is also mac and cheese. Jack stuffs himself at dinner and then heads to the shelter. Wow.

The shelter has changed since I've been here. The walls have been painted and new cots look amazing. Not a dirty place before, but it is spotless now. James is doing paperwork in his office. I hate to disturb him.

"Hey James, how have you been?"

"Pretty well. I haven't talked to you in a while. I guess you are doing well," James replies.

"I'm doing ok. But I need my old job back. I got injured and I need a non-physically demanding job. At least until my injury heals."

"Sure, you can have your old job back. It seemed like you really enjoyed it. I was surprised that you stopped doing it."

"Well, I wanted more money. But now I want a steady income until I can get back on my feet."

"As a matter of fact, you can start working tomorrow morning. Most of the people here would love to hear a good story," James says with a smile.

I don't remember James ever being this calm and understanding. They say people can change.

"I'll be here in the morning then."

"I'll see who wants to be read to at 8:00 AM and you can begin then," James replies.

They shake on it and Jack is so relieved. I may not get paid as well as the marine construction job, but reading to people is more satisfying. It's getting late, so I'll head home and do some writing.

At home, David is watching tv. He is too relaxed for a man who has been through so much. Oh well. At least he is safe- for now. Next time he gets in trouble he's on his own. Thinking about him makes me upset. I'll write a poem to calm down:

> What do when someone works your nerves, and it seems that you have the urge, to slap them silly, not to hurt them, but to make them change really, yet you know that's wrong, so it's the same song, they annoy me what should I do, I guess I'll pray for him, that he'll change one day, nonviolence is always the right way,

Not my best poem. Now, I'll work on my novel until I get sleepy. At least I don't have to set my alarm clock so early in the morning. My hand is sore, so it's time to stop writing and get some sleep.

I hear my alarm clock, but I want more sleep. Oh well, it's time to rise. I don't know why I'm so sleepy. It's 7:30 AM so I had a good night's rest. Anyway, I'm ready to read to some people at the shelter. I'm hungry so I'll eat at the soup kitchen.

Breakfast is as appetizing as usual. This omelet is excellent. It's full of sausage, bacon, peppers, and cheese. A restaurant couldn't do it any better. Now that I have a full stomach, I'm ready for a day's work.

"Welcome back!" James says emphatically as Jack enters the shelter.

"Yep. I plan to read to people for a while," Jack replies.

A man is already waiting on the couch: ready to hear a good book. He has the Bible in his hand, and he looks anxious. He can't keep his legs still. He stares at me as if waiting for me to speak first. Well, that's no problem.

"Hey, my name is Jack and I'm reading to you today."

"Yes, I figured out who you are. Your face is unfamiliar around here. My name is Zach. I would like you to read some of the Bible."

"Where should I start?" Jack asks.

"Psalms."

"Which verses?"

"You can start from the first chapter," Zach says.

After reading a few chapters, it is obvious to Jack that Zach loves this book of the Bible. He is seriously thinking about each verse and looks to be memorizing every verse.

I take a short break from reading and ask Zach, "Are you memorizing the lines.?"

"Why yes. It's a mental exercise. I already memorized some of the first chapter of Psalms. I may not be able to read all that well, but my memory is very strong. I memorize books because it's easier than to read them," Zach says.

"Well, that's the opposite for me. Reading is very easy, but I'm not great at memorizing things."

"We can teach each other things then. You can help me to read well, and I'll show you how to improve your memory," Zach says.

"So, Jack the first thing to memorize a chapter is to visualize what's being presented in the verse. Then it's just about repetition. You repeat a verse day in and day out. Until the verse sticks in your mind. It's not that hard. Why do you want to memorize verses?" Zach asks.

"I figured that if I memorize verses, it will help me write better poems and novels."

"Sounds good. Anyway, can you read more of Psalms?" Zach asks.

"Sure."

Jack spends all morning reading Psalms and Proverbs to Zach. Zach asks a lot of questions that Jack can't answer.

"I don't read much of the Bible daily. I'm just reading it to you. I hadn't opened a Bible in quite some time until now.

But there is a church about a quarter block away. I used to go there sometimes when I was living on the streets. Especially during bad weather," Jack says.

"I may talk to the preacher someday soon," Zach says.

"I'll chat and read to you later because my voice is hoarse," Jack says.

Maybe I should visit Pastor Jenkins. Trying to save David from disaster is stressing me out. And I'm angry that he walks around like everything is normal. I don't know if he is dense or just not thinking about the consequences. But he is still in serious trouble. Anyway, I'm hungry and it's lunch time.

Chapter 28

I'll grab a bite to eat at the soup kitchen. Then, I'll come back to the shelter to read to someone else. This Philly cheesesteak is fattening, but good, nonetheless. It could use a little more cheese, but the meat is so tender. After gobbling this up, Jack is back at the shelter reading a novel for his own enjoyment. Jack reads about 15 pages and then he sees Kent enter the shelter.

"Hey buddy, why are you here?" Jack inquires.

"Just bored while on vacation. I visited some of the city's museums to pass the time. I kinda want to go back to school to occupy my mind. My instructors didn't assign any homework. I'm not going to the public library, so I have nothing that I want to read," Kent says.

"I know what you can do. You can read to the next person that comes around. Because I'm a little hoarse."

"Sure. I can do that," Kent says.

A young boy hands Jack a Physics book.

"Aren't you a little young to learn about this subject? Do you even know who Isaac Newton is?" Jack asks.

"Well, no but my brother left this book for me before he went to college. I want to impress him with my knowledge when he comes back home."

"My throat is sore. So, my friend, Kent, will read this book to you," Jack says.

"Here we go!" Kent says.

This boy is so different than my son, Brent. Brent just wanted to fit in. He was basically the class clown. Which is strange because his mom is serious about education just like me. But I still love him anyway. I'm so frustrated not being able to see him. Maybe I should give up contacting him. He'll understand more when he's older. Worked up from thinking about Brent, Jack takes a walk outside. Maybe it will calm me down.

"I'm getting some air," Jack says quietly to Kent.

The weather is fair with hardly any clouds in the sky. I want some coffee. I'll walk to the coffee shop. The coffee is excellent. Although a bit pricey. With a little milk it is just right. I need to work on my novel so I can save David. It's so stressful writing now knowing what is at stake. But I promised to help him in any way that I can. Wow, this coffee is relaxing. It doesn't get much better than this.

I've been in the coffee shop longer than I thought. I'll head back to the shelter now. Kent is still reading to the boy wonder. I won't disturb them. I'll have a chat with James who is in his office.

"Hey James, how is it going?"

"Fine Jack. Everything at the shelter is fine. We may be getting more money from the government. We are looking at building another shelter. Like I said, everything is fine."

"That's great. These shelters are beneficial. I still recall being in my Cardboard Palace, scrambling to find a decent street to sleep on. Not only did the shelter provide me with a place to stay, but I also met good people here. I'm glad to hear this," Jack says emphatically.

"On a different note, Jack- I don't know about your friend, David. He supposedly has a job. Yet when I called his so-called employer, no one has heard of him. I'm thinking of kicking him out of public housing. Well, what do you think I should do with him, Jack?"

"Give him a chance to find a real job. If that goes wrong, do what you must," Jack replies.

"All right. All right. But if he messes up again, may God help him because he's done in public housing," James says.

All I can do is sigh. David man, I've got to talk to you.

I'll try to talk some sense into him," Jack replies.

James nods as Jack leaves his office. I'll see how far Kent has read in that Physics book.

"F=ma and that's the end of the chapter. I'm finished reading out loud for the day. I'm losing my voice," Kent says to the boy wonder.

The boy wonder nods, shakes Kent's hand and takes the book with him to his cot.

"How was it?" Jack asks.

"Entertaining. That little guy knows more about Physics than me. Well, maybe not me now, but when I was his age. I didn't know most of the things he knows by heart," Kent says.

"It is amazing what he can do already," Jack says.

Although Jack is worried about him. Will he fit in with kids because he is so advanced. My childhood was normal until high school. Then I started to take education seriously. However, I wasn't studying so far ahead of everyone else. I would read magazines and newspapers. But I wasn't studying Physics. In fact, I knew little about the subject until my junior year of high school. I had some fun in school. I played varsity basketball averaging 10 points per game.

Now I can't touch the rim. I'm so used to lifting weights that I've lost most of my athleticism. My chest is strained but I'm not going to the doctor.

The rest of the workday is uneventful. Jack and Kent take turns reading to others until it's time to go to the gym.

"I'll walk on the track, and I may watch you lift weights," Jack says.

"You know, you could work your legs now. It's not like you can't do anything with your hurt chest," Kent says.

"No, you don't understand. Every time I make any chest movement I can feel pain. It's best for me to rest. Anyway, are you playing basketball today?" Jack asks.

"No way. The boarding school doesn't want me to lift weights here for fear of injury. But hey, I'm young so I should be ok. Plus, lifting weights this week will keep my conditioning intact. Also, it's boring reading all day. Don't get me wrong- I love helping others, but reading every day gets old quickly," Kent says.

"I want to see you play ball in person, but I can't afford to visit you right now," Jack says.

"You can stream games live, but I have 3 ½ years left at the boarding school. I'm sure you'll make it there for one game within that time span," Kent says.

"I should have some money coming in from my novel. I really believe that I'll make it rich," Jack says.

"I know you will, Jack. All the time that you put in must pay off someday soon," Kent says.

"I sure hope so. I'm ready to change my life. Living on the margins like this is stressful. I'll get there," Jack says confidently.

At the gym, Jack walks the indoor track while Kent lifts weights. The track is very comfortable on my feet. It's so spongy. I'm starting to get tired. I'll see what type of exercises Kent is doing. I see Kent doing biceps curls with light weight.

"Now lifting weight that light can't be doing much," Jack says.

"You're wrong Jack. At school, we don't use heavy weights to gain strength. Using light weights can increase strength and is safer. You should try using them when your chest heals," Kent says.

Kent continues curling 10 pounds in each arm. Which isn't much for a person of Kent's strength. Jack recalls Kent curling 80 pounds in each arm before he went to boarding school. Kent claims he hasn't gained any weight, but he looks more muscular now. Looking in the mirror, Jack can see that he too is muscled up.

Man, my chest is broad, and my arms are very defined. This type of musculature gives me an incentive to keep exercising. Because I can see significant progress.

Jack and Kent go to the sauna for old times' sake. I'm sleepy now- feeling the warmth in this room. Although it is time to get out because my skin is pruning. Then they get into the jacuzzi. I can't stay in here long since my skin is already pruned. It is no longer comfortable in the jacuzzi.

"I'm almost done with my first novel. I've gotten my writings back from David."

"Can I read one of your poems? Or better yet can you recite one from memory? Kent asks.

"Yes. I'll recite one poem that I've memorized:

> From the streets of a city, to a Benz sitting pretty, all from being witty, skip the pity, it was hard work yes, now I'm the best of the best, full of zest, not worried about the rest, focused on my goal, I'm on a roll, large money soon to come, and I'm having fun,

no pardon the pun, no accidental wordplays,
what can they say, but good things from what
I've been through,

"Pretty good. I've been so busy at school that I haven't had time to write much. Wow. You have skill in putting together poetry," Kent says.

"Yeah, thanks. I've been writing almost every day. I've gotten better. It used to be a pain writing poems. But now it is easy. Plus, it is fun seeing my progress."

They leave the gym and Kent goes back to his parents' house. Jack goes back home to do some writing. I guess I have Writer's Block. I don't know what I want to write for my next scene. I've been brainstorming for 30 minutes, and I have not written a sentence. This is very unusual.

Chapter 29

DAVID COMES BUMBLING IN the house looking nervous. He looks like he wants to talk, but Jack doesn't want to be bothered. He pretends to be concentrating on his writing. David goes to his room and shuts the door. Good. Jack thinks as ideas begin to come to his head. He writes for 30 minutes feeling confident about his work. After a quick reread of what he just scribbled down, Jack puts his writings aside and turns on the tv.

It's almost time for dinner and Jack watches the news. There is nothing positive going on. A bad storm hit eastern Canada and a few people lost their homes. Also, one of Jack's favorite athletes was hurt in a car accident. Fortunately, he'll be ready to play soon because he sustained a minor injury. A former prime minister passed away from natural causes. Jack hadn't heard of this man. Jack grew up in the USA not Canada. Just as Jack is turning the channel, David pops out of his room.

Looking sad, he asks, "Hey Jack, can I talk to you for a minute?"

"Go ahead."

"Well, I'm thankful that you are helping me. Or rather saving me. But I want to run away to Europe and hide out."

"But how? You have no money. And these guys that you

owe money to are very powerful. They'll hunt you down like a dog. Just relax. I'll pay them once my novel sells. Everything will be fine," Jack says.

David seems to take these words to heart. A spark comes into his eye. Jack notices the tension leaving David's body. It must be hard not knowing what may happen to you. David and Jack talk about what they see on the news- nothing positive. The time passes quickly and now it's time for dinner.

On the way to the soup kitchen, Jack says, "David, don't ever put yourself through these problems again. Just stick to making an honest living."

David just nods. Leaving Jack to believe that his words are going in one ear and out the other. David looks embarrassed about what has gone on. But there's something about him that could get him into trouble. Something just isn't right about him, Jack thinks.

At dinner, Jack zones out. He is caught up in his novel figuring out where to take his plot next. He usually doesn't think about these things unless he's writing. But this part of the book is extremely important. It includes the climax, so I must get it right.

Kent is at the soup kitchen entertaining everyone with events that occurred at school. He has the entire table laughing about the time one of the students came to class with a faded shirt. The shirt was bleached when the student washed his whites and his colors together with warm water.

This boarding school simulates life at college. Jack remembers some funny incidents when he was in college. Pretty much just silly pranks. While everyone else is laughing at Kent's tales, Jack is laughing about the crazy things that happened in college.

Kent can tell stories. He has the attention of practically

everyone at the table. His cliffhangers are excellent and the inflection in his voice is well used. He's as good as that guy who does movie previews. He's almost as good as me. I'm a great storyteller.

Mainly from reading to others so much, I have a good ear for what sounds right. I'm almost as good as this turkey sandwich. The lettuce is fresh, and the onions have a strong taste. But not too strong as to make my breath stink.

The potato chips are also fresh and good. In fact, all the food is top notch. Even the drinks are not the typical fountain sodas. Jack orders freshly made cranberry juice. It's supposed to be healthy for you, but Jack just loves the tart yet surprisingly sweet taste.

After devouring his entrée, Jack wonders if he should eat dessert. The kitchen is serving cheesecake, but Jack wants to stay in shape. I usually think about how much I exercise to avoid eating sweets. But I really want cheesecake. Oh well, I'll give in this time. I've been working hard in the gym. I can eat one slice of cake without it decreasing my fitness.

Jack grabs a slice and goes to work. He eats it in about a minute. I want another piece, but I must control myself. I'll eat celery now to balance out this dessert. Celery doesn't fill anyone up, but hey, it's better than eating more cake after more cake. Through all of this, Kent is still telling stories about the boarding school. How can they still be interested, Jack thinks.

That's why I zoned out. The stories are intriguing to a certain extent. But c'mon- he's been going on for 30 minutes. Jack thinks about how his son is doing. He still won't answer Jack's emails. And Jack believes this is due to his ex-wife telling Brent lies about him. That really boils my blood. But getting mad won't help the situation. I need to calm down.

Jack takes deep breaths and tries to relax. Kent is still telling stories, so no one notices how mad Jack is. Until it's time to go back home.

David asks, "Hey Jack, what's wrong?"

Maybe I should lie to him- I don't want to hear advice. But I would rather tell the truth.

"Honestly David, my son won't answer my emails even though I love him dearly."

David nods his head, and says, "You may not have guessed it, but I had a similar problem. My daughter refused to talk to me for years. After she had a baby, now she wants to talk to me every day. He'll come around as he grows older. Just don't stop emailing him. He'll realize it's not your fault for whatever has happened in his life."

"Thanks David. What a great thing to say."

That's deep. How can he understand so much and yet get in trouble over money with a criminal organization? I want to ask David this question, but he may get upset. I'll listen more to whatever he says. Because he knows something.

"So, how are you coming along with your novel?"

"I'm almost done. I must edit a little bit more of it. Then I'll submit it to Jacob Price. He's been wanting to see my novel edited for some time. I'm confident that my novel will sell well. I don't think you have anything to worry about." Jack says.

"I'm not a religious man, but I've been praying daily that everything works out. My life may depend on it. I have no options," David says.

"Well, I'm going back to writing now," Jack says.

"I guess that's my cue to leave you alone. I'll go to my room and watch tv," David replies.

Jack sits down at the kitchen table and lets his instincts guide him. As he puts down words on the paper. Jack is in the zone, so he writes for 2 hours straight. And every idea fits into his story. Meaning, he doesn't edit much- everything flows logically. This is wonderful. Usually, I must cut out one third of what I write because it doesn't make sense.

Jack only stops writing because his hand is tired. This happens when he gets into this mode of extreme creativity. It's getting late and I must read to a middle-aged man in the morning. I'll watch a little bit of tv and then tuck it in. After watching some sports, Jack heads to his room and calls it a night.

The next day, Jack wakes up on time and heads to the shelter right away. Damon, a middle-aged man, is waiting with a classic novel in his hand. The novel is Around the World In 80 Days. Damon is looking like a child at Christmas time. Who can't wait to open his gifts.

"Hey Jack, I heard you are the greatest reader around," Damon says.

"Yeah, I'm ok. Do you want me to start now?"

"Yes, go right ahead," Damon says.

After clearing his throat, Jack begins. Damon is initially relaxed as he listens to Jack. But he looks nervous as it is almost time for him to go to work. Jack is engrossed in reading the book that he doesn't notice how anxious Damon has become.

"Sorry to interrupt Jack, but I've got to go to work," Damon says as he gathers his workbag and then brushes his teeth.

"Thanks Jack, please read to me again whenever you get the chance."

Jack nods and walks back to his house to take a nap. After napping for a while, Jack walks back to the shelter. He reads to others all day. Jack leaves work early to see Kent off. Kent is returning to boarding school.

"All right Jack, I've got to get back to school. Hopefully, I'll see you again soon," Kent says.

"Yeah. It was fun hanging out. I'll stay in touch," Jack replies.

A tear forms in one of his eyes like a proud parent. He's doing so well. He gets straight A's while being the best athlete at school. Hopefully, I can see one of his games live. I have some money saved up. And if I buy a plane ticket way in advance, I may be able to afford to travel to Kent's boarding school. However, I need money to stay in a hotel for a few days. Maybe I can get James to loan me money. He has deep pockets. I may ask him for money tomorrow. Right now, I just want to have some peace and quiet.

Jack falls asleep in his favorite chair. He wakes up to work on his novel before going to dinner. Wow, I've been looking at the same page for 15 minutes and I have no idea what to write. It's like I'm going through Writer's Block again. I'll go for a short walk and maybe this will spur my creativity. It has worked before. It's a cold, rainy night. But I have my raincoat on and my scarf so I should be ok.

The streets are crowded. Maybe I can get inspiration by observing people. I used to observe people all the time when I lived on the street. I wonder what everyone is in a rush to do. Watching people is a good way to pass the time. Especially when you are bored.

One woman is walking a big dog that looks as though it is walking her. She is about 110 pound and so is her Rottweiler. I guess it is for protection. But if someone wants to rob her, what good is a dog? Robbers carry guns. Well, she thinks she's protected and that makes her feel good.

Man, that's a big dog though. His chest is muscled up like a professional bodybuilder's or something. But this dog doesn't scare Jack. Yes, a dog can outrun a man, but a man can still beat up a dog. Because in quick sidesteps, a dog is not as quick as a man. And Jack knows this.

He beat up a pit bull while living on the street. The dog growled at him and then jumped for Jack's neck. Jack punched the dog in the throat. This stunned the dog and the pit bull ended up running away. Instead of standing up to such a formidable opponent.

Before that incident, he had heard stories of people defeating awesome animals. But he wasn't sure that a person could really hurt a big dog. I've got goosebumps thinking about that pit bull. Man, I can really fight.

Jack then turns his attention to the hotdog vendor. The aroma coming from his stand is captivating to say the least. I'm ready to pay for overpriced food after getting a whiff. But the vendor looks dirty.

He is smoking a cigar, and he handles the hotdogs without any gloves or hairnet. There is a line at his hotdog stand. So, these people must not care much about unsanitary conditions. I can imagine getting sick from consuming that food. Well, it's time for dinner.

I'll head to the soup kitchen right now. Out of the corner of his right eye, he spots that unmistakable black Benz. He pretends not to notice it, but he is frustrated. I told them I'll pay off David's debt when my novel sells. They are so impatient. My first impulse is to contact Officer Johnson. But that can only lead to something unfortunate.

The police still don't know the full extent of what's happening. Because no one will tell them that out of fear of the mob. David never told the police how stealing Jack's novel was to appease the mob. I'm worried. What if my novel doesn't sell? No! I won't let my emotions get the best of me.

Jack, calm down. But what will they do to me? I know the face of a mobster. I'm in big trouble too if I don't make any money.

Forget about staying calm. I've got to come up with a plan in case I don't make enough money from my book. I don't know what to do. Jack sits at his usual table in the soup kitchen.

He then gets in line behind David and whispers, "That mob guy is tailing me again."

David tries to keep his facial expressions in check. Because he knows other people are watching him closely. The other people don't know his exact situation, but clearly something is going on. So, David looks down, takes a deep breath and walks like that. As he walks to the table, Jack senses everyone there watching David closely.

Shirley is staring at David. Trying to decipher anything from David's body language. This makes me nervous because I haven't explained to anyone what's really going on. Now I must tell my friends something. It's obvious that they want answers. True answers. I see them whispering to each other.

After dinner, Shirley asks Jack bluntly," What's going on?"

I pause for a second to gather my thoughts and then say, "Well, David is in trouble. My novel must sell so I can pay someone to get off his back."

"Why don't you go to the police?" Shirley inquires.

"It's not that simple. David has the wrong type of people against him. I shouldn't be telling you this, because if these people find out you know something, you could be in a lot of trouble. So, don't tell anyone what I told you. If you value your health."

Shirley looks worried. She is breathing heavily.

"Should I avoid you, Jack? Are these people really that bad?"

"They said not to contact the police. They probably have connections in law enforcement. I'm thinking they have a few spies in their network," Jack responds.

"In that case your secret is safe with me," Shirley says.

Jack nods and then walks home. To his surprise, no one is tailing him. But the hair on the back of his neck is standing up. Living like this is bad for my nerves. I've got to get this stress off me somehow. Once at home, Jack decides to write something to get his mind off this stress. But I'm not working on my novel tonight. I'll write this poem instead:

> Stress can really put one in a bind, the amount of pressure it can put on your mind, that's why I'm sighing, so I write lying, to myself like, doing this will take away all of the pain, it's getting hard to maintain, some degree of sanity, dealing with a misfortune is devastating, is the creator mad at me, how to fully get out of this situation, I cannot see, I'll be rich but will these negative people, still have a hold on me, it's only a matter of time, until the negative thoughts become reality, so I pray to the Holy One, even though I'm not that religious, my enemy has an appetite for destruction, to him this tastes delicious, watching me squirm, I can just tell he loves it, maybe more than even the profit, once my book sells, I may move across the pond, just to avoid his influence, I'll be affluent, yet something tells me he has connects, where I may go, even to some, remote island in the Pacific, so I must hope that he is a man of

his word, he said when I pay him his due, my
time haunting you is through,

Jack writes more poems until he looks at the clock. Wow! It's time for me to get some sleep. My hand is tired anyway. But my mind is restless. I can't sleep. I might as well watch tv. Just in time for the local news.

The headline reads, "Mob boss is locked up for money laundering."

It's him! The man behind the plot against David has been detained. Jack jumps out of his chair and knocks on David's bedroom door.

"Hey David, wake up! I've got great news!"

"Yeah ok, Jack I'm up."

David opens the door to see an ecstatic Jack. Barely able to speak because he is so excited.

"The mob guy who sent his underling to blackmail us has been locked up," Jack says.

David's face lights up immediately. Tears of joy stream down his face.

David keeps repeating, "I can't believe it."

Good. Now I can keep all the profit from my book if it sells.

The news anchor says, "This mob boss, who was captured this evening, faces 20 years for the crime of money laundering. Police have been investigating him for 4 years and their hard work has finally paid off. Many familiar with the case expect the boss to expose his associates for lesser jail time."

Now Jack and David are celebrating. After about 20 minutes, they calm down. David goes back to his room while Jack watches tv. There's nothing good on late night. So, I'll turn the tv off and try to write more poems. What should I write about? While brainstorming, Jack's thoughts turn dark.

Chapter 30

I'M TIRED OF NOT hearing from my son. Maybe I should save up money to go to my ex-wife's house and have a word with her. No. I don't want any trouble. But I miss my son. I wonder what lies she is feeding him. She must be telling him lies because I'm not that bad of a guy. What have I done so wrong to keep me from my son? He's at an impressionable age. So, I may have to wait until he grows up to understand my side of the story. The we can have an honest conversation. I wonder how he is adjusting to high school and such.

My high school days didn't mean much. Just studying to prepare for college. I had so much homework that I didn't have time to party. I had some fun. But my focus was academics.

I recall spending my Saturday nights memorizing words for vocabulary tests for English classes. And other nights working math problems. I also played a few sports. But not because I enjoyed them. But to have extracurricular activities to put on college applications.

I didn't know what type of fun I was missing until college. Yet, after one semester, I was able to return to studying almost every day. I hope my son will be disciplined at both levels like me. Yes, it can be boring studying all the time. But it's better than partying all the time. No bad habits. They always say that children need a dad present in their life. That's what I'm trying to do. I hope that if he is mad at me, his anger doesn't last for long. Life is short. He'll miss me when I'm gone. I guess I'll write a poem about my frustration:

> Does my son even love me anymore, I left him and his mom of course, he may be mad, but he doesn't understand, the anger between me and his mother, I wasn't happy so I needed another woman to show me some attention, I did not have an affair, I left before cheating, that is clear, at least to my ex-wife, but she hates me despite, my faithfulness, I can't help if her attitude drew us apart, I should've never married her from the start, no one warned me though, so I learned a hard lesson, in life, I can't live in an environment with so much strife, I had to say bye, and at least try, to find happiness somewhere,

Tears being to stream down Jack's face. From thinking about how bad-tempered his ex-wife is. And how bad he misses his son. I'm not going to keep sobbing. I must suck it up. I'll be ok. Writing is therapeutic. In a weird way, I feel a bit better. Jack is in and out of sleep when he hears a knock on the door. It's Officer Johnson.

"Hey Jack, sorry to bother you at this time of night. But this is very important. I want you to be the first to hear this. The mob boss claims David is involved in the money laundering case. I am personally investigating David because I believe he is innocent. But we will be taking him into custody if things stay the way they are. He is facing a long jail sentence unless he can clear himself. Or talk about who else is in the organization."

"Wow, David told me he owed the syndicate gambling debts. I'm sure that's all. He is more careless than criminal. That I'm sure of," Jack says.

"I hope you are right for his sake. Protective custody can only do so much," Officer Johnson explains.

Just as I thought I could get David out of one sticky situation, something else pops up.

"Thanks, Officer."

Jack closes the door and grabs something to drink. Nothing alcoholic, but a drink to distract his mind. David is sleeping soundly. I don't think I should tell him about seeing Officer Johnson tonight. I won't tell anyone. Hopefully, David's name will be cleared before the police have to bring him in for questioning. Officer Johnson said they may bring him in, but nothing is certain.

Everything will be fine. At least that's what I want to think. I can't stop my eye from twitching due to stress. This drink isn't helping. I don't know how I'm going to sleep now. I guess I'll go for a short walk around the block.

It's a clear night but because of light pollution, it's difficult to see any stars. It's not like Jack cares anyway. He isn't even looking around. Just thinking about David's bad luck.

I've got to get this off my mind. Jack sits on a bench and begins to relax. Hardly anyone is walking on the street during this time of night. This night reminds me of the last night I was homeless. I had tried to get into shelters for weeks. But they were all either full or for women and children only. I went to a church, said some prayers, and stumbled upon a shelter that would take in practically anybody. At the front door I knocked, and James answered. James didn't even greet me.

He said, "If you don't cause any trouble, you can stay here as long as you like."

I nodded and from then on, the shelter has been my home. James can be irritable, but I'll never forget what he did. Even though there aren't may snowstorms here, it still gets cold on a person with no place to stay. I came to the shelter with the clothes on my back and my writing notebooks. Look how far I've come.

Now I have a home and a literary agent in Jacob Price. After pumping himself up, Jack feels better and heads back home. As soon as he arrives home, David is up with a perplexed look on his face.

"Where have you been?"

"I went for a walk. Why do you ask?"

"I was half asleep when I heard you talking to someone. Who was it?" David asks.

I want to lie to him, but I can't.

"Officer Johnson. You are still in big trouble. The syndicate mentioned you as a worker. Unless you can clear your name and/or tell on your associates, you will be spending a long time in jail.?

David puts his hands on his hips.

David takes a deep breath and says, "I know what I did. I may have to do some time, but I'm not telling on the syndicate. I'd rather do time and come out with a clear conscience."

He's so confident in his decision. I wish I could help him. I'm tired of thinking. I'll sleep now.

The night flies by. It's time to get up already. Oh well. At least I have an easy job now. At the soup kitchen, Jack eats cereal and heads to the shelter to read to others. As requested, he I reading to children.

"Hey kids. Today, I'll be reading Harry Potter!"

They all respond, "Yay!"

"All right. Let's get started."

With a bottle of water next to him, Jack reads for an hour before needing a break. None of the kids look bored and none talk. Their full attention is on this book. The book is good- great.

"Well, that's all for today kids."

"Awe!" They all exclaim.

I'm tired now. And I'm hoarse. I wonder what James wants me to do next. Oh well. I'm going to a restaurant for lunch. I love eating at the soup kitchen, but I have a taste for Greek food. I need space to think, so I don't want any company. I've only been to this restaurant one time and the food was amazing. It's not crowded so I should get back to the shelter in no time. But I'm not on the clock or anything. I like to work when it's my time to do a job.

Jack sips green tea. That reminds me- I need to email Jacob Price. I'll see if he likes any of my latest poems. He really wants a complete novel from me. But it's not quite ready yet.

As soon as Jack enters the shelter, James approaches him and says, "Great job this morning. The kids really appreciate that book. Thanks a lot for the work you've done."

"Thanks." Jack replies.

"This afternoon, I want you to read to a group of elderly people. Not at the shelter, but at a nursing home. They really need attention, and I think you would be perfect for the job," James says.

"How far do I have to travel? I didn't expect to go anywhere," Jack replies.

"It's within walking distance. It's a few blocks away. They want you there soon. Once you get off Main Street up by the Chinese restaurant, you'll see it. See you later," James says smartly.

And I was starting to like this guy. At least my job is easy. I'm sure these seniors won't be rude at all. Plus, reading might be uplifting to the elderly people. They probably don't have many visitors.

Following James's instructions, Jack arrives at the nursing home 10 minutes later. The nursing home doesn't look like it's being taken care of. There are dark spots on the walls and the floor doesn't look clean. The whole place smells like ammonia.

A middle-aged lady approaches Jack and says, "Hi, you must be the reader that we have been requesting. Follow me to the dayroom. Everybody is waiting."

"Hi everyone, this is Jack. He'll be reading to you all today. So don't talk loudly and make him feel comfortable."

The staff already picked out a book for Jack to read- the Bible. Where should I start? I guess Genesis. Half of the audience looks sleepy. So, they won't care if I'm nervous. And this is the King James version. Who really understands everything in that version?

After reading the first chapter, Jack looks at his audience. They are into this. All of them are watching and listening closely.

"Amen." Says a member of the audience as Jack really gets into this book. I haven't read the Bible in a long time. I may read more of it later just for me. Because it's interesting. Well. I've read a few chapters, and my throat is sore.

"Well, everyone, I'm done," Jack says.

Groans come from the audience. Obviously, they are upset that the reading is cut short.

"Will you be here tomorrow?" An elderly man asks.

"I'm not sure yet. I don't know my schedule."

Leaving the nursing home, Jack's mind is still on some of the verses he read. I've never been this into the Bible even when I used to attend church. I could use some prayer. All this stress from looking out for David. Oh well. There's nothing more I can do except maybe pray. I'm done reading earlier than expected. So, I'm not going back to the shelter yet.

James may put me to work if I come back to the shelter right now. I could window shop. I might as well check out the latest fashions. Jack stops in the Ferragamo store. It's too pricey for working class people, but Jack wants to look.

That doesn't make sense. $500 shoes? The shirts are well made. In fact, if my novel sells, I'm going to shop at this store. I'll make it big. I can see it now. Anyway, I'll go to a shoe store.

I may buy walking shoes since I no longer play basketball for cardio. Because Kent is at boarding school. I don't see any shoes I like. I'm losing track of time. I'll go back to the shelter now.

At the shelter, James says, "Hey, Jack, I heard they loved you at the nursing home."

"I don't know about loved. But they enjoyed the Bible," Jack replies.

James smiles and says, "Do you want to go back there tomorrow?"

"I don't know. Do I have to?" Jack inquires.

"No, you don't have to go back there. But who else do you want to read to?" James asks.

"No preference, I guess I'll go back there tomorrow afternoon," Jack says.

James smiles again and says, "Well, your workday is over. See you tomorrow."

Jack leaves the shelter and heads home. What an interesting day. I could use some of this material in my writings. As soon as I get home, I'll do some writing. Jack sits at his kitchen table and writes this poem:

so I might, still have my faculties at the ripe,
age of eighty, doctors claim they have the
reason, a great diet with less meat and sweet
treats, but I saw what some of the elderly eat,
no prunes or beets, but pork chops and pig
feet, yet they seemed, relaxed and stress free,
that seems to be the way to be,

Not a bad poem. I could do better. I may write another poem later. Then Jack works on his novel. The phone rings.

"Hey Jack, it's Jacob Price. Are you almost done with your book?"

"Yes Jacob, I'm nearly done. I'll have it ready for you very soon," Jack says.

"Ok Jack, I'll talk to you later," Jacob says.

I really need to get this thing finished. I know he is irritated that I still don't have a finished product. Hey, I'm doing the best I can do. I might even switch agents if he pushes be too hard. Anyway, back to writing.

I have a few hours until I go to the gym. I might as well be productive. Perfecting this novel is challenging. I'm rewriting so many parts of it. Should I write a poem to vent my frustration? Doing this can't hurt anything.

I'm writing to be the best, but the pressure for
greatness causes stress, I feel obsessed, with
every letter of the alphabet, perfecting every
line at the most basic level, I will not settle,
for a lukewarm piece of work, a masterpiece,
pretty good at the least, writing now reminds
me, of hardship on the streets, abject poverty,
I'm not rich yet, but soon to be, I feel it in

> my bones, owning multiple foreign cars and
> homes,

This poem motivates me to work on my novel again. Well, time to go to the gym. The gym is empty. So, Jack can use all the exercise equipment without having to wait for anyone. Now, it's time to hit the sauna.

To Jack's dismay, the sauna is crowded. I wanted to be in here alone to relax and meditate. Oh well. At least being in the sauna feels good. Thankfully, no one is talking so I can relax. Jack is lost in his thoughts and takes a nap. I'm on a beach somewhere warm- enjoying the weather.

Suddenly, a man appears trying to choke me. Before he can get his hands around my throat, I open my eyes and punch him in the nose. As soon as Jack envisions striking the man, he wakes up and is still in the sauna. What an odd dream. I rarely think about anything violent when I relax in the sauna. I don't know what is going on. I'll get in the jacuzzi now.

He's the only one in the jacuzzi and Jack relishes this. But he can't relax. Instead, he thinks about all the things he needs to do. I've got to write more, email Kent, and maybe email Brent. There are more things to do, but I can't remember them. It's time to get out of the jacuzzi. My skin is pruning.

This reminds me of bathing Brent when he was a baby. He loved staying in the bathtub for as long as I allowed him. He cared more about that than any toy I ever bought him. Even when he could bathe himself, he would stay in the shower until the hot water ran out. Since I had a great job then, a high-water bill was no problem. If my son was happy. One day he'll write back. I'm sure of it. So, when I get back home, I'll email him.

Jack is now home and emails Brent immediately. Not wanting to upset his ex-wife, he doesn't ask about her. He asks

Brent how he is doing. Nothing that would rile anyone up. All right I composed this email. I'll watch tv until it's time for dinner. There's not much on tv. While flipping through the channels, David comes home.

"I just got back from the public library. What a treat. It's so high tech."

"How long did you stay? Jack asks.

"For about half the day. I studied different subjects. I was thinking of becoming a write like you. Maybe you can teach me something?"

"Teach you? I'm not accomplished yet. I haven't sold a book. Hopefully, I will soon, but you can learn a lot on your own. I'm still a beginner."

David sighs and then goes to his room. How is this guy going to act if I make it big? I may distance myself from him if I become rich. I can't trust him. He's prone to doing odd things. I can see him going back to gambling. Getting back into trouble. I'm tired of watching over him. I'm tired of worrying about what he'll do next. I'll write a poem about David and this situation to settle my nerves.

> I know we are supposed to forgive others, but this guy is really pushing it, you want me to teach you something, after you stole my manuscript, but I stay composed, keep my anger in check, yet I really want to wring his neck, put some sense in him, because what he does is bs and, and other synonyms, but I'll stop attacking the man, ad hominem, and concentrate on the good in him, he does work he says for Helping Hands, helping those who literally need a hand, or arm, or leg,

prosthetics, so he must have a good heart, but
he's really pushing it, like I said,

I feel much better. A few months later... Jack gets an email from his literary agent, Jacob Price. A major publisher picks up Jack's book. It looks as though he's on the road to riches.

The End.

Printed in the United States
by Baker & Taylor Publisher Services